BON AND LESLEY

Also by Shaun Prescott

The Town

SHAUN PRESCOTT

BON AND LESLEY

FICTION

Published 2022
from the Writing and Society Research Centre
at Western Sydney University
by the Giramondo Publishing Company
PO Box 752
Artarmon NSW 1570 Australia
www.giramondopublishing.com

Cover image: Tony Garifalakis, *Untitled*, 2018–19, from *Garage Romance*
Courtesy of the artist and Hugo Michell Gallery

Designed by Jenny Grigg
Typeset by Andrew Davies
in Tiempos Regular 9/15pt

Printed and bound by Ligare Book Printers
Distributed in Australia by NewSouth Books

A catalogue record for this book is available from the National Library of Australia.

ISBN 978-1-922725-25-7

9 8 7 6 5 4 3 2 1

The Giramondo Publishing Company acknowledges the support of Western Sydney
University in the implementation of its book publishing program.

This project has been assisted by the Commonwealth Government through the
Australia Council, its arts funding and advisory body.

I climbed the rocky hill in front of me and came to a large stone house lying well back among the trees, the trees of my dream. I walked in. Beyond the cold darkness engendered by the leaves, the sun shone strong, and the mossy joints of the stone veranda steamed. Then I heard the bees, and their voices were like the sun singing aloud down through many flutes; long, low and banked by the fires of work were their murmurs, as they streamed out of an empty room in which they had their hives. This old house was a mingling of wet mossy stone and dry wood; little cell-like rooms lay along its passages; blue glass doors locked the halls, and over all lay the silence of distillation. Everything that could have been taken from those who lived there once had been taken and now was breathed out again. The human life in that house was still active. Yes, from old books that I saw scattered around, from old rags and bits of crockery, an oblique sort of family was formed by the house in its loneliness.

Eve Langley, *The Pea-Pickers*

1

Bon

It was an ugly and unfussy town, a town no one would visit, and during the years Bon had spent passing through on the train every weekday, he had sometimes dreamed of disembarking there and never returning home.

How had Newnes appeared in Bon's dreams? There had been homes and factory buildings, sallow and unmanned. There had been a row of shops, several pubs, and a little pedestrian square. There must have been people in the town, in the back rooms and first floors, behind the venetians of modern brick homes. But what kind of people, and what kept them living there? Bon didn't know.

In the middle of autumn during the worst year yet, Bon disembarked at the town. And brushed his hands clean of it all.

He passed through a small station arcade into the main street proper. Orange and white construction mesh barricaded the road, and dirt had caked around the tyres of local council earth movers. As in his dream, no people were around. The smell of smoke suffused the air, and the footpaths were dusty with ash. The footpath cement seemed luminescent in the softening light and the silence ceremonial. An old Harvey Norman across the street lay shut, as it should have been, for the thoroughfare was funereal, the town felt closed. A billboard for weight-loss supplement shadowed the footpath: two muscular and trim figures, a man and a woman, stood side by side brandishing the packet. Pictures of everyday people were scattered below, big before and smaller after. All shops except a corner petrol station were shuttered.

Inside the petrol station, pop music emitted softly through torrential radio static. Bon bought a pie from an old woman at the counter. Then he turned around, hurried back up the street and through the arcade, descended the steps onto the platform two at a time, and urged the arrival of the next city-bound train home.

He awakened later to a deep orange dusk. The stationmaster stood over him with a jabbing stick, said that a fire in the mountains had stopped the trains. You can get a bus, the stationmaster said, waving his stick, but you'll have to wait: it might take several hours. After that, best-case scenario the trains will run again tomorrow morning.

And you can take your attitude elsewhere, the stationmaster added.

For a while Bon sat, until the stationmaster returned. There's no point sitting there, he said, jabbing with his jabbing stick. It's an offence for you to keep sitting there.

Bon had found he didn't have the courage to linger in the quiet town. A bus waited near the northern station exit, so he got on it, nodded at the driver, and sat four rows down. Three other people were seated already, mere shadows in the dim interior light, each staring out the window. The door closed, the motor idled for a while, and then without warning the bus pulled away from the kerb.

It travelled west, across an old cement overpass and past the barricaded main street. The sun spilled orange in the west, but didn't reach as far as the black above the mountains. A fluorescent Dominos sign and white-lit interior glowed at the intersection with the barricaded main street, but no other shops were alive, aside from the petrol station he'd visited before. And anyway, rows of homes soon replaced landmarks, all space-blue with the light of screens.

Settling in for a long journey, he undid his top button, untucked his shirt, retrieved his phone, and texted home that he'd be late. Replacement buses were circuitous, far less direct than the trains, beholden to traffic conditions. It was likely he'd be home a mere five hours before it was time to set off again. But it didn't matter. Setting off wasn't the problem and had never been the problem. Bon shut his eyes and tried to will back sleep.

But the bus pulled up minutes later.

The driver was already up, an unlit cigarette in his mouth. He yelled last stop. The bus was stopped in a large open-air car park, and in the near distance loomed a giant cement box, Coles and Liquorland branding near its peak. Beyond the tarmac of the empty car park the night obscured all further land.

This is no replacement bus, the driver said – this is just the bus. He dragged on his cigarette, closed the sliding doors, and walked away.

After school Bon had gone to work, and then worked. He had worked in the day and then worked in the night. Arriving in Newnes is when that stopped.

On one of Bon's final commutes before disembarking at the Newnes station, he had stared out the train window for hours. He had rarely stared like this before, preferring to sleep or watch movies or sometimes tackle a book. Staring out this window as the train rolled through the countryside, he had imagined what the whole Central Western expanse might look like if, for example, the train line ran north to south. What if the city was inland? What if the Great Western Highway pivoted off into the calm farmland around Bathurst and Orange, veering from its current destination? He had travelled roads all his life, roads and train lines, and had rarely, if ever, strayed from them. But that's not what troubled him. He knew that only the roads, the trains, the maps and the fences domesticated the land. Not just this land but any land. That was not what troubled him.

What troubled Bon was that it wasn't going to be this way for much longer. He might have been among the last to realise it. But he might have been among a small number to acknowledge that actually, *it's time*. It's time, Bon thought, to stop dreaming of plans he could not afford. It's time to stop keeping on, keeping on, back and forth, as if there remained any nobility or dignity in it. It's time to stop hoping that he was suffering a paralysis that he – and they, everyone – would soon awaken from. It's time to stop fearing failure, or worse, feeling like an imposition, a lingering superfluity. It's time to stop aspiring to even a sufficient kind of wealth.

And so, newly counting himself among the small number to believe, for different reasons or the same, that actually, *it's time*, he figured himself no longer obligated to catch any train or replacement bus home.

A radio ballad decades old, swathed in lavish echo, aired faintly from the ceiling in the Newnes Valley Plaza. Bon listened as it echoed through the central thoroughfare, the harmonised voices warped and the melodies frayed. He had heard this song countless times before, but it had never sounded so old.

The shops were all shuttered and everyone gone. It wasn't a modern plaza, nor an especially old one, yet it resembled some vast memorabilia, it felt like a video. The windows in the Reject Shop needed a wipe, and blowflies were trapped in toy vending machines. Some ceiling panels had collapsed, revealing giant webbed tubes, and several of the lights either flickered or had blown. Bon could sense life, though. He wandered where he thought he sensed it, down the large corridor and around a bend.

A Coles and Liquorland both stood open, surgically lit and blinding with all the colours of groceries. In front of these a food court opened out, fanning from a central, totemic, dormant Donut King. At the table closest to the supermarket a single man sat eating from a grey plastic bag.

The man must have been around Bon's age, approaching his mid-thirties, but he dressed younger, in an oversized branded shirt and frayed black cargo pants. He made no effort to look old like Bon had learned to do. Bon's clothing made him disappear when he dressed of a morning. He lived in poorly ironed shirts and creaseless trousers, with pockets full of laundry-mulched tissues and breakfast receipts. The man at the table looked like he'd never stooped to wearing something uncomfortable.

The seated man yelled out. He motioned at Bon, and Bon, fearing a bashing if he didn't obey, approached.

It's time for me to go home, the man said.

He was grabbing at handfuls of bread roll from inside his plastic bag, nibbling.

It's time to go back to my house, he continued, only I can't now, because you've turned up. I was all ready to get up right before you arrived.

But now I can't, he sighed theatrically. Who knows what I might miss? I can't walk home alone, on just another weeknight, wondering what I might have missed leaving you here all alone. What if you thieve from the bottle-o? What if you have something to say? I've never seen you before. I'll wait here until you're done.

Bon nodded. He entered the Coles, retrieved a box of muesli bars and two cheese rolls. He would need to eat while searching for somewhere to stay. He would need to navigate on foot, somehow, the labyrinthine route the bus had taken from the centre of town to this shopping outpost. Approaching the check-out, he saw no clerks, but instead a self-serve bay monitored by a lone standing woman.

Thank god you're finished, the man yelled. Bon had tried to leave unnoticed, but hadn't been forgotten.

What are you going to do now? the man said.

Bon said he was going to walk back to town and find a room at a hotel or pub. And in the morning first thing, he would call in sick and catch the train home.

But the man just laughed: You can't walk back to town, you don't know the way. The way is complicated, and it's dark, and there are wild dogs and men.

Bon shrugged and kept marching, but the man stood and blocked his way.

That was how Bon came to move in with Steven Grady.

Bon could tell they were walking in the direction of the mountains because they moved towards the black, up gradually steeper hills. It was a poorly lit town. He couldn't tell how late it was, though the freestanding houses did not throw ambient light upon the streets.

Only Steven's cigarette, its cherry swaying at waist level and then, briskly, swollen and high, emitted any distinct light.

I've been to see my brother today, Steven said on the way. He's pulling through, but I can tell he's frightened still. He should leave town, move to the city. I always say to Jack: it's dangerous for you here, people know it's where you are. But he only shrugs. He doesn't care. He doesn't admit it, but I know he doesn't care, or else he'd be over the mountains. But you don't want to know why. No one would want to know why. It's disturbing. It's like a horror movie. I used to like watching horror movies, I used to love feeling scared. But nowadays I don't want to watch anything, I don't want to watch any new movies or new TV programs and especially not the news, and I don't want to talk to anyone who does. Do you watch TV, Bon? Best not mention what you see on it to me, because I don't want to know, unless you're talking about the classics. Nothing is as interesting as what my brother thinks, nothing is as fictional, his mind and phone are full of indescribable evil. Thanks to him, I know what can be shown on screens. I know the worst of what can be described. And I bet you're wondering what my brother has thought, and seen, and described, and shown me, but let me tell you, it makes perfect sense not to know. They say that all the time nowadays, *it's better not to know*, but they're being insincere, they're just pandering. They say it when they know you already know. And who are they, you're probably going to ask? Of course *they* don't say it, I'm only guessing that's what *they'd* say, *they* being logical people you've never met, people who enjoy being wise. But there are things that no one should know happens in the world, Bon. The world has gotten to that stage. And it's probably always been at that stage, but who are we to know, we're not *meant* to know, no one's *meant* to know, and it's of the utmost importance that we try not to know. There's no harm in knowing as little as possible. They say: learn. I say: pull your head in. It's now too easy to know.

Steven continued, like they were old friends: My brother still lives with my mother. He sits in his bedroom playing *Counter-Strike* against bots. He won't connect to the internet anymore. There was a time when Mum had tried to wean him off the screen, had tried to retrieve him from the forums and chat rooms, it came to be a problem, no one knew how to fix it. But there's not even a modem in the house now, no cabling. There's no data. But the problem hasn't gone away. He was stalked by him for months, a very stubbled, very large, very swollen-faced, very colossal man, his shadow would be everywhere and you could even see his features in it. This colossal man is a beast, he has too much hair, he has too much girth, he is incredibly large he's a filthy man. He always wears trackpants and sandals even in winter, and a simple fleece too large for him, its cuffs reach the tip of his longest finger, he wipes his nose with it. His hair wisps and weaves even on a still day, even when seated in his car. He always drives his car very slowly, a hatchback, its back window obscured by piles of boxes and tools and rubbish, torn and soiled rags, tied-off plastic bags full of who knows what. He's the Colossal Man, that's what I call him now. His face is either enraged or placid, never in-between, the latter always worse. But don't ask how Jack came to know or be targeted by the Colossal Man, Bon, ask only how he managed to lose his scent.

Bon wanted the man's rambling monologue to end. He wanted to make a polite getaway.

But he dutifully asked: how did Jack manage to lose the Colossal Man's scent?

Well, you have to keep it a secret, Steven said. After who knows how long of his lazy haunting, we followed him in his car one day, easy enough because he always drove slow enough to walk behind. We followed him from the plaza, and then up this hill and past my house, and then further up the last of the town's inclines into the mountains, and then onto an unsealed road between types of trees that we had never seen before, onto a road that we're sure had never been there on any day previous. We paced unseen among the tall trees and brambles as he drove very slowly up this rocky road, through dips of mud and low-hanging branches, occasionally around fallen rocks from the steep cliff to the south. Sometimes the brambles and foliage were so thick we'd need to take detours hundreds of metres off the road northerly, down the hill and then back up, crawling under and over fallen trunks, but when we re-emerged onto the side of the road the car was always there, it was impossible to lose it. And it was a long march in pursuit of the Colossal Man, it took some fifty minutes, but finally the hatchback stopped in a clearing before an old wooden cabin, surrounded by old barrels, old baths and random old mess. For a while he didn't get out of the car, which gave us time to take stock of the environment. It didn't look much like the scrub around here, it was denser and darker than even in the upper mountains, there was more mist. It felt as if, turning onto the Colossal Man's hidden unsealed road, we had crossed into a nether region of some kind, we were guided slowly into it, we had entered an invisible portal, the portal being the otherwise invisible or non-existent turn-off into the forest. It was a pretty average world into which to cross, it wasn't amazing. The trees seemed different but very little else did. If pushed to imagine what a world reached via portal would look like, I would have once guessed that everything would seem much stranger. I would have imagined a different civilisation. I would have imagined this civilisation not seeing us but being aware of us, and wanting somehow to dress us down.

Finally the Colossal Man squeezed out of his car, which was comically small for the size of this man. He carried his plastic bags of groceries towards the door of the cabin, stopping to take a breath every ten paces or so. When he went inside the cabin Jack and I crept around to the side without a window, waded through the trash – there was rubbish everywhere, grocery rubbish, empty packaging and leechlike plastic – and we listened for a while. The Colossal Man was just walking around the house, but we heard a generator loudly power on, and the noise gave us more freedom with our movement. After taking stock of the situation and psyching each other up, we crawled to the front of the house, crouched beneath the windowsill, and inched towards the front door. I picked up a nearby fence stake and gave Jack a large rock. Jack didn't know what to do with it. I told him to use his instinct. Then we hid them behind our backs, and I knocked.

It was a silly tactic because the Colossal Man surely never had visitors. The Colossal Man lived on a road which didn't and doesn't exist. It's not on maps, paper or online, and satellite images don't show a clearing. I knocked again and there was shuffling inside, so I called out: police! and there was more shuffling inside. And then I counted down from five in a dramatic military way: five, four, three, two...but I didn't count to one because that's a strategy, you see, a single moment off guard can be useful during a confrontation.

I crashed through the door and Jack stepped over me, but he was too stupid or too cool to act confrontational. Inside there was a large bed and a small kitchenette and a computer, but everywhere else there was just trash, food scraps, tossed wrappings and soiled clothes, and probably the corpses of rats because it stank like death. A mat on the ground had been pulled aside and a trapdoor lifted, the Colossal Man had escaped into the earth. But before we followed I addressed the computer, spent a full half-hour smashing it to pieces, breaking its three solid-state drives up into the smallest pieces I could manage, submerging the pieces in a bucket of water and then, outside, while Jack sentried the trapdoor, piling the refuse into one of the old drums and siphoning a bit of petrol out of the Colossal Man's hatchback with my mouth and a bit of hose. I set the barrel alight. During the long period I spent at work my adrenaline wore off, and Jack made it clear that following the Colossal Man down the trapdoor, and into the dark unknown of whatever lay down there, might not be such a good idea. So what do you suggest, I yelled at him when I finally managed to speak. The Colossal Man will just re-emerge, I had said, and follow more doggedly than ever before. He'll seek compensation for our having destroyed the computer.

It's true we didn't approach it wisely. We hadn't factored in the possibility that the Colossal Man might have an opportunity to outmanoeuvre us. But had I meant to kill him? I don't know. Jack reckons I did and it freaked him out, he's still freaked out. Merely bashing him wouldn't have helped much. We sat at the mouth of the trapdoor and had a smoke. I yelled down some profanity, Jack played calm. I told the Colossal Man that staying down there would mean certain death because we wouldn't leave until he climbed back out – you'll starve down there, I yelled. But there was no sound or evidence of movement, we didn't know how deep the trapdoor went, or where it went. And besides, the sun outside was going to set, soon. We turned on the cabin light and the room lit up a harsh blue fluorescent, but it didn't illuminate the hole at all. So what I did was I dragged the Colossal Man's bed onto the closed trapdoor, and then stacked every large and loose belonging I could find on top of it.

We left the cabin and started in the direction from which we had come. But Jack wanted to explore beyond the cabin, he must have wanted to see what lay at the far edge of the small clearing. Maybe he was too psyched up to go home and drink beer, but maybe he also expected to find something down there. Or, maybe he knew it would be a shortcut – you never know what Jack knows. So we walked down the decent slope, and came upon another little track leading farther into the woods, wide and clear enough that it must surely have led somewhere. The sky was a dull orange and we only had a matter of time, so we sprinted for a while down this track, racing the sun, compelled towards this investigation because though we never discussed it, we both believed the Colossal Man's hidden road would no longer exist the next day. We ran but mostly fell, the track was steep and winding, and it felt like our bodies had become vehicles we could barely control, until finally the path flattened out, and then, at the foot of this track, a dead end of brambles appeared. We pushed or fell through and then, to our surprise, emerged onto the football field of the Catholic school. It was a fortunate shortcut because the night had fallen proper.

We exited the portal there, Steven said. That's what I reckon. But it didn't take us back to our origin, the portal didn't return us, but rather, it led us into yet another region. We're living in a different version of the town now, a version that you (what's your name? Bon), must be a native of. And that's why I'm being so nice to you, Bon, because I'm a visitor in your land. And you're a visitor in my land, except it's a different version of my land. I know the layout, the street map, the illusions. But neither of us are where we think we are, though you haven't even stopped to wonder, I bet, whether you're where you're meant to be or not.

Steven asked Bon, as he turned his key in the door of a weatherboard house, and pushed it open onto a pitch-black hall: Do you remember having passed through any portals? Do you remember anything changing?

Bon considered it for a moment, and for the growing duration of the moment, lost track of what he'd been asked. From the rubble of all he could remember of Steven's speech, he started to compose a response that seemed fitting.

But in the end, failing that, he just said: Yes.

Steven could have passed for a teenager if not for his balding scalp. He never walked, he scrambled, usually he was seated. He smoked with his thumb and index finger and he never listened, though he always sat forward with furrowed brows. His eyes conspired and he was eager to confide, giant oaken pupils burst against their sockets, and in his red-coursed whites there was a stubborn kind of lack.

In the windowless lounge room, a mantelpiece over the disused fireplace displayed carefully placed spirits bottles, red and black candle wax melted down the sides. It was otherwise barren, save a mattress re-purposed as a couch, stacked with pillows and cushions and junk. A framed hand-drawn illustration of Chewbacca hung above the mattress, and just to its left, a crooked old magazine poster depicted five men in rap metal garb hunched over low-rider bicycles. Steven collapsed onto the mattress, patted the clearing besides, and muttered 'fuck me dead'. Bon sat and folded his hands. Whenever Steven lit a smoke he guarded the flame tense as if against a gale. Then he exhaled serene, and from a navy plastic bag tore out two stubbies of beer, opened both with the butt of a lighter, and passed one to Bon.

So you got off the train in Newnes, Steven said.

Bon responded yes in a formal kind of voice.

Far be it from me to tell you what's on your mind, Steven continued. But I reckon if you've gotten off the train now then you've made a decision to stay. I've seen it before. People always get off the train here, but only once they notice the stop exists at all. It takes a certain kind of looking, a certain mood, to notice the train stopping here. But they get back on for whatever reason.

He blew smoke through pursed lips.

I know you won't though, not that it matters to me. I'm just saying that I can tell you won't. I couldn't care less why you got off the train in Newnes and that's me being honest. I'm not polite you'll need to accept that. I say whatever's on my mind politically correct or not. Don't tell me why you got off the train, I've heard people's reasons before and none have ever needed to justify themselves to me.

He picked up a guitar and played an elaborate riff, then put it down again. It would have been a polite time for Bon to leave, but it was past midnight, and far too late to board a train or replacement bus. Anyway, the beer had gone straight to his head.

I've caught the train before, Steven said. Up and down the

mountains and even into the city. In the city they get loose, but in the mountains they get looser still, they're all so keen to get hammered. Boy did we used to get hammered, Steven said. And you could say we're getting hammered at this very moment, because I've already swilled four beers with no sign of stopping. But we're not getting hammered at all. This is not getting hammered, Steven said, this is getting drunk.

They sat side by side staring at the wall.

Steven said that at some indistinguishable point in the not-too-distant past, his drinking sessions had come to result in drunkenness rather than the effect of being hammered. Bon asked what the difference was, though he thought he had an idea. But Steven said that once upon a time, getting hammered seemed a vehicle for something, seemed to drive him towards some transcendental moment. Maybe love, he said. Maybe fame in a globally popular metal band. But a grey pallor had coated everything. You know what I mean? Steven said. It could have been for a number of reasons that 'a grey pallor had coated everything', but Bon didn't press Steven and never would, because Steven preferred to be understood.

The problem is I left and came back, Steven said. I left, moved to Orange to work at the mines. I had a nice rental property in a nice new suburb off the Northern Distributor. I could decorate it however I wanted. I was making enough that eventually I could start to pay off a similar house of my own, with three bedrooms and a nice open-plan living area so that I could watch TV while cooking. I made some friends at the mines, some that even liked music. I worked shifts – seven days on then seven days off – and during the seven straight days off I spent my time in the backyards of all the men I had met on my shifts, drinking and watching football games. Or else we'd gather in their garages, decorated with the posters of liquor brands and motorsport legends, usually also a dartboard. I wasn't unhappy in the job because it was a job, and everyone has a job. Not having a job is worse than having one, people look down on you if you're without. Having a job is a normal part of life. Rich people, poor people...they have jobs. It's part of what they mean by freedom. Freedom is not running naked in fields, it's not driving a convertible with the roof down, wind in your hair, blaring techno on your way to a party. That is only in film clips and dreams. Freedom is having a job and not being bashed. And that's fine, money is what makes the world go around and that's just that. At some early stage I would have thought to myself: wouldn't it be nice to have lots of money, but equally, at some early stage I would have thought: wouldn't it be nice to live a life of pure chaos, as part of a major metal band in the global metal industry, or even just as a loser with no job. You see what I mean? Life is all about rhythm if you ask me, it's all about tension and release, repetition, inter-cut with the occasional wild night. Your rhythm is either a speed metal song or it's a doom metal song.

Steven said he and Bon were living a doom metal kind of life.

He picked his guitar up, hit a deep chord, and let it ring dim for some thirty seconds. Then he hit it again.

You have to admit, Steven said, that we're living a doom metal kind of life. And that's fine, he said. But I wanted to live a speed metal kind of life. It was possible to imagine back at the mines that I was made for this, that one day I would no longer be working at the mines. And if this had come to pass – which it did, but not in the manner I had hoped – then it would give people cause to think: isn't it great, isn't it noble, that this person once worked at the little old mines. Chipping away (it's not a matter of chipping away anymore, Steven added) and then later, a hero among those remaining, among those who continue to chip away. I would become a kind of hero, so heroic, so capable of carrying myself in the correct fashion, that my former colleagues and others would never detect some air that made me seem above it all. I would always be tipping my hat to them in my proper speed metal life, in a language not so different to this, one which could not be mistaken as smarter or better. Even the bosses, the corporate movers-and-shakers, the stakeholders and potentially the CEO, would think to themselves: there are people in this mine who are overall more interesting and talented than us, and so we should stop doing random drug tests and we should stop laying people off. They might announce it at some symposium: *We have generated among our staff a man so capable, so intelligent and talented, that it would only make sense, from this day forward, for us to place the utmost faith in every person willing to work at this mine.* From then on, they would no longer believe the miners to be mere workers: they'd believe them to be up-and-coming go-getters, specialists in a field, disruptors in a field. The bosses, corporate movers-and-shakers, stakeholders and CEO would make an effort to dine with me, and at first I would be sceptical and dismissive, but eventually I'd have to submit, because it would be my responsibility to the miners. On the night of my scheduled dinner with these vaunted figures, all the various miners and workers, the administrators and electricians and diggers, the cleaners and et cetera, would fantasise about how the dinner might play out. And I would be sure to make their fantasies close to the truth.

He paused his speech to play an especially complex passage on the guitar. His nostrils flared and his eyes locked onto the collar around Bon's shirt. It was another cue for Bon to leave, only if he left now, he'd be sleeping in a park.

Sleeping in the park might be preferable. Bon sat up, dusted his legs, and stood to leave, but the beer rushed to his head so he sat back down.

Then Steven said: You know how everything has changed and we're only now noticing? You know how we've quietly passed into a new real? I'm not an idiot, Bon, I know there's something sinister about the mood around town. My dreams are violent, and I dream them every night. Even when I'm drunk. Sometimes there's a certain type of breeze in the air that terrifies me. And the faces of people in the street seem mortified, don't you think? They seem desperate, like hungry dogs. It's true that something has happened.

He pushed the guitar off his lap. His head fell onto Bon's shoulder, and he closed his eyes.

Bon woke in horror well past midday. After a long time dreading it, he looked at his phone. There were dozens of missed calls, many texts he feared to read, and the working day had long started. Steven had toppled over sideways on the couch, and when Bon got up, he mercifully didn't stir.

He crept for the front door. From Steven's hilltop front yard, the lower part of town was submerged in a spectral morning mist. Bon followed the street towards the town, around a cliff-side bend, then down another hill between rows of webbed terrace houses. After this hill, the road flattened and the houses looked more modern: brick and single-storey with browned grass yards. Newnes was cement still, only the thrum of distant highway traffic animated it.

The old blast-furnace ruins were his guide and he weaved through the streets towards them, but in his way were grids of homes and closed dusty shopfronts, empty lots and overgrown lawn. Wending through the suburbs he became lost, and the ruins had sunk out of view. Train brakes wheezed in the distance and he couldn't tell their direction. But it didn't matter: he had all afternoon to jump aboard.

Soon the streets began to widen. A long half-moon road led out of the residential area and onto a four-lane artery, lined on one side with featureless grass and on the other, the interminable asphalt fields surrounding the Newnes Valley Plaza. It seemed to take a good half-hour to clear the area around the plaza, and despite the early autumn cold a strange heat emanated from it. But Bon endured, past the plaza, through another canyon of terraces, and onto the west end of the long main street, where a rare lush green park framed a disused theatre across the road. It was here where, having barely reached the centre of town proper, Bon felt a familiar presence. Steven was standing directly behind him, hand shading brow. He took Bon by the wrist, held it for a while, then trapped him in a pitiful embrace.

Locked inside this hug – not a pleasant hug, but not an alarming one – Bon tried to formulate a valid excuse in the event he boarded the train again. But there was no making excuses nowadays. They probably somehow knew, already, that he had voluntarily left the station. He would need to live with everyone knowing he had voluntarily left the station, and he would become not a hidden but a known problem case. All trust and faith: lost, just like that. He was too far gone. He'd done his dash.

With barely a word they turned around and walked back up the hill.

Bon wiped his phone, removed the sim, dropped it in a Salvos bin.

Bon had sometimes daydreamed about disembarking at Newnes and getting drunk alone. In his fantasy, he would walk into the closest pub. It was a grandiose pub split over many levels, but still retaining the lazy mood common in regional pubs. In his fantasy, the pub had an outdoor smoking area at the back, and in his fantasy he'd buy a full jug of beer and take his chances, hoping he would find a seat in the smoking area and not have to stand. In his fantasy he always found a seat in the smoking area, a corrugated-iron-fenced concrete courtyard, abuzz with all the various machinery required to operate pubs. Out there, in the smoking area, Bon would have a whole table to himself. He would take a seat, pour his beer, light his smoke, browse a newspaper, maybe even a book, and drink the beer as quickly or slowly as he desired. In his fantasy, the beer garden would not be so busy that he'd need to strategise leaving his sought-after seat to go to the bar. He would sit at this table alone and drink two whole jugs or maybe more, while reading a newspaper or a book. Occasionally he'd stare into the distance, ruminating on what he had read, and whatever he happened to stare at would seem awash in melting calm. Then, at exactly the time he might start to become bored or lonely, a person or maybe two would request to share his table, a person or two not too drunk and not too boring – a person or two who comprised his vision of an ideal companion, or companions, at a pub. Then, after some preliminary banter with these strangers, possibly about sports or TV but ideally not current affairs, Bon would have an opportunity to explain, at great length, his position in the world and how he had arrived at it. In reality, he'd never been capable of holding forth in this way, he'd never had sufficient reason to explain himself to anyone. But under these circumstances, in his fantasy, he is given the floor; maybe one of these ideal companions would say: I can detect a glare in your eye that foretells a lesson learned. And he would have to say in response to this, that no lessons can be learned from me, that I am no authority, that I can only provide the raw facts and have you – the ideal companions – draw your own conclusions. He would do so offhandedly and not in an arrogant or wise kind of way. But these ideal companions would beckon him to start right from the very beginning, they would want his whole story, every possible detail, with some window-dressing to boot (go nuts, they might say), and so he would submit. How did you get here, they might ask, to this concrete beer garden, and what were the circumstances that gave rise to you getting here? Bon would make an effort to oblige them, but instead of plainly stating his story he would make an effort to tell them about everything he had once thought himself capable of, and how he had been proved wrong. And then he would add that, actually, it's not worthwhile studying oneself too closely, and his manner of not self-studying – when you think about it – is the way it should be. He hoped his telling them this would prove that he was not as selfish as he must surely appear. He had tried his best, he would say to the ideal companions. He used to try his very best. They'd only coax him to continue though, at which point, he would tell them that no story of his was worth their time. But they would persevere: What were the circumstances ('and tell us in great detail') that led to you drinking these numerous jugs in this concrete beer garden in a town you have no life in? Reluctantly but eagerly he could only tell them that, come to think of it, it was because of a critical failing. And in response to this the ideal companions would only want to know him even more, they would admire his confession. But Bon would shake his head. He would instead deliver a casual epitaph, so casual as to not resemble one, an epitaph for the dream version of himself, a version that can see far into his future and others' futures, the futures of loved ones and even disliked ones, and not detect a boundary. Maybe it would be something as simple as: I only wanted for things to stay normal.

Evenings they drank beer and Steven would talk. He would cycle through a list of topics ranging across his brother, his work prospects, and the end of the world. Sometimes his speeches arrived at questions, but Bon would always say he didn't know.

I don't know, Bon would say. Or else he'd say: I'm not sure. Sometimes he'd shrug in an empathetic kind of way, or so he thought. And Steven would appear satisfied.

They'd start drinking around three in the afternoon and keep doing so until nine. It was around this time when Steven would pick up his guitar and muddle his words trying to speak and play at the same time. This was Bon's signal to go to bed, though he'd always need to tear himself away from Steven's clutches, because Steven never liked a cosy moment to end.

Bon was content to listen to Steven, though to call it listening was wrong: Steven's speech passed over him like the din of rapids. He begged no response, though sometimes he dropped a rhetorical question, an answer for which Bon would momentarily struggle towards. Steven always saved him the effort by continuing on, and this suited Bon, because he had never been happy with anything he had said in his adult life.

But there was always still a time for bed. After much complaint, Steven would let him sleep.

Of a morning they'd lurch out of bed and sit in the lounge room. They'd sit there quiet and sick. After half an hour or sometimes more, Steven would announce his intention to go on some excursion, usually to search for hidden roads and pathways. Later on he'd return hungry, and they'd walk together to the Newnes Valley Plaza, which held within its walls everything one could ever desire. The men didn't keep groceries in the house, they preferred to make daily trips to the plaza, for cheese rolls or half-chickens or plastic tubs of tabouli. They'd eat these in the food court, a shadow of its former self, for the surrounding restaurants and eateries had long shut, save a bakery and a café, the latter stocked with sponge rolls and quiches and Danish tarts.

But the food court was, at least, a vast open area in the centre of the plaza, filled with seats and tables, designed to be sat in. And so they sat in it, even while few others did: mainly the elderly catching their breath, one hand on their canvas wheel bags, or mothers with children shouting over reverberant shopping centre music.

Steven announced one day, as he brushed Coles's donut cinnamon onto the tiles of the Newnes Valley Plaza food court, that secret roads and pathways appear, but then they close up.

There's no route to the Colossal Man anymore, he said. I can no longer find the road we took. And I've since discovered, or rather I've remembered, that roads and pathways have been opening and then closing again all my life. Hidden roads and pathways don't register to most, but now I'm on the lookout. I know to pay attention, because unlike most others I've actually wandered one, I've actually sprinted one. Strange roads and pathways have been appearing all my life: memories of them appearing, previously lost to time, are newly recollected. Having wandered and sprinted a spectral road and then a spectral pathway, I've since been capable of remembering all of the times in my life when I've seen – not noticed, but *seen* without *noticing* – avenues and routes that aren't officially there, roads and pathways that don't exist confidently. Now that I tell you this, Bon, now that I've revealed to you the existence of these roads and pathways, you might even remember having seen one yourself. You might have been in the backseat of your mother's car, in the distant past, on the way home from the shops, peering out the window – maybe you were strapped into a booster seat – and maybe you felt rather than saw that something was amiss, or rather, that something had been added. Am I conjuring buried memories in you now, Bon? Have you known the way to the shops but never cared to pay attention to the way an expanse is patched together? If you've ever quietly noticed a road or pathway that you'd never previously noticed, did you ever return to that spot, did you ever confirm that it was confidently there?

Bon had to admit, with utmost confidence, having spent a moment thinking, that he didn't know whether he'd ever seen a road or pathway that wasn't confidently there.

Well now you know to keep an eye out, Steven said. They definitely exist. Look at the bigger picture: maps can't be accurate, they simply can't be. Cartographers may argue otherwise, and it's true that satellite maps seem to corroborate the lay of the land as depicted on public maps. But why does everything feel different now? The feeling that things are different, in theory, doesn't mean the world is actually different. Feelings versus facts, I understand the difference, everyone understands the difference, we're always told: look at the facts, forget your feelings. At most, a feeling might mean that something has changed. But the world is not just changed *it's different*, everything *is different*, it's a different world. Nothing: no object, no building, no road, no face, no origin or destination is reliably familiar. The world looks the same but it's foreign: I can't possibly be in the same place that I was some twenty years ago, back when I was a child and the streets felt alive. At the very least, maps should nowadays be viewed upside down or from a certain different angle. Have you ever wondered how a map would look if it oriented west at the bottom, north to the left?

Bon, shaken, scrambled to reply, but needn't have bothered.

I can't be in the same place I was back then, Steven continued, riding in the backseat of my mother's car, a child strapped into its booster seat, looking out upon a world which, trust me on this, is simply gone. And we wouldn't be having this conversation, Bon, were it not for the fact that I have wandered and sprinted hidden roads and pathways. Were it not for the fact that I have and that I did – and that since then, everything has been different – we would not be having this conversation.

Bon and Steven stared at the muted food-court TV. A montage of yacht-race disasters aired on the screen.

In the afternoons Newnes bore the air of exhaustion; in the absence of mist its truth was revealed. Bon would buy them beer because they always needed it. They'd break the carton apart on the tarmac of the car park and separate the six-packs into manageable canvas shopping bags. It was always an event to see passers-by, Steven never failed to comment. Maybe a woman carried more than was healthy for her back. Maybe Steven had known someone who had put their back out. He might have done so himself, before. Maybe the labouring woman used to work at the Cignall.

By mid-afternoon they'd wander back up the hill. If Bon needed to drop his bags and take a break, Steven would pat him on the back.

It's okay to take a rest, Steven always said.

We'll get this beer up the hill eventually, we won't be killed or hospitalised. And then we'll have a drink.

Whenever Bon doubted Steven's sincerity he only needed look him in the face. His face was unhinged for its sincerity, and his words abruptly turned from candid fool to grand recital. It took a while before Bon was certain of its truth. Somehow, all the preliminaries between them had been skipped, and in a funny way, it felt as if Steven inhabited a region of Bon's interior, or at the very least had visited it. In light of this natural affinity, and for lack of need to dally on neutral ground, Bon came to look upon Steven as a plant, a struggling yet enduring, ornamental kind of plant. He could take pleasure in watching as circumstances brushed against him.

Steven's eyes and words lurched through emotions like a plant bends and folds with a breeze. It was more interesting to watch Steven than it was to hear whatever he said. Steven's collaborations with breezes compelled Bon towards an awkward type of affection.

Even when Steven became angry or frustrated, as during one evening when his fingers were too cold to roll a smoke, Bon felt a flurry in his chest – the flurry of amused affection. He watched as Steven struggled. As frustration ascended to rage Bon refrained from intervention. He watched as Steven scrunched the paper and tobacco in his fist and tossed it indignantly into the air. Then, without teaching or guiding him – without a word at all – Bon would roll one and pass it.

In the weeks that followed his disembarking the train, Bon's dreams were gradually accompanied by versions of Steven. Even his most elliptical and nonsensical dreams featured varieties of him. Steven was never a subject, more an omnipresent ally.

Bon did not dream in first nor third person but rather somewhere indescribably between, and even if Steven's body and face were absent he was always there, never as a shape, usually as a gentle directive. Bon never remembered the events of his dreams, but in Newnes dreams he always recalled being in lock step with Steven, that was his only recollection. It wasn't for the love of Steven's person in particular, it wasn't for the love of his skin. It was for a love that yearned for a dream version of Steven, his dream smell and his dream being, his plant being, his child version. In the light of day he couldn't exactly describe that dream smell nor the dream being, and if he was being honest with himself (it took concerted effort) he could see how, within dreams, it was possible to reach a certain apex of sensation with regards to Steven, an insoluble kind of love. A plant kind of love, a swollen fondness, an affection, something that *only just* catalysed a drive towards intervention. It spilled over into waking life, despite the man's body and his face.

And it appeared as if Steven loved him too. The way he latched at the end of their binges, and the way he'd always be there in the morning at the foot of the bed, ushering him to rise. What a hopeless man, Bon would think. What a thoroughly harmless man.

Every morning Steven would say that his brother Jack was moving in that day. Steven had to go and pick him up, and each afternoon was reserved for it. But whenever the time arrived there seemed a decent enough reason to delay it.

Bon hadn't met Jack but didn't look forward to it, even after Steven had explained that his presence wouldn't make much difference, because Jack barely said a word. It wasn't because he had nothing to say – Steven reckoned he had a lot to say. The reason Jack didn't speak, theorised Steven, was because every sequence of words he uttered seemed derived from an influence he wasn't fond of. And through the saying of words, the substance of them deteriorated.

He thinks everything he says sounds too much like something else, Steven said. If Jack were to express anger in any kind of way, the mere expressing of it would make him more angry. If he stubs his toe, his instinct might be to keel over and grab it, and possibly to swear. But that's the way people in films behave when they stub their toe. So instead of keeling over, swearing, nursing the toe... he *almost does it,* but resists, stands there, fumes. And it's not just extreme emotions. You can't blame Jack for feeling reluctant to say, for example, 'I love you', or 'I'm sorry'. He might mean it, but the moment he says it, he realises that the way he's said it is derivative. People have feared saying those things incorrectly since the beginning of time, but for Jack, he fears that he might be mistaken for referencing some moment. He is petrified of the glint of recognition in another's eyes. What if the person on the receiving end of that 'I love you', or that 'I'm sorry', is put in mind of a similar moment in a film? Or worse, a similar moment enacted by a father or a brother? That's punishing to Jack, he cannot tolerate it. He hates not being original.

Think of the way people say things in films, Steven said. They say things between profound silences. Jack hates profound silences and he hates for his words to culminate in climax or significance. Significance, climaxes and profound silences all belong to films and the elderly. He can't transcend words, Bon, but text can transcend words – Jack loves to type. But the moment he vocalises something he means, it ceases to be meaningful. I say to Jack: Yes, maybe us bantering together sounds like a movie where two brothers banter, and maybe there's not much we can do about that. But then I say to Jack: Silence is the most laboured kind of significance! Think of all the silence in films! Think of all the instances in books where there's 'a moment of silence'! My theory makes him rage, Bon, only he's getting better and better every day at not appearing enraged.

Bon couldn't sit at home alone while Steven searched for hidden roads and pathways. Some mornings they'd emerge onto the front steps together, mop poles hung over shoulders.

These were the mornings their drinking started early. They'd walk down the hill and into the side streets, beers in hand towards the forest exterior. At the sight of a gum-green barrier Steven would march. He'd thresh the poles of mops or rakes or brooms through brambles at the foot of freshly guttered cul-de-sac streets. He searched lazily, did so out of habit. Bon suspected Steven only ever threshed and pulled when he was present – in Bon's absence he probably just sat and smoked. But whenever Bon did join Steven, the latter selected a random route through the sloped streets, following no clues nor hunches. He'd beat the foliage until spent.

During one of their expeditions, Bon and Steven turned off the road linking the highway to the town centre proper. They passed through an arched brick train-line underpass, and on the other side was a beautiful, winding, softly sandy road. It was a beautiful road, Bon thought, because along each side were lines of giant trees, thick and vibrant, with shades of green rarely seen west of the mountains. The trunks were a mellow brown. These trees – he didn't know what kind of trees they were – seemed likely to house small communities of furry animals. They were the type of tree illustrated in children's picture books. Standing at the foot of this winding road, the sun shone directly through the thinner edges of the branches and into Bon's eyes. Around these thinner edges, the deep green leaves surrendered to the oncoming winter, bunches appeared to glow with a regal shade of orange. And on the far side of each of these lines of trees lay immaculate fields of grass.

Bon was so paralysed by the sight he didn't want to walk further. He feared the ethereal filtered sunlight might too quickly be dispelled. Steven stood too. Bon gestured at the road, raised a brow at Steven. Steven shook his head, but continued to just stand.

It's the most beautiful road in Newnes, Steven said. He took a few steps to the left, to stand firmly in the centre of the foot of the beautiful road.

It's a magical road, isn't it Bon? And magical all the more for the fact that there's nothing to do here, magical all the more for the fact it goes nowhere. The road just peters off into rough grass and then there's a stormwater drain. Across the stormwater drain, there's a strip of brown grass and a line of Colorbond fence and then some houses. Whoever built this road, Bon, did so because they knew this to be a beautiful location for a road, and likewise, they must have known that it was a beautiful and suitable place for these trees. Never mind that this road could not possibly go anywhere, because it would be a waste of this space not to have such a beautiful road. There are no statues or signs or anything else celebrating what this road commemorates. It's just here, beautifully commemorating nothing.

Steven sat down, crossed his legs, started to roll a smoke.

I'm sorry I haven't shown you this road before, he said. I've led you to gullies and to overgrown abandoned backyards, I've led you to the empty ratty terrace lots, all in search of hidden roads and pathways. We lunch on donuts at the food court, but I never once thought to lunch beside this beautiful road. I'm glad you love this road. But also, what's the point of seeing it? Do you think you might pitch a tent here and live forever? It's a long walk from my house to this road, a good half-hour. Odds are, you'll love and appreciate the beauty of this road, but you'll rarely or never visit it again. The walk to this road might be full of anticipation and joy, but once reached, and once this road is merely looked at, you'll need to walk back home, and the walk home will frustrate you. You'll continue to know the road's here, but knowing this will only cause you pain, because you'll look at our street and our house and our weeded backyard and think: this is a pathetic sight, I want to be closer to the beautiful road. So maybe, if you still had your phone you would take a photo of it. And you would look at your photo while sitting in our lounge room drinking beer of an evening. And maybe you'd spark a conversation: how about that beautiful road? But fuck the road, Bon. It's frustrating that the road leads nowhere, it's frustrating that I have no reason to walk it. I have to go out of my way to see this road, it's not a part of my environment, and it's not on the way to anywhere I could go. More frustrating is that I don't own the road. How can you continue to love this beautiful road if you cannot inhabit it forever? You'll never have your fill of this beautiful road...the moment we turn away to walk back into town, you'll feel wistful about leaving the road, and you'll want to come back. But there's no bed in the road, there's no roof and there's nowhere to sit. The moment you get here is the moment you wanted, and if you linger – like we are now – you'll only be forcing yourself to appreciate the road, you'll only be pretending. You'll be underwhelmed by the beautiful road. It's an underwhelming road.

Steven got up and dusted himself off. They turned back towards the major road. Bon was determined not to explain that he had never seen this beautiful road, nor the vast green fields, when he'd previously passed daily from the vantage point of the train line.

Bon woke late one morning because Steven didn't wake him. He rested for a while, tried to appreciate resting. The light outside scolded, a certain throb of guilt commenced. Then came the sound of glass shattering, so he got up.

It was Steven's weekly routine, ever since the garbage removal trucks had stopped coming, to shatter all their empties on the cement in the backyard. He'd sweep the shards into a great pile, collect them with dustpan and broom, and launch them into the rusted garden shed at the back of the yard.

There was a woman outside diligently sweeping. Steven watched her with two bottles in hand, both raised to his shoulders. When Bon emerged no introductions were made. Steven looked at him with faint alarm; the woman just nodded. Bon nodded back, watched for a while, then retreated to his room. It had been over a month since he had spoken to anyone but Steven. And when it came to speaking to Steven, one rarely spoke at all.

Later she was still there. Steven hadn't left to find hidden roads and pathways, he sat in the lounge room with the woman, who listened as he delivered his speech about the difference between doom and speed metal types of lives. Bon had wasted all those hours standing in his bedroom: he could have used the time to formulate his sentences, he could have figured out what he would say. He had wasted all that time, rehearsing how to walk with seeming confidence into the room.

So he improvised a practical reason to interrupt: he told Steven that it was getting near evening and soon the hot food at Coles would be reduced.

Steven looked at him as if for the first time. And then seemed to remember.

We don't need to go to the plaza today, he said, because last night after you went to bed I felt lonely, so I walked down there by myself. Lesley was there, she got off the train like you. She bought these finger buns on special, a packet of cabanossi and this bag of lettuce leaves. Not a feast, but neither are muesli bars and cheese rolls. So we're sorted for food, Bon, and Lesley helped me carry this whole carton of beer up the hill last night. Didn't you, Lesley?

She nodded and said yes.

Bon looked her in the eyes for an acceptable length of time, or so he thought. But she was unwilling or unable to explain any further.

She wore stern expressions with soft eyes and she often just stared. For the first few nights, Bon and Lesley sat shoulder-to-shoulder facing Steven. They didn't speak at length; Steven was the focus. Bon couldn't tell whether Lesley liked him or not, her attitude towards him was unclear. The fact of her being there warranted no mention, and during the times when he found himself alone with Steven, Bon couldn't muster the courage to question it. If he grovelled for answers all might irrevocably change.

Lesley was about their age, with curly brown hair tied back

functionally, and a lock or two always in her face. Bon and Steven towered over her but she looked formidably strong. Her face betrayed a tiredness she tried to hide, and she wore all blue: jeans, blouse, and cardigan.

She wasn't the kind of person Bon would ever notice – she was an invisible shade of blue. She was as inconspicuous as his adult self had ended up, but she wasn't dressed for any kind of work – she had turned up on a Sunday. Wherever her previous stops had been on the train ride, neither had demanded appearances.

Bon sat and listened and Lesley listened too. She listened closer to Steven than Bon ever had. She sat upright and forward, and her expressions reacted tactfully to everything he said. That she managed to do so was impressive. She navigated Steven's sudden shifts and rhetorical traps with a grace verging balletic. Bon, on the other hand, had taken to slumping, and becoming transfixed by the walls. It was ludicrous that Lesley tried so hard, or at all.

Steven made no effort to acquaint them, though he appeared to scrutinise the way they interacted. Bon could have sworn, when receiving a cigarette lighter from Lesley, when feeling her hand against his, that Steven studied this action. But it wasn't consistent with other patterns.

As much as Bon would have liked to ask, *why is there a woman now*, the topic never arose at the plaza, and it never arose when they searched for hidden roads and pathways. Steven would bloom and flourish or else darken and wilt in keeping with patterns long established. He'd collapse into laughter at the slightest thing, such as the hapless demeanour of an old man. And he'd incessantly reveal himself in every which way, though rare were the references to his material life. It was as if he and Bon inhabited parallel worlds, separate worlds so perfectly aligned that they communed seamlessly across an existential gulf. Far be it from Bon to cast a rock into the whirlwind of Steven, far be it from him to disturb his plane. It wasn't his role to select the topics of conversation, so he could only wait and see whether Steven found the woman's presence as strange as Bon did. Because there was a certain bend in his shoulder blades, a certain hollow in his neck, an aloofness in his gait, that made Bon want to keep him just the way he was.

One morning soon after her arrival, Bon found Lesley sitting on the front steps browsing through a catalogue. It was one of the dozens of catalogues that had accumulated at the doorstep and around the garden path; she perused its bright pages with Omo and Cheetos and Macro Organics branding. Bon had already formulated what he would say to Lesley, and felt so confident in his formulation that he dared initiate the conversation. In keeping with his long-gestated plan, Bon listed off all the major topics pertaining to Steven: the Colossal Man, the hidden roads and pathways, and his brother Jack. He asked Lesley for her opinion on each of these. She said she supposed that some of it, if not all of it, was of great concern indeed. But how could anything be of great concern to her anymore, Bon wondered, if she had disembarked at Newnes?

She was seated on the steps and Bon was standing over her. He crept into her line of sight and squatted in the grass, started fiddling with it. He couldn't figure out whether she really thought it was of great concern indeed. He couldn't tell what her face was trying to convey. When she tossed the catalogue aside it was an invitation for Bon to keep talking, but he couldn't improvise, he'd spent his reserve.

All these deals have expired, he said.

So they collected some catalogues up and tossed them into the shed.

She was on the steps again the morning after, reading another catalogue. He sat beside her and delivered what he had rehearsed.

He said that he'd once daydreamed about building his own hidden road or pathway for Steven. He had envisioned waking in the dead of night, retrieving a pair of hedge-clippers, and dashing off to the forest at the top of the road. In his imagination he didn't need a light: he would simply feel with his hands and his legs the thickest and most impenetrable wall of foliage. He would start snipping away at this foliage, in and through. He would continue to do so for many evenings, and then he would spend many evenings after that snipping a large clearing, a substantial destination. And then, on the day he was satisfied that his hidden road or pathway was long enough, and that the destination at the end was substantial enough, he would suggest to Steven that they should search up the hill, rather than down. Steven would protest, he reckoned, because Steven doesn't like to walk up hills. But Bon would gently insist, and because Steven wasn't used to anyone gently insisting, he would submit. Eventually they would discover this new route torn afresh in the otherwise thick green wall around the cul-de-sac.

I couldn't even imagine his relief, Bon said to Lesley, absorbed by his role-play. Can you imagine it? When I try to imagine it, it fills me with satisfaction. I start to imagine doing it, actually going out there and building a hidden road or pathway. And it wouldn't be an illusion, it wouldn't be a trick, because the road and the clearing would exist, and having cut a path into a clearing, into a destination previously absent, the mere existence of it might help him see what's next. He could feel changed, and so, be changed.

But in reality, I would need far more than a hedge trimmer, Bon sighed, with well-meaning futility. And I would need far more muscle than a single man can have. The forests are full of fallen branches and rotted trunks; foxes, snakes and vagrants too. And anyway, what would I put in the clearing?

Lesley nodded. Her languor had turned into genuine curiosity and Bon felt victorious. It was interesting to see these movements across her face, because her face normally rested just north of despondence, or else shone with a dim sentimentality. Bon wondered whether he hadn't misinterpreted her: maybe it was *her* who was the desperate one. Maybe she desired *his* welcome. Suddenly, Bon saw in her something akin to a lone child kicking dirt in a field.

You'd definitely need to have something for him to find in the clearing, Lesley said.

Bon laughed nervously, but Lesley didn't look amused.

When they met on the steps each morning, Bon was inclined to tell Lesley everything about himself, because unlike Steven, she left silences he felt pressured to fill.

The whole scenario had changed with her arrival. He didn't understand her; he didn't know what to do or say around her. He was troubled by her listening, her interest, her *trying*. Sometimes Bon would ambush her with a glance, and noticing this, Lesley would rapidly adopt a peaceable expression, something gentler than the sad frown she wore when she thought no one was watching. It was near impossible to block her out, harder still to resist trying to earn her respect, because it wouldn't do to be disliked, especially by a woman. Especially by a woman who, despite her seeming meekness – and herein lay the rub, for Bon – could still make him feel small.

So he had to say something, probably something about himself. But there wasn't much to say that was flattering. He wanted nothing more than to list the most unflattering aspects of himself, but to do so, he needed a few – just one or two – superbly flattering features for balance.

He hadn't lived an especially unflattering life, or so he had thought. The version of himself that he inhabited then, there in Newnes with Steven and Lesley, was a section excised from a larger and more conventional whole. It wasn't a reduction born of some conventional trauma, not the swift and violent kind. But it was nevertheless a reduction, and he suspected that he wasn't alone in now inhabiting a kind of shadow version of his previous self.

Before disembarking the train he'd had no greater desire, within the realm of possibility, than to be on it. He had refused to sleep on the train, for sleeping would only speed up its journey. When seated on the train, whether into the country for work or city-bound home, Bon would concentrate on the fact of his being on it, and he would carefully inhabit each passing minute. These several hours of daily train travel were his most alert, for he could not be touched on the train, and he himself could do no touching. It was not possible to be responsible for anything on the train, impossible to disappoint on it, and he had no chance to behave in any way that might sour through time. On the train, it was possible to forget the present and the future. Likewise, it was possible to ignore the insurmountable pressure of home and the monotony of work. Splayed impolitely across the purple leatherette seats, he could not have attended to anyone or anything, even had he wanted to. He was guarded from action on the train; in all honesty he was trapped. The train was stolen time, substantial portions of his life were surrendered to it, but he was numb to this injustice because life was not – so it had slowly dawned on him – a barrel of well-earned laughs. On the train he was just there being seated, moving from one point to another, and whenever it was delayed he would rejoice. Whenever the eight-car train languished on the tracks, waiting for a signal to change or a disaster to run its course, Bon would stretch his legs and he would relax, for there were few things more welcome in his life than bonus time on the train. His enjoyment of train travel became fraught with anxiety, for Bon would spend most of a trip willing a signal failure, hoping for a disruption. Uneventful trips would leave him feeling tense, often angry, so that eventually, he would spend the trip coaching himself to deal with disappointment. His long train trips – odysseys by many commuter's standards – grew to feel fleeting. There were a few occasions, he had to admit, when he had disembarked at a stop midway through the journey. During these occasions he had sat on the platform for half an hour, usually at a quiet station in the middle of the mountains, and then boarded the next. But while this increased the duration of the commute, it did not prolong his time spent on a train. Train platforms did not have the same mood of containment, of concealment, that train carriages did. Nor did every single moment spent on a train platform feel inevitable, safely inevitable, for every moment spent on a train platform could lead to the result that – in a worst-case scenario – the next train and all trains were cancelled. No, Bon had quickly discovered after a few experiments that it was better to stay on the train, even if that train might by some miracle or disaster arrive sooner than scheduled. Bon had no longer cared that he couldn't afford to live where he wanted, he had no longer cared where they might end up. Let the housing crisis spread beyond the mountains, he had thought, let it spread throughout the Central West, let it spread until the desert. Then he would have even more time on the train and it might even be practical never to leave it. When he caught upon this thought he let his fantasy wander further, imagining that due to some climate cataclysm, the government might one day suggest adding extra hours to a day to accommodate the blaze. A thirty-hour day, eight hours to work, eight hours working, eight hours back. Seven hours at home. To live sixteen hours a day on the train, where he could not be touched nor do any touching, was a dream so impossible it taxed him, it made him pent up, and it did so for long enough that his desire no longer seemed unreasonable. And yet, the circumstances that forced him to travel a mere six hours a day, had introduced a whole other set of once unthinkable convictions. It was true that Bon hated the government, it was true he wanted some of them dead. He was so enraged by the government that he dreamed of murdering some of them, and it no longer seemed unreasonable for him to harbour these fantasies, it no longer felt important to suppress this ideation. These fantasies had become so deeply entrenched that he had sometimes openly admitted to them. God I would love to kill that so-and-so minister, he would say during light political discussions at work. God does the Parliament House need a good bombing, he would mildly interject. And he would be laughed at, and it would come as a relief. But little did those lightly complaining work colleagues know that he felt this desire for violence towards power more strongly than he had ever dared let on. Or maybe they knew this about him, this potent frustration, because once, during an unusually protracted cooler-side session of grievance one-upmanship, he had boasted that he no longer voted, flatly refused to do it, scribbled on the ballot paper, because the system is rotten, fleeced by opportunists, thuggish capitalists on all sides, ugly rich men and women the likes of whom he'd never actually met or even seen in public, wealthy wraith-like scum who role-played the argot and mannerisms of their oafish subjects (poorly, he digressed), all the while openly demonstrating that it was all a game, a power struggle god-granted to them and their ilk. *Notice how they don't pretend it's not a game anymore?* His fellow complaining colleagues had scolded him for not exercising his hallowed democratic right. It was inconceivable to them that one might abstain from participating, so he'd walked it back, he'd laughed it off, *of course he voted*, he'd said – hadn't even scribbled on the ballot – only what was the point? What was the point indeed, the fellow complaining colleagues had agreed, but would you prefer China? Maybe he would. *Do they vote in China?* Maybe he wished he was Chinese. The world had him trapped, and he hated it, but also – and herein lay the greatest indignity – he found it fairly accommodating. Even now, in the town Newnes, having shed everything – even the train, but much more besides – he could scarcely find reason to complain about his comfort. Now was the time to withdraw one's deposits, now was the time to find shelter and wait.

Lesley had disembarked at Newnes too, so it was possible she would agree if he said all this aloud. But he really no longer wanted to speak, because his speech only ever seemed to simplify him. It turned him into a type, easily lambasted. So he remained silent.

It wasn't a matter of practicality that Bon and Lesley came to share a room and a bed, there was another logic at play. When Jack moved in – which he would, very soon – it was important to create an environment similar to the one he had enjoyed as a child.

It's not for my sake, Steven said. And don't you dare say I'm coddling the prick.

They both agreed that Steven wasn't coddling Jack.

It was awkward for Bon. He dressed in the bathroom and so did she. He would do so even if Lesley was at the plaza. During the evenings, when all three were seated in the lounge room drinking beers, he would retire to the room before Lesley. He loathed the thought of appearing to follow her. Alive with drink and not at all tired, he would lay there in silence until Lesley crept in. When she did, he would pretend to stir. She would get into the bed and lie flat on her chest.

He wanted Lesley to talk to him in the dark. He would always whisper or mutter that he hadn't fallen asleep. And anyway, he would add, I can sleep all day if I want, here in Newnes. It'd be cheaper if I did.

Just as he had done in the days after his own arrival, Lesley must have considered leaving. He could tell by the way she stood rather than sat on the steps one morning, staring at the road outside. Steven was up early and noticed her staring too.

You didn't have to get off the train here, Steven said.

The three of them stood on the front steps. The morning mist had yet to lift in that higher part of town, it amplified the smell of smoke.

The train stops every daylight hour, Steven said. It can take you to towns and it can take you to cities. It's not like you were lacking choices, Lesley.

Trains don't go everywhere though, he added. I'll grant you that. Not every town has a train. Sometimes the best towns don't have them. Grandma took Jack and I to Sofala once. Neither of you have been there, I can tell. If you had cars, you wouldn't have caught the train, and you can only get to Sofala with a car.

You have to see it, Steven said, lifting a hood over his receding hairline. He rubbed his hands together and pulled at the waistband of his pyjama pants.

You take the highway to Mudgee, he said, and after a half-hour or so, once you've passed the power plant and a couple of ugly roadside towns, you turn left. Then you travel for a whole other half-hour, across the ridges of mountains, the plains and bush stretching beneath. Finally you glide down a steep hill and across a narrow bridge of stone. To the left you enter a tiny town where everything is old. No plazas, no traffic lights, no Bunnings. There's no phone reception, but it doesn't matter because no emergency could ever happen there. People drink during the day or else they tend to the earth, managing vineyards and gardens. There's a bakery too, it sells sourdough and croissants and bullshit like that. The handful of uneven roads run narrow between old stone and wood houses that appear to be sinking into the Earth. If that's the fate of all old buildings, then the Earth never successfully swallowed the old houses in Sofala, because nothing ever happens there: especially not emergencies, especially not catastrophes. When you enter this town it's impossible to believe that all the worries we have in this world – the real world, this present one, connected to the major roads and within range of internet and hearsay – truly exist. When you enter this beautiful and perfect town, this idyllic town, with its quaint bakery and *ye olde* pub full of pictures of gruffly smiling old men, you come to understand that a scary future is not a dead universal certainty but instead, a neurosis born of just knowing. In this town no one knows anything. You stop someone in the street: What's going on. To which they would reply: Nothing at all, my friend, nothing at all, I'm just walking down the middle of this road for no pressing reason at all. You might be curious whether they know how things truly are, but it's impossible to ask them; it would be like punching a child. It would be interesting, Steven said, to go out there and start a fire. It'd be interesting to go out there and toss a brick through one of the townsfolk's windscreens. Would the fire start, would the brick bounce back? It'd be interesting to give it a go, Steven said, it'd be interesting to go out there and start a brawl, blare grindcore out across the precious little park beside the creek, sprint at passers-by and scream mercilessly into their faces, just scream. It'd be interesting to run a car straight through the little old antiques shop, and then scream. Wouldn't it be interesting to see if I was intercepted, to see if some visible or invisible force was protecting the town? Maybe I would evaporate the moment I turned the steering wheel off course.

Steven fell quiet. He turned to go back into the weatherboard, but stopped.

I can imagine Sofala in flames but it's a biblical vision, he said. Not at all similar to a news story on the TV. It's a vision that cannot be depicted, only imagined. I'd like to move out to Sofala one day, Steven said, when I'm old. But I'm not going to get old, not in any manner befitting that town. That town is ostentatious in its graceful oldness, it's old in the way all of us hope to be old: quietly resigned among the quiet wilderness of the Central West, secreted out of phone range, with not a care in the world for imminent death because every day is long and uneventful, every day is beautiful and green, every day is old-looking. Every day, they wake up and the hours pass and there's no problem with that. In Sofala hours passing meaninglessly is fine, nothing needs to happen in them, and despite how the hours blend together into days, weeks, years, lifetimes, it still doesn't matter, because all that matters is that you're alive, in such a picturesque, beautiful town. They are happy to just be alive, Steven said, in a town like that. Because it looks nice. Everyone's unimportant there. And probably for that very reason, most of the houses in Sofala are empty; you could just go ahead and live there, if you had a car. And why wouldn't you: they can wake up, no food in the pantry, no milk in the fridge, the bakery shut, their roof collapsed, distant hills ablaze, but who the hell cares. It would matter, of course, Steven said, on a certain level. You'd need to fix the roof, find bread or bake it, milk a cow, all those things. Someone would need to put out the fire. But not as much as it would matter here, because house or not, full belly or otherwise, everything is beautiful in Sofala. You'd want to go outdoors, into that beauty, you'd not feel so bad having to improvise. You've got to want to go out, haven't you?

Lesley nodded. It sounds beautiful there, she said. And then added: Unrealistic.

It's real, Steven said. I've been there. And it's the most amazing little town in the countryside, bar none. You've never seen anything like it. Let's go there one day, and have a beer in their quaint little pub.

Bon slept sounder knowing Lesley was beside him. He dreamed more vividly, and in most of his dreams they were husband and wife. Lesley was usually pregnant with their second baby. She was rosier, more tranquil, and kinder towards him. The dreams did not splinter and morph: they were simple and vivid dreams, as commonplace as waking life. In one example, Bon and Lesley sat on a park bench making lunch while Steven scaled a nearby climbing frame. As they buttered the white buns and tore apart the Coles chicken, they kept an eye on climbing Steven. The climbing frame was shaped like an old-fashioned space rocket, and at its pinnacle was a metal landing with a steering wheel. Steven reached the pinnacle, stood proudly, panned the view of the park and the disused theatre across the road. Then he took hold of the steering wheel and slapped it repeatedly, so that it rotated loudly on its axle. It rattled and screeched on the rusted pole. In his dream, Bon knew the boy-man would tumble for the excitement, and when he did, Bon yelled but did not run, because his hands were lathered in chicken grease. Steven was splayed across the soft woodchips beneath the bars, rubbing the calf of one leg, screaming with the severity of a child but with the gravel of a smoking man. From his vantage point at the park bench, Bon watched as Lesley took their child in her arms, she kissed his forehead and rocked the man gently. When Steven had finished screaming he stood and kicked the lower rungs of the climbing frame in a rage.

In Bon's dreams he and Lesley were life partners. They had an intimately entwined history and he was able to recall moments when they had previously discussed, in bed and in unknown homes and in other unknown locations besides, how accident-prone and how given to violent rages their son Steven Grady was. Sometimes in these dreams, Lesley would ask Bon: What are we to do with this child? And in the dream, Bon would say he did not know. In the dream, there lingered a remote awareness of his waking life, in which he would need to have delivered an answer to any question, and to have improvised a plan on the spot. But in his dream, his admitting that he did not know would be respected for its truthfulness, maybe even received as wise, because it was actually very wise not to know – intelligence knew its boundaries – and to speculate blindly was the pastime of idiots.

Lesley smoked cigarettes with her left hand, she cradled her left wrist in her right. When she spoke – far less than Steven but far more than Bon – she did so with a deep voice, it was a philosophical-sounding voice. In the lounge room of an evening, she offered comforting speculations. Bon couldn't tell at times whether she was speaking metaphorically, and he was sure that Steven couldn't tell either. With his doubt applied, and an equal measure of faith applied, and with various measures of other forms of misgiving and approval applied, her voice acquired the quality of ambience.

She only ever spoke at length after several beers, and she was capable of reasoning any weakness into a strength. According to her logic, it was noble and healthy to be forthright about one's weaknesses, and failing to wear one's weaknesses openly was the one and only damning weakness. She was always soliciting admissions and confessions. She held her left wrist with her right hand whenever she smoked and it lent her the air of a sage.

If Steven, but sometimes Bon, made a sincere declaration about a weakness they believed wasn't already obvious, Lesley would treat them with the utmost affection and reward them with praise.

One evening, after countless bottles of beer, and after several familiar speeches, Steven felt pressed to admit that he had been a bad brother.

He was once a cheerful and intelligent child, Steven said, but now he's reclusive and afraid. He's hounded by the Colossal Man. If I hadn't wasted my late teenage years taking drugs and running amok, Steven said, I would have had time to cultivate Jack in the way a younger brother should be cultivated. My brother Jack, Steven said. He should be married to an attractive woman, he should be hosting elaborate and expensive children's birthday parties. He should have an attractive wife and two children, maybe even a third. He should be driving a nice car to a lucrative job five mornings a week, and then cracking open a beer – if he's feeling lavish, two – on balmy Friday nights. If you saw his face when he was a child, you couldn't have imagined any other fate. At the very least, he should have become a mediocre but satisfied man. But he got led astray, let himself adopt some worldviews, made it his job to spread them for a while – not just one worldview, several – and believe you me, his wasn't just a position, he wasn't taking a position, it wasn't a part of any kind of debate normal people ever have. Not even I understand his bullshit, and I'm the kind of person – and I don't have tickets on myself – but I'm the kind of person who tends to understand things. I understand what people are saying, even if I disagree. And I'm the kind of person who wants to enact change too! You Bon, you Lesley, me, my mum, the people at the plaza: all would make changes. Name me someone who wouldn't. Not on this scale though, not this, real barbaric shit, him and all the other lackeys, directed by the fat bastard up the hill, the Colossal Man. None of it for the betterment – all for the worsening, rip it all apart, they reckon. You've got to read the book they made – it was even too much for Jack, that's when Jack had enough. He's just a hectic, curious child. But hut boy and his soldiers won't let him off scot-free. I know that. He knows that.

Steven's speech had gone on too long for Bon to follow. Lesley shook her head and muttered objections, as she was wont to do, whenever someone spoke fatalistically. It wasn't Steven's fault that he had been a bad brother, she said, he hadn't been a bad brother at all. There were many unassailable reasons for why Jack would have met his fate anyway, and an equal number of unassailable reasons for why being a bad brother was, in fact, a perfectly normal thing. Every responsibility fell to the world, according to Lesley.

But what did she mean by this? Was nothing Steven's (or Bon's) choice? It was hard to tell if this is what she meant. Bon wasn't inclined to give Lesley the benefit of the doubt when it came to questions of her worldliness, because she seemed weak pretending to be strong, with the air of someone harangued by middle-managers in a middling life, just like himself. But there she was, and she was saying what she said, and they were listening, and although what she said was slight, it was spoken with utmost stumbling conviction. He heard it, and it wasn't provably wrong – actually, it had the ring of common sense about it – so it endeared her to him.

Every life is a story, she said. There are ups and downs and dizzying plot beats. Jack's story is a much more interesting story compared to ours; his has an antagonist. Some people enjoy calm stories where not much happens, others enjoy stories punctuated by explosions and extraordinary events. So it stands to reason, said Lesley, that maybe you, Steven, have been an exceptionally good brother, for the fact that you have loved your brother but done so at a distance, you've allowed him to live a different story to your own. Jack's life is a story punctuated by explosions and extraordinary events. Who are we to know whether that detracts from the overall quality of his life, when he reviews it from his deathbed? How can you be sure, Steven, that you're a critical component in Jack's story? There's no guarantee that you are, maybe you're even a minor character. No one is one's own minor character, you're naturally inclined to overestimate your importance. Jack's situation may not be one that anyone desires, she said, but it's not your fault. It's not your story. When you assess it from this angle, you're an exceptionally good brother. You've done the least you can do, and that's actually good.

Bon nodded in fierce agreement, because it was actually true: Steven was incapable of directing his brother onto a course. And it was unimaginable that Steven would steer the course in any better direction anyway. Bon nodded in fierce agreement, because he understood what Lesley was saying.

Newnes was all hills up and down, full of illogical turns. There was a severe beauty about the town but it was always contaminated with nearby contrasting mundanities. Old terraces and worker cottages were abutted by squat modern brick homes, dead grass out front. Lush parks were partially shaded by towering red-brick warehouse buildings for companies long faded from the sheet metal signage. The main street, a long snaking strip which started at the highway McDonalds and finished at the closed Courthouse Hotel, could sometimes carry the air of a regional European town, but its hodge-podge plainness always lurked at the periphery. No photograph could capture the essence of Newnes. One needed to see the whole dissonant expanse.

Jack was a man or boy ten years Bon and Steven's junior. He's a rat, Steven said. He's a rat, but he can't stay at home anymore, down on one of the old roads towards the water treatment plant. Mum's sick of the bastard, he needs to go, he needs to get out of the smoke, out of the black clouds emitted by the burning. That whole part of town stinks like death, Steven said. It stinks like a stroke.

It was time to pick up Jack. They walked down the hill past the plaza, past the Supercheap Auto and H&R Block, up the lower half of the main street and through the arcade into the train station, where a four-carriage 11:20 was waiting to depart. Seeing the train there waiting, and having all his required belongings with him, Bon was tempted to dash aboard. Because it wasn't exactly stress-free anymore, there in Newnes, with Lesley wooden in his bed and a troubled brother moving in. Only he couldn't be sure how he'd be received, and it was definitely too late for excuses.

They passed through the station and onto the other side, walked for a long time, through the part of town closest to the old mines, the old mines now a museum, where the single-storey townhouses opened straight onto the footpath, where the elderly sat on balconies staring at the train line, staring at the distant ruins of the old blast furnace. Bon thought it was nice. He said to Steven: This part of town is nice and old. But Steven scoffed at this: It's Newnes, Steven said, everyone hates Newnes. In Orange, Bathurst, Mudgee, further afield, even in the shit-heap towns with no petrol station along the minor highways...they all take the piss out of Newnes, they all think we're trash. They drive through on their way to the city, to take their kids to the aquarium or the beach, or Luna Park, and they see Newnes and they think: This is hell. But they don't know shit about Newnes.

Steven's mum and Jack lived in a narrow freestanding two-storey brick house. Trains coursed along a fenced-off crest directly behind. In the driveway a webbed old caravan was barricaded by stacks of mildewed cardboard boxes. The yard was long and tangled but it looked peacefully wild rather than neglected. Steven leapt the front steps and flung the door open. The front room was thickly carpeted, and smelled of decades of smoke, meat and boy. In the centre was a couch where his mother was sitting.

Steven yelled: I'm here. His mother said: I know. She was browsing a Coles catalogue. The house was cluttered with a half-generation of family keepsakes, and there were pictures of young boys though none resembled Steven.

Mother Grady put the catalogue aside, stood, offered herself to be hugged. Steven put his arms lazily around her.

He's upstairs and his bags are packed, she said. And then she noticed Bon, raised her chin and whispered specifically to him: They've been packed for weeks.

The men went upstairs and down a narrow windowless hall. Bon could hear automatic rifles and explosions. Steven barged into a dark room where the silhouette of a figure sat poised in front of two large screens. One screen bobbed through a war-torn urban setting, swaying rifle in the foreground. The other was filled with browser windows populated with thumbnail images and short lines of text. From a small Bluetooth speaker on the desk a high-pitched abrasion aired, a blizzard-like ambience. The desk was elsewhere strewn with boyhood ornaments, video game controllers and books, and flimsy monochrome paperbacks the likes of which didn't exist in libraries. White Germanic font on coal-black cardboard, images that didn't coalesce into shapes, one with lethal barbed wire in the foreground and a ruined tower behind. Within this mess were a handful of toppled cartoon figurines, long-legged bulging-eyed cartoon women, lightly dressed and wielding oversize claymores. The bed in the corner was double-bunked and speckled with Pokémon stickers.

Okay cunt, let's go, Steven said. It stinks in here, your farts smell like chops.

He roared at his joke. And I thought Mum cut the internet, he said. You could have told me there was internet again, I could have been looking for jobs.

Jack looked over his shoulder and raised his eyes and then looked back at the monitor. After a long half-minute handling the mouse, closing windows, the stick-thin boy rose, pulled the cords from an oversized laptop, tucked it into a pouch and slipped it under his bed. Jack was tall, but the kind of tall undermined by his features elsewhere. The hair on his small round head was closely cropped, and his shoulders were almost non-existent over his bizarrely thin frame. The petulant wariness of a teen was preserved in his face, and his tracksuit pants were worn and stained. As he lifted a backpack onto his shoulders, his eyes met Bon's with a dim kind of amusement. Steven hugged the boy, punched him gently – much harder and he'd break – and told him he was a fucking idiot.

You're a fucking idiot, Steven said. You could have just come when I told you the address.

The three of them descended the stairs, where at the foot Mother Grady was waiting. She held another larger backpack by the handle, waved a shrink-wrapped Styrofoam tray of meat with the other.

Well here it is, she said to Jack. Your brother's finally pulled his finger out.

She laughed and Steven laughed, Bon chuckled too.

I've been busy, Steven said. Trying to figure out my next move.

You'll get there, she said. She briskly hugged him again, stood aside, and told him he was allowed to visit even for no reason.

But Steven was already out of the room and in the kitchen, rifling through cupboards. Jack was cross-legged in the front yard smoking.

We'll just get his stuff up to ours today, Steven yelled. We've got a bit on, lugging this stuff up the hill.

And I've got a bit on too, she answered. I'm taking the caravan and I'm going on a trip to the desert. I always promised to myself that I would, once you boys left. Now it's finally time. I'd love to see the desert.

Bon stood awkwardly next to Mother Grady. He looked at her and he straightened his back because he always felt more confident around older women. He smiled and said he was share-housing with Steven. But she seemed to be aware of everything and more.

Sorry about Jack, she said. I hope it's not imposing.

He said it didn't matter to him either way, that he seemed really nice.

It'll be nice to have him around, he added.

I thought they'd have kids and lawns and gutters to clear by now, she said. I thought I'd be visiting their houses and looking after their children, swapping war stories with their wives. I thought I'd be awaiting their calls. I thought I'd be off in that caravan, travelling the country, reacquainting with myself. But they're sticky, these bastards – she waved in both directions at her sons – they don't seem to want to do anything. They just want to drink and then come home, or else never leave at all. They want me to cook them chops every night. I'm done with cooking chops.

She proffered the tray of chops to Bon.

I'm sick of bloody chops, she said. And don't thank me I don't deserve it, because I'm off to see the desert. You get sick of trees and cliffs. And don't think I'm kicking them out because I'm not. They're always welcome and I've always told Steven that. But I have to make them live.

You do, Bon said.

I never thought I'd want them gone, I thought I'd try to keep them lock-and-chain.

You can't.

They're not boys anymore, Mother Grady sighed. And I've cooked tens of thousands of chops. I loved them and I still love them but the truth is, I love my memory of them, I love their baby faces and their wondering at everything. Their precocious role-playing, their wanting to be big...it was cute but you held them back, you'd say: just wait, it'll happen, you'll be adult in good time. In the meantime, play with your toys but learn to put them away. But now they've grown and I still love them but between you and me, I loved them more while I still shaped them. I don't shape them anymore, and when I did I didn't do a good job.

That's not right, Bon said.

Well there may not be much work around, Mother Grady said, and Newnes may not be what it once was, but people make more money now than ever, and besides everyone works, working is easy, everyone does it, even idiots. Meet a woman, fix things, innovate, conduct the trains if you have to.

She collapsed onto the couch.

I know it's not easy, she said. The path from child to adult seemed fixed. The milestones seemed universal. The shape of my lifetime felt like the shape of lifetimes centuries past and forever to come. Not long ago it felt as if time had ground to a peaceful holding pattern, it had stopped throwing curveballs, curveballs were obsolete. Their father left but people leave, that's not what I'm talking about. A mysterious kind of change is underway and I'm horribly under-qualified. In a strange way, I feel that I've outlived my own life. Maybe if I'd died at the threshold of their coming of age, they would have blossomed into suitable kinds of adult. But instead I have endured and my endurance has stymied them. My milieu, my generation is a kind of haunting, it blocks their passage.

Bon reckoned aloud that she was probably reading too much into it.

I'm not being unkind to myself or even to them, she said. I'm not being one way or the other I'm just being truthful.

He nodded at her, and she nodded back at him. He couldn't tell whether she expected him to keep talking or not, and anyway, he was at a total loss for words. But he was nevertheless locked in meaningful eye contact with Mother Grady.

It's normal, he said. And then added: I hear what you're saying.

Jack dawdled in silence behind Bon and Steven. Not many people walked the streets of Newnes, but the few they passed threw interested stares at Steven's brother. He bore an anxious kind of intensity; his presence felt debatable.

Mum talks a bit of shit doesn't she, Steven said. And he assured Jack, on the way up the hill, that his arrival in the weatherboard was cause for celebration. We're going to get some beers and we're going to get obliterated, Steven said. There was a crazed brightness in his eyes.

They bought a whole carton of Tsingtao beer at the Newnes Valley Plaza. Bon monitored Jack for signs of feeling, but the young man, a boy of around twenty-one, no doubt intended to understand the territory first. It wasn't a juvenile rudeness and it wasn't exactly superiority either, but Jack's face operated as if its every expression pivoted around an essence utterly foreign to Bon.

They all drank together that night: Bon, Steven, Lesley and Jack, the former two on the couch, the others cross-legged around the ashtray on the ground.

You and me Jack, Steven said, arms aloft. Christ Jack, you and me. Could you find two more loving brothers? You as a baby, Jack, there wasn't any funnier kid. I remember holding your hands as you learned to walk. You stumbled like a drunk, grinned like an idiot, you were the cutest thing. I hope you don't mind me saying you were cute, Jack. But you were, you were a soft and kind and loving boy. You used to admire me, I could always see it in your eyes. When you were really young, one year old, thereabouts, I'd snatch your toys off you as an experiment. But you'd only watch with interest, you thought I snatched from you kindly, you thought I wanted to show you something. You were in thrall to me, Jack, you were such a little monkey. You'd stand up in your highchair and shake your head, mimicking Mum's reaction, thinking it was a game. I remember you then, I was eleven and you were one. I was a bossy child, I know that, Mum always says that. But I wasn't being malicious. And I know you know that, otherwise we'd be distant from one another. But look at us now, Jack. Living together. It's unreal.

We used to chase the chickens in the yard. Once one of them died. It died from terror. The other two didn't lay eggs for months after. Mum was pissed off, I thought she was going to skin us. But even Mum couldn't be pissed off with you for too long, Jack, you were placid and smiled at everything, even the wind, even the ants. Your smile could melt the gruffest of men. I was bossy and loud and always screamed, I was a shit of a child, I admit it. But Jack...I don't know if you ever knew this, but Mum reckons you saved our family. After a problem child, a child that made her anxious, a child that made her think she'd done something wrong...your arrival was a blessing. And you weren't even a wanted birth, you were an accident. But you were beautiful and placid and your smile could save the world. That's what Mum once said, I remember hearing her say it.

Back in the 1990s, what a time to be alive. Jack, remember the time you wandered off? Mum and I called and wailed for a good hour, knocked on each door surrounding, called the police, called the radio...only to find you playing with snails behind the garden shed in the yard. God, I was petrified Jack, I couldn't imagine life without you, I remember the feeling and it's going to make me cry. My little cherubic Jack, run over by a car, dead. If you were dead I too wanted to die, I couldn't have lived without you.

Do you remember the year we got a PlayStation? I can't think of a better feeling in my life. We were in the lounge room on Christmas morning. Mum was adamant for weeks before: you're not getting a PlayStation, boys, I can't afford it, you can get electronic sets. Remember electronic sets? On Christmas morning we sat down and unwrapped our presents and sure enough, both of us got an electronic set, and we pretended to be surprised and happy because Mum always taught us to be grateful...but we didn't really want electronic sets. Nevertheless we started to unbox them so that we could see what the deal was with electronic sets, we set them side-by-side in the lounge room and started to connect the wires with the little metal springs in order to spark a light...and then *boom*. Mum knelt before us, brandishing a wrapped box: 'What on earth is this, this must be a secret present, who could this be from... it must be a special bonus gift from Santa!' And we unwrapped it thinking it was just another puzzle or just another Meccano set or else another minor present, but no, it was a goddamn fucking PlayStation. My god, the joy in your eyes Jack, I can't even describe it, and my body was in convulsions. I think I even cried. Did I cry, Jack? I know I gritted my teeth, and squeezed my fists, and screamed, and I also wanted to throw my body around the room. Do you remember that? You're fucked if that wasn't the happiest moment in my life.

That reminds me of when you first started school. I was in year ten at the high school, I had to walk you to kindergarten. Mum wanted to take you for your first day, but you said: 'No, I'm big now, I have to walk to school with Stevie.' So after much fuss we set out, you with a backpack larger than your body, eager to hold my hand. Along the way I wanted to hide in the park and have a bong. So I said to you, Jack, that on the way to school it's sometimes fun to go on the swings. I put you on the swings, and said I'd be off talking to friends around the bushes for a while. You loved the swings, and you weren't scared of anything, least of all being left alone in a park, because nothing had ever touched you before. Terrible things were impossible to you – didn't the world seem greener then, Jack? So I made off with my backpack and hunched down in the bushes to chuff my bong. I monitored you as I did so, and you just sat there swinging, like some kind of extra in a film, completely oblivious and seemingly without a thought in the world, you did exactly as I had instructed: you went back and forth on the swing, going higher and higher and then twisting around and kicking the poles. You smiled. You smiled, even though no one was watching you smile. And I thought to myself then, as a teenager with scant familiarity with remorse, that I really shouldn't smoke weed, because what if I died? What if I got addicted and went insane, and it ruined my poor brother Jack's life? I wanted to cry then. I wanted to cry because I knew at that moment, me hiding in the bushes, you pushing hard on the swing, that at some point in the near future, nearer than I could have imagined, everything was going to change. I would leave home and get a job, and then you might do the same, and then we would live separately, in different houses, with girlfriends and wives and kids of our own, and we'd always have to act like adults around one another...so what of that particular moment, the morning before your first day at school, a special moment, you in a uniform so tiny and strange? You were about to set out on the next big step in your life...and rather than go with Mum you'd selected me. The enormity of it overwhelmed me. What if I died, and you, Jack, forever remembered the day when your brother had been smoking drugs, killing his brain, instead of appreciating every fleeting second of this threshold between your babyhood and childhood? Teenagehood is crazy, isn't it, Jack? The emotions. I packed the bong up and I jogged back towards you. Because Jack, you were a gift of a child. I'm almost going to cry just thinking about it.

But it wasn't always beautiful. One time Mum had to run to the shops. You were about three. I was always good with you Jack, Mum knew it, she'd let me mind you for a half-hour here and there. So Mum was out and we were home alone, watching Austar in the lounge room. And I can't remember what prompted it, Jack, but you got angry and indignant. I tried to reason with you, but sometimes children can't be reasoned with. It escalated and escalated, until finally you charged at me and scratched my face. I picked you up angrily, marched to our bedroom, tossed you inside, closed the door. You banged and screamed at the door, at the highest and most desperate pitch imaginable. You kicked and tore and wailed, your scream became deep and guttural. I flung the door open in a panic, the knob hit your forehead, you collapsed onto the floor and somehow, impossibly, you screamed, kicked and wailed much more intensely than before, you threw your body around the room, dragged the quilt off your bed, punched the wall, pulled your hair. And I punched you: right on the chest, not hard but hard enough, I punched you and I told you to shut the fuck up. I spat it at you: shut the fuck up. I pinned you to the ground, and I whispered it again. Shut the fuck up. And you fell silent.

But no one's telling you to shut the fuck up now, Jack! Why don't you talk to me anymore? I know things aren't the way we'd always hoped. Things are actually a nightmare compared to then. My best years are gone, everyone my age knows that, unless they're filthy rich. We're going to be left to drown, or else to burn, or else to murder one another – I know you think that. So Jack, it's time to make the best of all this together. I want the old Jack back, the one before the brainwash.

Steven was sitting forward now, had spent the last ten minutes rolling a smoke. Bon had gotten the drift of it. Lesley's face was shining, and her eyes had softened.

Jack struggled to contain the expressions that unfolded on his face. He was always struggling against his jaws, and even his blinking was self-conscious, like he was labouring to do so naturally. His cheekbones creased erratically; sometimes he'd bear his teeth in seeming frustration at the futility of his efforts.

Would you prefer that I sent you an email Jack, Steven said, while Bon rolled him the smoke, supportively.

Jack Grady was bored, that's what Bon decided. He'd sit in the lounge room or else on the front steps, he'd smoke most of their tobacco. Jack's phone was off-limits by command of Steven, but Jack still kept it, and it was easy to catch him using it. He'd peek at it even if his brother was around.

The phone infuriated Bon, he felt betrayed on Steven's behalf. He'd stand in the doorway while Jack sat on the steps, to spy the illegible text. Occasionally there was an image on that screen, low-res and incomprehensible, and whenever Bon approached an understanding of it – during moments when he could get a stealthy vantage point – it would disappear. What was this ceaselessly scrolling shadow document? Based on his half-understandings of the images, it was a document concerned with outlandish proportion and excess, it was shaded in rash pinks and greys.

He only ate chips, he only drank Coke or beer. He was rake thin and sallow. Bon feared him all the more, for the fact he carried no firm air of depression or resignation. Actually, his face was doe-eyed and harmless, it was his body that alarmed. Jack's body was a carrier and not much more, it appeared superfluous, a perfunctory substantiation. He didn't drag his feet, he moved through the house in perfect silence, but it appeared as if his whole body, his head and his face included, dragged or struggled through resistant air, so that his movement between rooms, between the lounge room and the front steps, resembled that of an automaton, a disadvantaged kind.

Bon had no reason to think about Jack during the day. He'd go with Steven to the plaza, or they'd traipse through the forest together sticks in hand. But of an afternoon he'd find Jack seated on the front steps with Lesley, and it was always dispiriting to find him there. Lesley had found an inroad with Jack; Bon conspicuously hadn't. Lesley and Jack would stay up late and talk, and in the musty, creaky old weatherboard, it was impossible to eavesdrop unnoticed. Bon had tried, of course. All he had managed to hear was the rhythm of Lesley's coarse orations. She spoke like a mother persuading a stubborn teen to elaborate, with tender guile. She spoke like a mother did – so Bon supposed, so he vaguely remembered – when she wanted to hide some penetrating ulterior motive. As for Jack, he spoke too quietly, if at all.

It's crown forest land in three directions, Steven said as he threshed the forest. Hundreds of square kilometres of tangled wild forest and range. In the fourth direction there's a clean flat passage into the country. It may seem calm here at the edge of the forest, where the McDonalds rubbish collects, but further in and east there are great canyons, deadly valleys, subterranean cave systems. You know you're in dangerous uncharted land if you can't see the rubbish, because there are secrets beneath the canopy that are undetectable by satellite. There's depravity in the forest, Bon, it beats me why they built a town at the edge of it. Who can know what emerges from it in stark daylight, let alone by night? There are no sentries, there are no rules: anyone's allowed to hide in there.

Bon was tempted to ask Steven what he thought hid in the forest, but by the time he'd decided against it, the topic was long forgotten.

The town no longer has families to protect, Steven was saying. It's been that way ever since I've been adult. Everyone's disconnected, at best acquainted, everyone has come from somewhere else, everyone has fled from somewhere else. Not one of these houses – and he waved at the cul-de-sac – are home to what you'd call a family, either the kids have moved away or disappeared, or a lonely person has arrived, and they've not arrived for the love of mist and smoke. Children aren't conceived here, they are brought in from somewhere else, by fleeing mothers or renegade fathers, they arrive for the collapse of best-laid plans made elsewhere. There are no Sunday lunches, no children at cricket or ballet.

But it wasn't like this when I was a kid, Steven said. Jack would agree.

At the mention of Jack, Bon drove his rake into the dirt.

He asked what exactly was the go with Jack.

Well he thinks he knows what goes on in there, Steven motioned at the brambles. And he thinks he knows what goes on everywhere else. He thinks he knows everything. And he knows that no one will protect him and that anyway, he doesn't deserve it. And he doesn't believe we should hold on, he's not a believer in salvaging anything, not a believer in course correction. Jack wants chaos and madness, you won't believe it but it's true. He's subject to a powerful force, him and many others, they're directed by the big bastard in the hut. I don't like it, but it might as well be him, because all the old logicians are bogus, bought, secretly antagonistic. But Jack and his so-called friends, they reckon there's going to be a war, not in decades but any day now. They could be compelled to take up arms tomorrow, the sooner the better, rip the bandage clean. He *wants* to go to war, Bon, he doesn't want to join the army, he just wants there to be war, and he wants to be in the middle of it, a tragic free-for-all, no allegiances. Mind you, there are plenty like Jack who want it too, and the funny thing is they argue about it – not soldiers, not commanders or governments, just hundreds of dickheads like him, they argue about wars and what might best give rise to them. And it's not for want of freedom or anything like that. And it's not for the acceptance that there's no other thing to do. Jack won't tell you why, he won't tell me, it'd no doubt sound stupid if he spoke it aloud, everything sounds stupid when spoken aloud. You probably don't even believe me.

I don't follow you at all, Bon said.

Steven laughed and slapped Bon on the chest. Bon gently punched him back, and they smoked seated against the trunks of ancient gum.

Jack and Lesley were on the front steps when they got home. Bon thought he could detect some self-satisfaction in Lesley's eyes, an expression that vaguely said, *I have mastered the spiky one.* She seemed to brood on top of him, waiting for him to hatch. Bon avoided eye contact with her, landing instead on Jack, who never looked at him anyway.

A familiar, blizzard-like ambience emitted from Jack's speaker. Bon could hear voices in it now, calm speaking voices, too baritone and too low in the mix to be legible. Lesley stared at her shoes, performing an appreciation of the music. She occasionally nodded approvingly and Jack watched her do it, his lips were pursed, it looked like he was silently giving her cheek.

Steven and Bon stood at the gate.

He can't even stomach normal music, Steven whispered. It has to be this bullshit, as far from normality as possible. He's an absolute piece of work.

Bon crept to the speaker, squatted against it, furrowed his brows. It was indeed the same electronic kind of blizzard he'd heard in Jack's room. Inside the blizzard, fleeting notes resembled ghostly melodious foghorns. These notes seemed to press against the lower ebbs of the blizzard, and aired only during moments of relative calm. But no matter how closely he listened, he couldn't figure out the words. To Bon's ears, it was desperate and sinister music, though he wasn't one to take music seriously at all.

What's it saying, he said to Jack.

It's Jack's music, Lesley said, like she was his manager. He makes it on his phone.

You made this? Bon pointed at the speaker and tried to make eye contact with the boy.

It's impressive, he said.

It's very original, Lesley added.

Bullshit, Steven shouted. He was now squatted by the speaker too, hearing it for the first time.

You're telling me you made this, Jack?

He made it, Lesley said.

It's genius, Steven sighed. This is genuine art, Jack.

He sat next to the speaker, asked Bon to roll a smoke. His hands were pressed gently to the air, commanding stillness and silence.

The four of them sat on the steps of the weatherboard on that chilled autumn afternoon, staring sometimes at the cement, sometimes at the road. There was no birdsong, no passing traffic, but still no access to the substance of the words in the music. A train arrived and departed down the hill, the sound of brakes and the hum of the engine offered an informal intermission. When the train faded into the distance, Jack's music seemed to return with greater clarity, its buried foghorns began to make a more lucid musical sense.

After two smokes Jack's song still hadn't ended, and Bon became restless and self-conscious.

It's very impressive, he said, dusting his trousers. It's beyond me, really.

There's a lot to unpack, Lesley said.

So much, Bon agreed. You fit a lot into it, there's a lot going on.

Jack hung his head lower.

It's a shame you can't understand the words, Bon said. People would want to hear them.

It's deliberate, Lesley reckoned. Isn't it Jack? It's part of the artistry.

The boy turned his face away, scowled at the wall.

Jack doesn't care about artistry, Steven laughed. Don't say it's art, you'll piss him off.

He's pissed off already, she said. Sorry, Jack, it's beyond us. And it's not art.

Bon and Steven laughed, the former reluctantly, the latter joyously. Jack flared a nostril.

Bon would lie awake in bed and wait for Lesley to speak. Whenever she did, it was only after a period of silence spent working towards the heart of the matter. Bon wasn't ever sure what the matter was, or where the heart of it might be, hadn't even known how to start thinking about it.

Whenever he tried to understand the complexity suffered by others, he could only guess at what type of complexity it was. He would try to determine the category, and he would then determine a course of action based on courses of action he'd witnessed in movies and television programs, or courses of action vaguely reported second-hand by others. If called upon, he could offer second-hand advice. Few ever called upon Bon, though. Problems of people and problems of passion were tedious and enigmatic.

It had always seemed reasonable to believe that complexities were sometimes – more often than not – relished by those who suffered them. People found ways to exploit them. Those who dared articulate the details of their complexity only risked complicating things further. And anyway, the way to address complexities had already been consecrated, there were blueprints you could find, you couldn't innovate new solutions to complexities of the heart. Life was just a consultation with precedents; to live the life of Bon was to always be plundering popular wisdom. The body and the mind have keyholes you can turn and, so it had once seemed to Bon, the teeth on the keys never changed. But people seemed hell-bent on finding new ways to be complicated, they seemed to want it. Why, though? Everything was bad, yes, but it was likewise mostly okay. Meat in the supermarket rotted in its abundance, water poured hard and profuse from every tap. You're well off compared to others, Bon had often said, and he'd said it often enough to barely notice when he said it.

When Lesley spoke to him in bed, he knew it was because she'd found the heart of the matter. She seemed ever determined to reach it independently, the heart of the matter could not be debated. She always retired long after Bon, having waited for Jack to sleep. She'd lift the blanket and heave onto the mattress, then wriggle to secure her share of space. She'd then turn away, fold her pillow in half, and lay her head in one of her palms. Bon would make some apology, for example, that he hadn't deliberately taken most of the blanket, or that she should wake him if he snored. She'd say something like, 'don't worry', or 'that's no problem'. A silence would then endure. And after long minutes, her voice would puncture the quiet.

Steven's just a loon, she said. We can make him happy. But Jack needs more work.

Bon wasn't sure what she meant, and even felt faintly offended: of course she would say Steven was the loon, and not Jack, because she was better friends with Jack.

And anyway: why should they want to make them happy?

You won't believe me when I say it, she continued, but Jack's not stupid. He understands more than the both of us combined. We won't make him happy any time soon.

People are always thinking I won't believe what they say.

Bon scowled in the dark, he'd already derailed the discussion.

He probably just needs to get out into the world, he said. We've already gotten him away from his mum. He's still a teenager, he's still got that anger about him. He needs a girlfriend and a job. Or else he could start playing concerts, get his art out there. He's got his whole life ahead of him.

His art wouldn't make sense anywhere else, she said. In this town it has a certain kind of clarity, anywhere else it would barely be audible. Jack is officially a man, hard to believe, because he's a decade younger than us. But he is a boy, he is arrested in his boydom, and there is no escaping it, not in the material world. There is no way for men to avoid staying boys in this town, there is no way, he will be forever sullen, silently embittered, in many ways more childish than boys, unless the world changes, or unless – and this seems more feasible – he becomes a proper boy again.

This town isn't so different from anywhere else, we're still in the same country.

Bullshit it's not different, she said. Everyone here drinks and smokes themselves to death or wishes they could. If you think it's just us, you're dreaming.

What else are they going to do.

I don't know you, Bon, she said. I can guess that you were an elections and petitions kind of person. You'd vote and sign knowing it would change nothing, and you might have been privately glad that it wouldn't. The expression of the desire for change...what could be more gratifying, for people with no want? You photograph your sausage sandwich and barrack for a team. Your anger has never been real, you believe in the myth of your empowerment. Maybe you've felt indignant, but you are not contained inside of your rage or your fear, it doesn't consume you, rage is a kind of catharsis for you. Your rage recedes as quickly as it arises, you're left with a righteous afterglow. You're still young, but also you're spiritually too old, too old to feel as potent as they do this rage. You're too old to imagine a nation in flames. Your rage has never been for desperation, it's been for pity. Pity may compel the strongest and most passionate but it doesn't compel the public. You are exactly the public, Bon, no offense.

None taken.

And I'm not trying to make you feel small, because I got off the train here too. We're all learning to be alarmed, it's a hard threshold to cross, it takes a certain departure, a difficult, maybe inadvisable, voluntary derangement. I've considered going back, I know you have too. But we're here now, and we both know there's no going back. Nothing obscures our view from here, there's nothing on the horizon but the inevitable. And since neither of us are setting buildings alight, since neither of us will agitate, we must secure warmth or a semblance of it, wherever it can be found.

Bon felt indignant and thoroughly misunderstood; he'd never eaten a ceremonial sausage at a polling booth, had in fact meaningfully avoided it. Lesley hadn't been critical of him before – she had only been gentle, placating. She must have thought she was some kind of authority now, having been off the train for so long, and having endeared herself to Jack. But he wasn't going to explain himself to her. He didn't want to explain himself to anyone ever again. Why should he do so, there in Newnes? And especially to her? More than ever, but still not enough, he regretted getting off the train.

He folded his arms against his chest. Lesley squeezed his shoulder, and then she pressed herself against him in a motherly kind of hug.

I shouldn't have gotten off the train.

It's too late, she said.

Bon and Lesley dutifully wondered about Sofala. They wondered at first whether it existed at all. Deciding that it surely must, Lesley moved to wondering whether it might be practical to move there, for it was a matter beyond dispute that Sofala would be a more pleasant town than Newnes. This town was haunted by colossal men, drenched in the smoke of ominous distant fires; Sofala was reportedly immune to any event at all.

All of us can go, she said. We must.

Bon, terrified at the prospect of going anywhere ever again, wrote it off as impossible.

Lesley was the first to admit that it was in her best interests to be as far from her old life as possible. Bon was less sure, but he nodded when she said so. They discussed it once, as they cooked thin sausages on the electric stove. She said that her old life had been like spitting into the wind. She must have said it because the sausages were spitting fat in the pan. Bon didn't know what to say to make her say more than that. He supposed that if he allowed the silence to linger for a while, Lesley might continue talking. But she didn't and he flinched.

So once they had retreated to their bed that night, he asked her in a whisper. He had devised a way of asking it, and it was easier in the dark. Easier still, because talking to Lesley about himself had lost its appeal.

He said: Lesley, what are your best interests?

But she misunderstood. She listed the things she had been interested in once. She had been interested in travelling the interior of the country. That's how she put it, she called it the interior. She had been interested in living in a house permanently and knowing the names of her neighbours. She had been interested in moving to the city. As a girl and then a young woman, she had been interested in working in some kind of office environment in the city, overlooking a harbour or quay. She had wanted to go to bars of an evening and markets of a weekend. She had wanted to dine on affordable foreign cuisines. It had been a pipedream, she said. She had moved to the city, but even then, a life in the city had remained a pipedream, there was no way what she had there could be mistaken for a life.

She had never been interested in having a family, but then, suddenly, from one day to the next, she had wanted nothing more. It wasn't for having fallen in love, and it wasn't to do with hormones or nature. It's probably about time we stopped having families, she said, it's probably wise to spare children. But given how everyone alive now balances on a threshold, and given that none of us know just how thick or generous the threshold will prove to be...given that its edges are already coming into view for some of us, and given that children are beautiful beyond question, in the sense that they are yours and you theirs, and that they're only as evil as you allow them to be, it gives you cause for reassessment, you've got to admit. Urgency, resignation...which do you choose? They'll have you think one is more noble than the other. Nothing shits me more than the noble, but it gives you cause for reassessment.

And then she had been attacked by a dream, one where she had reared children who had disappeared.

Bon needed to improvise, he could not let the matter hang. She had plainly spoken what others had only ever alluded to, in his old life. He experienced a fleeting kinship with her.

So he said: I'm going to ask, right now, and pull me up if you feel uncomfortable, but I'm going to ask: where do you think the children went?

And then after a silence he construed as compliant, he asked again: Do you know where they must have went?

She didn't know. She didn't know where they were in the dream, nor did she know where she thought they were. Though it didn't need Bon asking, for it to be clear that they were somewhere, i.e., they had not died.

I was a mother in the dream, she said. I have inherited some of the knowledge of mothers. So now I know that when you are a parent rearing babies and then children, it doesn't seem possible from day to day that anything can change. And although things do change, very quickly, the moments between change proceed so slowly. You think you'll rock them to sleep and wipe their arses forever, but then they're suddenly complex, and then – she flung her left wrist up into the air, towards the ceiling – the next day they're gone. And there is pain in watching them blossom from animal into person. Most boil it down to nostalgia – that you'll never get your cute and helpless baby back – but actually, it's painful, watching tiny creatures become more like us.

In the dream, so unlike her usual ones, Lesley lived at the foot of a backstreet cul-de-sac in a town of the mountains, lined with interminable townhouses, footed by a gully of brambles and waste. They'd not gone missing in the brambles and waste, they'd not gone missing anywhere. They'd not gone missing from one place, only to be present in some other. My children were simply gone, she said. In the dream she'd awoken to the sound of morning cartoons, and thinking – or rather not thinking, just preternaturally sensing – that they were seated on the lounge watching TV, she had fallen back to sleep.

But this sleep, Lesley said, was a strange sleep. She could sense it even while she was sleeping. It was an odd sleep, a discomforted sleep, it was a sleep inside a dream, and it wasn't because of any dream within the dream (though she sensed that one had occurred), nor was it any low-flying plane throwing her senses off course. Certain vivid images pop into my mind that remind me of that sleep, she said, certain arrangements of shadow. She'd awoken again at ten past nine, and sensing that the TV was no longer airing cartoons (instead a loud, formal, adult-oriented bark) she had tossed her quilt onto the carpet and knocked over her glass of night-time water and not even checked her phone, only to find in the lounge room, and then the kitchen, and then the bedrooms, the backyard, the front yard, the street, the neighbouring homes, the local council area – no children.

These dream children, Lesley said – and she did say 'these dream children', in a manner removed – had shown no signs of wanting to pick up and leave, though she had to admit they might have been unhappy. In her dream she could remember often asking her thirteen-year-old 'Are you unhappy?', and he would always say no, even though it was likely that he was. And the eleven-year-old... she was eleven-years-bloody-old, she looked like her father though Lesley had never even met him – her father didn't exist. She was surely too young to fall into fits of depression, so it must have been – and she sighed – an especially bad depression they were in. You can suspect or know that children are in a depression, she said, but they're sheepish, they don't know whether it's allowed. I had always said to my dream children: tell me everything. You do not want to let bad feelings spread like wildfire inside of you. You want to tell someone while the chance remains to put them out.

Call me an idiot but I miss my dream children, Lesley said. I now have a mental image of their spirits and demeanours, I understand their sparks and their warning signals. They are more substantial than characters in stories or movies, more substantial than most people I have met. And you couldn't call them fictional, I never made them up...there was no fabrication. If they were merely fictional, I would have done what I've always secretly thought was the best thing to do with children: I would have been harsh and unforgiving. I would have been reluctant to permit them to fail, I would have enforced punishing moral regimes, I would have beat them into shape, I would not have allowed them to believe that the world was on their side. To be on the receiving end of gentleness...I would have sought to make them understand it is a rare privilege. I would have told them when the time was right, that their house might burn in fire, that they may one day die of thirst, or be maimed in the struggle to quench it. I would have done so in just the right, careful way.

Bon was disappointed that he'd been reported a dream. He searched for something to say, but it took too long, and sensing that it was taking too long, he said (empathetically, he thought): it's complicated.

Lesley agreed, because she was always willing to accede to the authority of complexity. Bon didn't mind her acting the sage – quite liked it, even, especially in the lounge room, and especially when it quelled Steven. For a long time there was silence, coloured only by the traffic on the highway. To Bon, it seemed a premature silence. She must have fallen to sleep, though maybe not quite; every five minutes or so her body shifted in a deliberate way.

When she finally spoke, he guessed it was only because she thought *he* had fallen asleep. At least, he couldn't understand why she would confide in him, of all people. She said, below the height of a murmur, that what she needed now, was some kind of family.

He didn't answer, because he thought she thought he was asleep.

The household had established an informal chore roster. Bon and Steven would retrieve provisions from the Newnes Valley Plaza one day, it was Lesley and Jack's turn the next.

Bon could not feel at ease with Jack around, because Lesley had bonded with him in a way verging on the conspiratorial. There appeared to be a silent consensus that Bon could never understand the boy. But Steven, Lesley, Jack...they didn't know anything, he had reserves of all kinds of openness and insight, it only required the right amount of time to let it all out.

Sometimes late at night, when Bon had retreated and when Steven had passed out, he'd hear Lesley and Jack in discussion. Lately, it had not been only Lesley's voice: he spoke too. Jack's voice was not one he had expected. It had a slight youthful affectation, belonging to the kind of voice that thought itself averse to affectations. It cycled through accents, slow and then fast, lacking a reliable source. It was higher pitched than he had expected. Whatever it expressed, he knew he was not invited to hear it.

Whenever he broached the topic with Lesley in the dark of their bed, she would pretend that she misunderstood, or that she hadn't noticed anything. In as subtle a way as he could manage, Bon would suggest that Lesley ought to tell him all of the boy's secrets. With her back turned deliberately towards him, she tactfully declined.

One night Bon dared suggest to Lesley that they swap boys now and then: Lesley would take Steven, Bon would take Jack. It wasn't met with the surprise he expected; he thought Lesley would be proud of his initiative. But she didn't put up any resistance, because it must have seemed a logical way for Bon to endear himself to the boy.

Of course there's no reason why we shouldn't swap the boys, she had said, with far too much sham confidence.

Bon gathered a fistful of canvas bags the next morning and bravely approached him. You and me, he said, are going on the daily shop. Lesley wants to help Steven find hidden roads and pathways. She wants to see what it's all about.

Jack, sitting on the front steps browsing his phone, delivered an expression he must have hoped looked bored rather than dismayed.

Bon wanted to say that it wasn't his idea. He wanted to tell Jack that this strange project was dreamed up by Lesley, and that they – men who must sometimes act subservient to the wily strategising of women – should just get it over with. But he had been warned that Jack was smarter than he appeared. The boy stood, dusted his tracksuit pants, stubbed his smoke, slotted the remaining length behind his ear, and indicated with his body that he was ready to follow.

They descended the hill into town. Bon couldn't tell whether he was walking at the optimum speed. He couldn't tell whether Jack was keeping up with him, or if he was keeping up with Jack. He had formulated several possible things to say to Jack, things that were mild and circumstantial but not too banal. He had wanted to mention that Steven should find another way to dispose of the empty beer bottles, he had wanted to say that the food they ate was crap. But he found himself incapable of saying anything, and as they approached their destination, Bon supposed that Jack perhaps admired his silence. No doubt, Jack had intuited that their sharing the shopping duties for that day was a strategy devised to bring them closer together, and no doubt, so Bon supposed, Jack felt understood and respected for the fact that Bon didn't seem to be trying to engage at all. Yes, maybe this is exactly what we need, thought Bon. We need to just do things together in silence. The silence would blossom into a form of understanding, maybe some day it would lead to speech.

They entered the plaza, wandered the hall of shuttered roller doors towards the supermarket. People stared at Jack but he paid them no attention. He was just going shopping, after all. He was just retrieving the only provisions he ever seemed to require: two 1.25 litre bottles of Coke, bread for Vegemite, and a bag of off-brand corn chips. Bon forgot what he wanted so improvised instead: another loaf of bread, some more bags of chips, pre-tossed salad sealed in plastic, a tray of sausages, and just in case: toothpaste. The self-serve checkout failed and the supervisor came to their aid. Bon was extra grateful to the supervisor – he wanted to show Jack that he was polite to checkout supervisors. Then they went to buy a carton of Tsingtao beer from the adjoining Liquorland.

A six-pack of beer each isn't enough, Jack said, speaking for the first time. He poked the stack of cartons for the least water damaged cardboard.

It used to be enough, but it's not anymore. We're hitting it pretty hard.

Bon had noticed this too – the men would end up drinking half of Lesley's share, and it was unfair on Lesley. He rejoiced in the opportunity to show warmth towards Lesley.

It's unfair on Lesley, Bon said.

We should get some rum to go with it, Jack suggested. A bit of rum a night would tip us nicely over the edge.

Bon couldn't agree more: he was delighted to be in discussion with the boy. They bought the cheapest bottle of rum they could find, and then they took a seat in the food court to catch their breath and figure out the logistics of carrying everything home. Jack would take the carton split up into bags, Bon would carry the groceries.

They lumbered out the sliding doors and onto the tarmac of the car park. There they were, Bon and Jack, the ice between them partially cracked. Soon enough, they might even leave the weatherboard and venture into town for the sheer pleasure of it. With this incision made, maybe they would go and have a midday beer and punt at the pub, or maybe they could sit on the train track overpass and ruminate as the sun set over the west. Maybe, some day in the future, Jack would venture to impart to Bon all that he had already imparted to Lesley. And by the time he did so, Bon would have formulated the precise thing to say in response, he would have found the correct order of words leading to just the right amount of empathy. It would no doubt be months before Jack felt comfortable enough to confide. And this being the case, Bon felt confident that if he applied all of his mental efforts to finding those correct words, then they would come. The words would not seek to solve any problem, they would not seek to philosophise, they would not dare suggest any understanding or comprehension...they would just be a sequence of words that perfectly fit the occasion. They might not be many words, maybe three or four. But how would he make his body cooperate with these words? Would he need to make his body appear nonplussed, vaguely accepting and fateful? Would a shrug of the shoulders suffice, or would he need to be standing upright at the time, in a posture showing both strength and sensitivity? Would his body need to adopt a part of the boy's seeming trauma, would it need to, in some way, mirror that of Jack's? They did after all, seem to share a motivating kind of resignation. But whose paled in comparison to whose? Maybe it would be best, so Bon speculated, weakly, unconvinced, that his own story should cut through the drama of Jack's, that his own voice should prove to be the most distraught. He had learned over the years that it's unwise to address someone's problems with problems of one's own. But under these circumstances, as a man talking to a boy, it might be different.

As they carted their provisions down the small flight of steps into the sun-blanched asphalt car park, all Bon needed to do was be silent, and whenever Jack happened to cast a look in his direction, he needed only appear occupied by the task at hand. The project was complete: he and Jack had passed time together.

Parked at the kerb of the Newnes Valley Plaza was a dusty old hatchback, mottled in grime, rear window barricaded by swollen plastic bags. In the passenger seat was the outline of the figure Steven's description had evoked. It was precisely the image Bon had imagined. It was less a body than a shape, details did not cohere, whether for a quirk in the light or the fissures in the glass, Bon couldn't tell.

Jack hadn't noticed: with the canvas bags full of beer hung from his shoulders, he was peering into his phone. Bon herded him in a wide arc around the hatchback and towards the hill. Jack wasn't the type to pay much attention to his surrounds, and Bon, taking care not to provoke the figure in the hatchback, looked intently forward as they struggled up the incline, he carried his body in a way he thought looked capable.

But upon reaching the first crest, where the road branched off into further winding inclines, he noticed the hatchback idling at the kerb of a nearby side street.

Bon grabbed Jack by the shoulders and turned him firmly around.

We can't go back home now, he said. I just remembered something.

Jack looked angry – they'd just mounted the first of three dramatic hills.

Lesley wants us to meet her at the RSL, Bon said. I just remembered.

Fuck off she does, Jack said. And you can't take six-packs into the RSL.

If they're sealed it's fine, I've done it before.

Jack didn't believe him, Bon knew he didn't. But Jack wouldn't stoop to arguing.

They paced down the hill and back onto the car park of the plaza. The hatchback was parked on the outskirts of the tarmac, but Jack wasn't looking, he was bent over gasping for air. Bon led them across the wide road, through a large vacant field of overgrown grass, then onto a cul-de-sac on the other side, where a naked terrace house splintered off into a deep gully. The RSL stood temple-like at the far end of this barren street, it wore a modern artificial sandstone facade, it was speckled with orange lights and the logos of gambling organisations. Aside from the terrace ruin, the RSL was the only maintained structure for hundreds of metres in all directions, it rose monolithic on land that was empty save the remnant brick foundations of long dismantled squats. It occupied its own pocket of town, invisible unless breached.

They passed through glass sliding doors into a spacious, tastefully brown lobby, bedecked with plaques listing men killed in wars. The sign-in desk wasn't attended, nor was the counter of the coat check. Beyond another set of sliding doors dozens of poker machines idled in rows, their vulgar jingles jovially entwined. TV screens hung from the rafters but all the screens were an idling blue; a wall-long bar to the right sat unattended. Above the cacophony of jingles a familiar radio song aired, shorn of bass and pulse, the wail of a yearning FM ballad. Within the confines of the room it was a languid Saturday night, the daylight at the entry was overcast and bleak, and anyway, partially obscured by the hatchback at the kerb.

He retrieved his wallet from one of the canvas bags and emptied its change into Jack's palms.

Have a punt, Bon shouted over the jingles. Lesley will be here soon.

Jack browsed the poker machines while scrolling on his phone. Bon waited until the boy was seated and engaged. He felt elated for a moment, then remembered that Lesley wouldn't arrive – realised he'd gradually taken refuge in his own lie. He turned towards the street and stared at the hatchback. He could see a face inside, the shape of a face that did not cohere into qualities.

I'm just going for a smoke, Bon yelled.

He passed through the first sliding door. The hatchback seemed to bulge, it seemed to become swollen and more forbidding. He dallied, pretended to read the sign-in sheet. He had hoped that other people would be in the RSL, and that somehow they would help. Because it wasn't his duty to protect recalcitrant men from their foes, and whatever happened couldn't be mistaken for his fault.

But the idling hatchback was the substantiation of myth or lunacy, he was compelled for this reason to approach it. It might then dematerialise, surely it wouldn't endure. Once he'd reached the footpath, and once he knew it wouldn't dematerialise, and once he'd stood so close to lay his hand on the bonnet, Bon began to choke. The figure inside lacked qualities, it was still with wide glazed eyes...was it dead? There was a bizarre dearth of perceptible quality in its face, and due to the dim in the cabin even its clothing was indeterminable. There were facts about the figure that were possible to describe, for example that its face was stubbled, that its forehead was lightly wrinkled and its scalp was bald, though hair grew wildly behind. But the figure didn't move nor express in Bon's direction – they did not interface – though it met him in the eyes. With a certain wry flatness of the lips, and a neutrality in the pupils, it resembled a heavy-breathing manikin.

Bon patted the bonnet to orient himself. And then he opened the passenger door and crouched. The smell of meat suffused the air. The figure was obscenely large, its head and its shoulders and the upper portion of its chest belied proportions elsewhere. What a hopeless man, Bon thought. What a tragic, harmless man.

The figure's mouth appeared to form a scowl, but its eyes and body didn't correspond. It's possible that the figure felt imposed upon, but Bon couldn't be certain of this, he'd never been certain of the meanings of expressions. It resembled an animal, Bon surmised. It was some kind of animal. Like a neglected dog. This analogy consumed him so that after some time, Bon emitted a brisk vocalisation, something resembling a bark, an experimental gesture. But the figure, whose eyes were partially buried by wrinkle and rolls, remained just as it was before.

Go on, Bon barked. Get.

He was suddenly disgusted by the figure.

The hatchback rolled slowly away, but fast enough that Bon didn't perceive the motion of arms handling gear stick or wheel. It turned left onto a road hidden by the RSL, passenger door swinging. The air was still; the smudge of tangled pokie medley sounded faintly from inside. Bon jogged around the corner in pursuit, onto a grey and potholed road, arid and exposed amid low brambled fields. There was no way to give chase unseen but Bon wasn't frightened, he now felt a morbid fascination – he now wished he had listened closer to Steven when he spoke. The hatchback turned right, in the direction of the main street, and Bon maintained a fifty-metre distance behind it, could do so at a brisk walk.

They were soon among houses, sullen front yards, ruined cars. Sun-faded flags curtained dusty windowpanes. The hatchback seemed to slow for the presence of homes, allowing Bon to adopt a regular shopping pace. The figure in the cabin didn't look left nor right through intersections, it didn't have to, for there was no other traffic on the roads that Thursday. The passenger door, still open, flapped lazily.

Together they reached the quieter part of the main street. That westerly end was lined with old warehouses and garages on one side, and the elevated train line opposite. The hatchback turned right towards town, and for the presence of light traffic, gained speed. It soon came to a halt at a streetlight intersection, close to the lush green park and disused theatre. And then, after the lights, it turned left down a narrow street and into the vast commuter car park of the train station. It parked carefully between the lines. The motor turned off.

Bon stood at a safe distance, monitoring the vehicle. A country-bound train came to a stop in the station, followed by a three-note chime signalling an announcement. From the station speakers a voice announced that, due to some unspecified emergency repairs, the train was terminating until further notice.

It was typical, Bon thought angrily. Though he'd grown to love and need train travel, he reserved his right to be enraged by trains. The audacity was what dismayed him: how dare they make a promise – train travel – and so frequently fail to deliver on it. How dare the trains behave with the capriciousness of weather, how dare the operators of trains allow it. The Oscars, the Tangaras, the Waratahs...failure was baked into their very function, as a means of sinister societal control, no doubt.

Figures started pouring from the station into the car park. At first a dozen appeared, mostly elderly. They stood dumb and tranquil in a loose crowd, looking around, waiting for further instruction. These were soon joined by even more, those who had, at first, simply denied the situation. Bon was familiar with this second type of person: those who have heard that the train will terminate, but linger in their seats all the same, for the remote chance that the announcement had been made in error. They joined the crowd, dropped bags sullenly, swatted away at mobile phones.

Then came the third wave, much larger than the first two combined. These were the people who must have had headphones in, watching movies or listening to music, those who would only ever disembark at the stern direct command of a station assistant. There were upwards of a hundred people in the car park now, most of them passionately texting missives to whoever expected them to arrive.

Then in dribs and drabs: the fourth wave, those inclined to linger on the platform, investigate the matter, to have the finer details explained to them by train station staff. This fourth wave roamed the vast car park apprising everyone else of the situation. Or else they stood inside the thickets of the crowd speaking loudly to themselves, soliloquising the matter, enlivened and sustained by the frustration of less proactive bystanders. It was business as usual, as far as Bon could tell. But it surprised him that none had seemed to notice they had terminated at a station missing from conventional timetables. What would become of these marooned people, this crowd that did not voluntarily alight?

A mild-mannered discontent was fermenting. Some people from the fourth wave were jogging up and down the station stairs, dutifully seeking status updates. Most of the third-wave people held their phones in a viewing position but nevertheless gazed, at a loss, into the nearby streets. Second-wave people spoke among themselves; first-wave people had taken up the closest steep gutter, seated and resigned. Bon was transfixed by this behaviour, it made him feel potently nostalgic, he smouldered with a sad remorse. There was a buried sensation slowly burrowing to the fore, it resembled jealousy, but not quite...it wasn't with certainty regret. Unbeknown to them, these people were at a crossroads of the most consequential kind. He identified with their plight and felt inclined to warn them what awaited them. If it were possible for them to have all the facts and possibilities laid nakedly out, then maybe those minutes, hours, spent waiting for retrieval on the commuter car park asphalt might be replaced by a frenzied kind of action. But they were not going to board a train ever again, and they did not yet know it. It was unclear to Bon whether it was possible for them to be salvaged.

Or did they know it? Was there a secret timetable, now, and a widescale subconscious observance of it? The prospect of people alighting didn't dismay Bon. If they had done so deliberately – subconsciously so – this granted him a sour vindication. Because one fear he felt with utmost clarity was the fear of possibly not threading into some universal pattern.

The train stationmaster was at the gutter, jabbing first-wave people with his jabbing stick. It was forbidden to sit in the gutter, and for that matter – he announced more broadly – it was forbidden to linger so scattershot across an area designated for vehicles. Public liability, he sang. Fourth-wavers bristled at this demand, but everyone else hoisted their bags over their shoulders, or else unlocked the brakes on their canvas wheel bags. A congested exodus ensued, led for the most part by those from the third wave, who had managed to maintain an air of ambivalence towards the situation. Others from the second wave followed and Bon joined their dawdle, up the street towards a bus idling at the kerb. He knew it wasn't the replacement bus, but he wasn't going to stop them from boarding it: he might appear unhinged. Many boarded it, but others didn't, and those who didn't turned left towards the main street, the one torn up and barricaded by mesh. Once they reached this area the group splintered. There was no solidarity among them, and many stood on the footpath gazing again into phones, perhaps believing that after a whole five minutes something might have changed. Bon watched a few dribble into the nearby petrol station as the afternoon faded. And for the apparent end of this spectacle, Bon remembered why he was there in the first place: the hatchback was gone, and no longer leading him by the nose.

He fled back to the rear of the station and boarded the bus. It was almost full with passengers, some staring out the window. As soon as he was aboard the engine roared, it pulled away, he stood in the aisle as it laboured over the bridge, between lines of homes, and then onto the tarmac of the Newnes Valley Plaza. The bus driver shouted last stop.

From there he sprinted across the vacant field towards the RSL. Jack was hunched on a stool at a machine themed as if from ancient Egypt. He'd won thirty dollars but lost it again.

Steven had gashed his finger smashing bottles while they were gone. He'd wailed, howled, punched the wall, and Lesley hadn't known how to calm him. So Bon had to rush back down the hill to buy band-aids.

In the Newnes Valley Plaza, dozens of stranded commuters languished in the food court. Scraps and plastic discards were strewn on the benches before them. Some of them appeared to stir at Bon's approach, but it must have been his appearance that forbade them making contact.

He wasn't the sort to come to people's aid, lest they feel condescended to. But he couldn't help but deliver an expression of acknowledgement as he passed, a wry pouting of the bottom lip, an ironic kind of sympathy. All the seated people, every one of them, traced with their eyes Bon's movements, like he was a native to this unknowable wild. As he searched the foot of the aisles for the health-section signage, Bon felt oddly lifted, unusually confident. It was true that he was a pioneer of sorts. Was he not the first to alight at the station for good? There was no way of knowing whether this was true, but equally, no way of confirming that it wasn't. He straightened his slouch, pursed his lips, affected an air of wise familiarity, then purchased two plastic trays of cinnamon donuts – they were reduced by fifty per cent. He placed them on an empty food court bench as he passed back through, pointed at them, opened them, gestured like a magician at them, and walked briskly away. He dared not linger to see the reaction he elicited.

Jack was seated on the front steps when he got home. Steven's finger blood was smeared across his face.

It's not a good look, Bon said.

Lesley said they'd come to blows because Steven thought Jack wasn't being sympathetic enough. She whispered it in the kitchen.

They're brothers and they'll fight, Bon said dismissively, exhausted by the day's events. No harm done, a bit of dust off the shoulders. Sisters, women, girls, they might be different, but brothers: they punch on sometimes.

Fuck brothers, Lesley said, still shaking.

Steven hurt himself, he said, and he badly wants Jack's attention.

Bon knew that expressing the harsh truth first, and then watering it down, still left the truth intact while absolving him of callous truthfulness.

Steven welcomed his return with more gusto than usual, whether for the moral support or the rum, Bon couldn't tell. The bleeding had stopped, but to bring the matter to a close, Bon applied two band-aids over the wound. They sat together in the lounge room, Steven's arm slung over Bon's shoulder, both sated. Lesley seemed to be avoiding them, and Jack was beholden to no patterns.

Bon snapped the rum open and poured them each a shot into coffee mugs. He wanted to tell Steven that he should just relax about his brother, that it wasn't a big deal. But he was too dedicated to the version of himself he had cultivated in Newnes.

Jack, come and have some rum, Steven barked.

The younger man actually came after a couple of minutes.

You dumb cunt, Steven seethed. I love you.

Jack rolled his eyes and hissed. He sipped rather than shot his rum, studiously ignoring Bon.

I've been pretty honest you have to admit, Steven was saying. And I'm sorry for punching you in the face, I didn't do it very hard. But you're not impressing anyone, being so cool. Being cool and ambivalent, being steely, is not in fashion anymore, I'm glad it isn't. It's actually lame, because everyone, nowadays, is saying exactly how they feel, and it's frowned upon not to have something to mourn or confess...I'm just saying this, Jack, in case you think we're still living in the old world. Everyone cares now, you're being a prick if you don't. But all that said, I love you, and fuck it for the time being anyway.

He cracked a beer with his lighter and flicked the bottle lid into the fireplace. Lesley came into the room, she was always the last to join them in their drinking sessions. She'd sidle in and stand at the periphery for a while, as if to pretend she had no intention of joining them. But eventually she'd say something that was sensible to say while seated, in order to be properly heard. Once she sat down, her expansiveness could rival Steven's.

How do you know that Jack doesn't care, she said, pouring a tad of the rum.

Lesley's presence always softened the mood, and Bon had come to look forward to her pouring her first drink. Booze brought her alive. After a couple of drinks she held herself more confidently, like she hadn't come to depend on alcohol, like it was still a lot of fun. It helped Bon pretend they were drinking for the joy of it. It also helped that she was the only soul in the house willing to challenge or talk back to Steven.

She continued: Do you think it's possible to care so much that you no longer care?

This was the kind of riddle Steven loved.

You've got a point, he said. I probably seem like I don't care too.

No, she said. You seem to care about everything, which is brilliant, and that's what we love about you. But maybe you care in different directions, or you're practising a kind of self-protection. Caring for yourself is caring for others too, you know.

You think I'm caring for myself? Steven flared.

No, I think you're caring in different directions, she said.

Jack was looking down into his lap, staring into the smoke he exhaled.

I'm definitely caring in different directions to Jack, he said. But Jack cares so much – he mimed scare quotes – that he doesn't mind if lots of people suffer or die. That's a strange kind of caring, isn't it, when all you're caring about is people who don't even exist yet? I care about people who don't exist yet, but I care more about people who do, shoot me for it I don't care. And I don't think there should be war.

There's not going to be a war, Lesley sighed.

Jack reckons there will be.

But whatever he reckons, it probably won't be in my lifetime, he added serenely.

Exactly, she said.

Bon watched Jack, who remained impassive.

There's not going to be wars, she said. No one needs to go to war with us, they can just prise what they want gently out of our hands. And if there is war, no one will care about Newnes. And you've got no kids to worry about.

Steven patted a cushion under his side, lazed into it. You're probably right, he said, but it's not like I just care about Newnes. Newnes is part of the world, isn't it? And who would start the war anyway? Not the likes of Jack, that's for sure.

Not Jack and not no one. She clapped her hands and brushed her waist. Everyone's too busy with their freedoms, she added.

They all sat there smoking silently for a while.

You know what I miss? Steven said. I miss doing my tax. And fuck off in advance, Jack. But I miss the forms and procedure, I miss that contact with higher operations. I'm just being honest. The forms are complex and their wordings are like puzzles. You'd spend several weeknights understanding the puzzles – what are annuities? Should I worry about employee share schemes? What are dividend deductions? The meanings of words on tax forms never match the meanings of words in dictionaries. The page dedicated to the Medicare levy surcharge...I can simply tick a box, but what does the rest of it mean, the parts that don't apply to me? And who will chase me if I tick the box and ignore the rest in error? The obscurity of it all is reassuring, you are lightly running your fingers along the exterior of a well-oiled civic machine...and it's not for having searched it out, it's not because you've hunted down this secret phenomenon in the interests of exposing it. The secret phenomenon waits for you, and it briefly exposes itself to you, it formally reminds. You're not even forced to do your tax, it's possible just not to do it, and being audited is as likely as getting cancer. But I reckon doing your tax is a bit like going to church, and don't get me wrong I don't believe in god. But god was obscure and beyond our comprehension, god was once a matter for endless internal debate and anxiety...and

I think that, ever since I stopped doing my tax – and it's been a while now – I've lost touch with god. To be honest, I would like to walk into the post office and pick up a handful of sternly coloured forms, and to be confused once again by their complexities. They're firm, unyielding, facts and figures oriented, seemingly remote from day-to-day but intrinsic. Reportable fringe benefits, deferral schemes, lump sums in arrears...freakish, impenetrable phenomena with eerie biblical resonance.

So do your tax then, Lesley said. Why don't you just do it, if you love it so much? You might get a return.

Steven smiled, and Bon smiled too (it was because Steven smiled). Lesley smiled because the others smiled.

It came to feel true that he and Lesley, Jack and Steven, were a family of the town. By the standards of the world he'd left, they were a very unconventional family indeed. But conventions in that other world were coming undone, newly ripped fissures demanded the reassessment of everything. Under the circumstances, the fact of an arrangement being conventional or true no longer carried as much weight as it had before. Maybe truths and conventions had never deserved his faith to begin with. They were an unconventional family by the measure of the world, but in Newnes they made a dim kind of sense, a residual kind of sense.

One day Lesley woke Bon at three in the morning and handed him a cup of instant coffee.

There's rum in it, she said.

There was a saw, secateurs, lopper and axe at the end of the bed. Bon's head throbbed, the coffee seemed to boil in his gut and then up his throat. She had warned him this was coming, but he had chosen not to believe. He got up, pulled his shoes on, and retrieved the torch from under the bed.

The streetlights were few and far between in their neighbourhood. Down the hill, Newnes was specked with waning lights, with a blinding BP sign raised above the cocooning highway. They turned in the opposite direction, up the hill, where the road tapered off into black endless forest.

They needed to weave through trees for a while, they needed to start at the end: the entry must not be visible until the pathway was complete. Bon had conceived the idea, but he had intended for the idea to be poetic. Anyway, he felt secure in the knowledge that Lesley would soon give up, because the trees were dense and the terrain was stony, criss-crossed with ancient fallen trunks. It was also perfectly dark in there, and his torch made no impression within the thickets.

It doesn't matter, said Lesley, whether we can see the trees we're chopping or not. Just close your eyes and whack.

The trees in that part of the forest were tough but thin. They found a small, unshapely clearing and set about expanding it. Lesley slapped the trunk of four surrounding trees: You chop, I'll push, she said.

He'd struggled to walk before, but with the swing of an axe a powerful adrenaline surged through his body. It felt good to be acting the man, especially in the presence of Lesley. Here he was, doing a man's job. He hadn't even needed to make a case for it being a man's job. His first half-dozen swings had been uncommitted, they'd been fake swings. But as his body came alive and his heartbeat quickened, he gave more thought to how he must appear, and applied more force to the arc of the blade. I must appear strong, Bon supposed. It was unlikely that Lesley had ever known a man so willing to expend this level of strength in the interests of something benign and unprofitable. At the heart of it all – all things considered – he must still be a decent man. He was good and he was capable. Lesley couldn't have had much contact with good men: likely she'd only known drunks, layabouts and abusers. In their respective former lives, Bon and Lesley would never have spoken; Lesley would have been a plain woman passing in the street with a trolley and a smoke. But there he was standing by her side, unquestioningly doing her bidding, and all things considered, he was being charitable. He received no praise or encouragement from Lesley and this was promising, for it meant that she'd known he was good and capable all along. His goodness and his strength didn't need mentioning, they were a foregone conclusion. He worked hard if called upon, capably to boot, motivated by good.

It was half an hour before his axe had cut far enough through the trunk for Lesley to push it into the clutches of nearby branches. His body suffered as he attacked the other three, his lungs felt blackened. The sky was a velvet bright in the east; neither had a phone or watch. Lesley reckoned they had at least five hours before the boys woke up. She slapped the trunks of three nearby trees and stepped away. Bon felt alarmingly virile, because he had noticed the way Lesley's shorts carried high on her thighs.

Let's lie down for a moment, he said. I need to catch my breath. With tasks at hand Lesley had adopted the tone of a shift manager. As long as you're quick, she said bossily, snipping away at nearby branches with the lopper. She seemed to want the clearing to resemble a cave. As the bright in the east intensified, it became clear that their labour had etched the beginnings of a canopied dome. She stood back and assessed her work. Bon stared at her as she observed her work.

This will be the boys' route to Sofala, Lesley said.

She retrieved the plastic bottle of rum from her back pocket and swigged it, then she tossed it at Bon, who stifled a laugh.

We don't have a car, Bon said. And anyway, what's so good about Sofala?

She seemed to struggle. It's an old town, she said, with no 4G range, and it's accessed via a hidden unsealed road. It's not part of the world or even this one. You wake up and you deal with what's in front of you. There are trees and hills, some shops, there's countryside. There's no desks, no tyrants, no threats. You don't hear about anything there.

You don't know anything about Sofala, Bon said. You're making it up. Steven was a kid when he went there. And anyway, we don't have a car.

Lesley looked briefly hurt, and then, eager to tell him off. But instead she insisted that they had lots of time to sort that out, and anyway, it was time to go home.

They were back at the weatherboard just before ten in the morning. Jack was passed out on the couch; Steven was asleep in his bed. They crept into their room. Rum-drunk and reckless, Bon removed his pants and then his shirt in full view of Lesley. Then he stripped his underpants and lay alertly on the bed. Lesley went about her business, filing the tools back under the bed, while he stared at the ceiling through partially drawn eyes, shocked by his own audacity.

Then came the familiar sound of Steven's heavy door scraping along the carpet.

One's awake, she said, dusting remnant splinters from her jumper onto the carpet.

You take Steven today, she went on. She was running her fingers through her hair, splinters and leaves were pouring out.

And remember, she added, let's not tamper with the routine again just yet. Jack's not ready.

Then she left the room. Bon dressed and lay on the bed again, unbearably ashamed.

During the years before he disembarked the train, Bon had felt that his life was full. Now it was filling up again, with characters, each with an interior life he could never properly know. All he could learn about characters was what they themselves said or what someone else reported about them – neither felt satisfactory. Maybe it was possible to glean insights based on behaviours and other subtleties – others seemed capable of this. But Bon was not capable. He was awash in the intricacies of others again. It would not do.

And Lesley, she had too much initiative; he didn't want to deal with initiative anymore. Frankly, she scared him, for the way she had undertaken – and apparently conquered – Jack, without making a single attempt to assure Bon against the boy's unexplained complications. It played on his mind every night. But Lesley scared him even more, for the way she plotted towards outcomes he did not desire at all, all with the veneer of exemplary benevolence. What if she succeeded? What hope did a woman like Lesley have? Neither pleasant nor repulsive, extremely navy in presentation, small of stature, with no obvious intelligence, and a voice well-practised in the modulations of imbecilic soothsaying...what hope did she have?

Probably none at all, Bon supposed. But he shouldn't take his chances. Possibly more concerning was that, despite all this, Bon didn't dislike the woman. Whether her care was genuine or a convincing act, it didn't matter: it had the same effect. Even her scolding, even her criticism, made him feel pathetically taken care of. And she had the minor kind of face that blossomed complexities with time, becoming something one could admire. She was too complex a matter by far.

He quietly left the room, crept out the back door, tiptoed down the side lane, and escaped through the front gate. He jogged down the hill. There was something prickly and leaden in the air, like airborne metal splinters. He coughed and retched as the miserable old street sank into the miserable old town. What a comically miserable town, Bon thought. What an atrocious dump. At the Newnes Valley Plaza car park, people loaded their substandard diets from trolleys into cars. They won't survive, Bon surmised. No one cares about their dumb little town.

He collapsed onto the ticket machine at the station. A woman stood there with a full and frayed ALDI bag, she told him that the trains had stopped.

Bon was furious. That's just typical, he said. It only takes a bit of grey weather. And the weather isn't even grey – is the winter sun too hot for the dear old train? Have the ancient sleepers bowed? Has the signal failed at Hornsby?

The woman affected an air of charity. The train has stopped forever, she explained. Try to buy a ticket – she patted the ticket machine – you can't because it's off. Try walking onto the platform – she spat at the platform stairs – you can't, because the platform's gated up. Everyone knows the trains are finished now. You must be the last to learn.

It wasn't unlikely that Bon should be the last to learn. Ever since he'd thrown his phone in the Salvos bin, he'd resolved to learn nothing new at all. But he wasn't inclined to trust the word of this woman, whose hair was wiry, who smelled of vegetable oil.

Who stopped the trains, he asked, affecting his own tone of charity. Was it the government? A catastrophic weather event? She barked back that it didn't matter who stopped them or why. Maybe they want us to drive, she said, or maybe they want us to appreciate the trains, now that they're gone. We've all bickered and moaned about trains every day since their arrival, it's a kind of ritual. Maybe they're just sick of us being ungrateful about trains. Or maybe they're just bluffing, showing their power, and the trains will start again after all, only in a diminished way. They might want to demonstrate that trains are a luxury and a privilege. They're always trying to make us feel grateful. And to be honest I am grateful, the woman said. What a miracle that trains ever operated at all. What a true show of benevolence, by the people who deigned to build, operate and maintain trains. What a privilege trains were! You didn't even have to show proof that you were using them to go to work, you could ride them for no reason at all. I long for those purple seats, she said, and the musty smell, and the view over the valleys as you pass through the upper mountains. I was never calmer than when I was on a train, she said. Fancy having the option to just sit on a train and bear witness to the world from a safe capsule, travelling at a safe speed, no risk of speeding off course.

She said that the trains had stopped, in all likelihood, because she had gotten off. She had no reason to be in Newnes, and anyway, she had thought it would be easy to get back on. She had disembarked for the realisation that there was nothing stopping her from getting off at Newnes, that there had been no reason not to.

Bon noticed the empty chip packets and the stubbed cigarettes on the cement. He noticed the system prompts on the timetable monitors. The train station wasn't being swept anymore – it stood to reason that the woman was telling the truth. He felt immense relief. It was impossible to do anything.

I'm not the only one stranded by the trains, the woman said. Over at the old blast furnace there's a bunch of us camping, waiting for something to happen. And don't tell me to get the bus – she wrinkled her nose – we've looked into it. We're all getting used to the old blast furnace, she said. It's quite nice, actually. I don't suppose you're looking for a place to hunker down?

Bon said he wasn't – he had disembarked the train and fallen immediately into the clutches of a strange man with a house.

I got lucky, he said. I suppose Steven got lucky too. And Lesley got lucky, she's living with us now. I got lucky, he added, but I'm not glad – there's a difference. All I wanted to do was stop off and have a beer. But you don't just stop off somewhere and get a beer anymore, you don't dare go off course, do you. I got off the train months ago, you could say I pioneered it.

She rolled her eyes. The first man to get off a train, she said.

Up the hill, Steven and Lesley were seated on the front steps. They weren't even browsing catalogues: they were waiting. Lesley stormed at him.

Where have you been, she roared. Steven stood nearby with his arms crossed in obstinate support. Lesley was furious – Bon hadn't thought it possible. He was too shocked to feel properly told off.

He said that he'd had a bad night's sleep – a private glare at Lesley – and that he'd taken a walk to clear his head.

Well you could have said goodbye, she said. And you could have brought some shopping. It's four in the afternoon, we've been scared stiff for you. The routine's all out of whack and Jack's already on the rum. We're hungry and scared.

Bon somehow resisted telling her that, actually, he could do whatever he pleased, that he was not accountable to anyone, that he hadn't disembarked the train for this. Since when was she entitled to him? He managed to resist, because her anger had quickly transformed into relief, maybe even gratitude. Her face was wet and her eyes were red. He suddenly wanted to show some gentle affection, such as a pat on the back.

Instead he threw his hands up in the air and stormed into the house. Inside, Jack was splayed out on the smoky lounge room floor, leaning on a cushion, Bunnings catalogue in hand. The rum bottle was wedged between his legs. Bon ripped the rum away and took a swig, then placed it next to the boy.

We're going shopping, he said to Jack and the room. Steven and Lesley watched.

Then he added, to Jack specifically: But you can say no. He added: No one is forcing you to come. He added: But there's no reason not to.

But it's my turn, Steven whinged. He took Bon by the wrist. I didn't go to the plaza at all yesterday, he said, and Jack doesn't even want to.

Bodies stirred for an oncoming tantrum.

Lesley intervened: We'll all have to go today.

Bon grimaced, Lesley bellowed: Shoes on! Steven was indignant

– he already had his shoes on. Jack slapped the catalogue onto the ground, rolled onto his belly, laboured onto his feet. Lesley found him his socks.

Down the hill they went, Lesley and Bon in front, with Steven and Jack ambling behind. There was another confrontation brewing and Bon wanted to have it out in the open, he was utterly confident that he would win. But he didn't want to be the kind of family who spat and screamed at each other in full view of the town. Lesley was flapping her arms around in the way she always did outdoors, left hand over squinting eyes, swatting the occasional fly, sandals flapping. Steven was talking as usual, but Bon couldn't hear and didn't care to try. Bon admired the way Jack ignored his brother, his flagrant apathy was one of his strongest qualities, he was the most dignified among them. The way Jack ignored and the way he walked – with no slouch, with his eyes set on the distant town and not the asphalt – lent him a strange, impressive dignity. That's the way I've always walked, Bon thought. But on the other hand, wasn't it endearing the way Steven never shut the hell up? Wasn't it overall positive the way he cast his every thought onto the world? Steven was a pleasure, just listen to him speak, the patterns of his speech. No family, Bon thought, could ever be quite like this. Even Lesley, the whip bearer, the manchild soothsayer, had her charms. But they were all still characters, shapes of beings, surfaces of lives. Bon couldn't understand any of them.

Did any of you know the trains have stopped for good, he yelled at Lesley and the boys. Lesley shook her head and cast a wry smile, Steven even laughed. Jack was staring at the distant town but there was amusement in his eyes.

What's so funny about it? Bon felt indignant but couldn't help but smile in response. Lesley punched him on the arm and said: The trains have been stopped for ages, you wing nut. Steven looked at her slyly. They must have discussed how strange it was that he had failed to notice.

Why didn't anyone say? Bon drew to a halt to show he was serious; Steven and Jack caught up, and they all stood in a circle in the middle of the decline. He needed them to know he was serious and he said as much: I'm being serious, why didn't anyone say?

Well, Lesley said, maybe pay closer attention to what is being said and who is saying it.

It might have hurt had the situation not turned comedic. Steven laughed so hard he was coughing up phlegm. Jack stood with his arms crossed but he no longer stared down the hill. He was looking into Bon's face, waiting with seeming eagerness for whatever the stupid man might say next. Bon stared the boy back and said: Why didn't you tell me?

This elicited reckless amounts of public mirth. Steven was coughing and choking on the sidewalk, and Lesley was laughing – he'd never heard her properly laugh before. It was definitely a funny thing to say, Bon thought. He was suddenly proud of himself – it was a genuinely funny question to ask of Jack. He half-wanted them to think it was deliberate. Steven wrapped a single arm around Bon's shoulder, and Lesley punched him in the arm again.

He's off with the fairies, she said.

They marched down the hill in concert now, the four of them side by side, Bon and Lesley in the middle. A car came up the road but they didn't move, it beeped and mounted the kerb to evade them. Steven yelled go and get fucked, Lesley gave the bird.

They reached the plaza in good spirits, roamed the supermarket aisles more methodically than usual, up and down each lane, while making stupid jokes. With the full crew spectating Steven turned hyperactive, loudly pointing out vaguely amusing groceries and even sometimes opening a sealed product to sample its content. At the foot of an aisle he kicked a tower of stacked toilet paper packets, shouted as the plastic cushions bounced across the laminate. Lesley was enfeebled with laughter, she scolded the boy but it only served as encouragement. And Bon struggled to keep his mouth flat, struggled to look stern, which made it even funnier.

As they left the self-serve checkout there was a small commotion at the Big W across the food court. A bird had wound up in the rafters, fluttering urgently above the kids' shoes section, colliding and then falling, saving itself, landing. There were people banked up in the lingerie section watching with concern, and the store manager stood nearby leaning on a broom.

You can't get a bird out once it's in, Steven whispered. It's in too deep, the route back out is too complex, it'll panic and die. No middling or great effort can save that bird, it's going to have to perish.

Lesley reckoned management would get it out but Steven was adamant. We can busybody beneath for hours at a time but it's trapped and scared, he said. What makes you think management is qualified? It's not part of their training, they can't solve every problem that might arise in department stores. Short of killing it, or evacuating the plaza and allowing it to wander on foot, there's nothing we can do.

They all watched the bird for a while. The manager acted concerned for the bird and concerned for customers. The pigeon was seated on a long strip of exposed white metal, frozen except for its throat, which appeared to occasionally convulse.

Well you have to understand, Lesley said, that this bird might have dreamed all its life of discovering the inside of buildings. It'll die happy, you know. Maybe it will die in here and maybe that's fine. It's a pioneer, a true renegade.

Steven wrapped an arm around Bon's shoulder, Lesley around Jack's. The store manager had been prodding uselessly with his broomstick but now tossed plastic coloured balls at the bird. They bounced away and down the aisles. Two toddlers gave chase and their mothers scampered to snuff the event. The toddlers squealed with unhinged pleasure, red faces and teary cheeks. With every new launch of a coloured ball the pleasure ascended, the din intensified.

One of these days we won't be hanging around this plaza anymore, Steven said. He gestured at the bird, and then out towards the plaza.

No matter how boring all this seems, he said, no matter how dull or disheartening, or depressing, or sad, it can seem, it will appear romantic by the measure of our future selves.

Bon couldn't have cared less about what Steven had to say. He was watching the toddlers evade the clutches of their mothers. The mothers were annoyed, but not too annoyed, because their children were cherubic and the only things that mattered. Both had fled to the whitegoods section, where most of the balls had ended up. The toddlers were so padded for winter they had limited command over their bodies, so that every lunge for their quarry caused a great imbalance. They tripped on the balls and set them rolling again, could not pick them up for the slipperiness of their puffer jackets. There in the whitegoods section the mothers were defeated, and Bon remembered what it was like to surrender to the disruptive joy of children.

It's not because things will get worse, Steven was saying, loud enough so the whole crowd could hear. Though in all likelihood things will, just ask Jack. Even if things get better, even if they become ideal, say perfect, and then keep getting more ideal and more perfect as new periods commence, there will always be parts of all this we will miss. That's the way the human mind works. Everything becomes coated in a certain lustrous colour scheme with recollection, you begin to see the profoundness of it all. And because you come to see the profoundness of it all, you come to have a bit more faith in that former self, living in that former life. You might not like that person, you might cringe at the thought of them, but they're an awkward ally. They lived in a particular era of this life and you have to respect that.

You do, Lesley said.

And there's satisfaction in demarcating eras, in being able to demarcate them. And demarcations happen, Steven said – now addressing the store manager – even if you try to stop them. The demarcations are what save us. So don't feel bad about yourself and your own demarcations. The end will be demarcated too, and even if you sense it's coming – which we do, all of us – it will arrive abruptly and it won't permit reflection.

The store manager nodded; Lesley said she agreed.

Bon watched the mothers as they carted underarm their children from the shop. They were freed in the food court, but demanded to be picked up again.

There in the Newnes weatherboard, it was impossible for Bon to imagine anything happening to them. Their present was different to their pasts – that much was easy to see. And just like everyone else, their every waking moment joined with younger living moments, sometimes occasioning quiet permanent shifts in routine.

But quiet permanent shifts in routine could not be the future. The future, he supposed, would remain a matter for speculation, a sandbox for dreams and anxieties. Only unthinkable shock, unthinkable violence, catastrophic shifts, could catapult someone – very briefly – into the future, and only for a brief moment, and even then, a moment so brief it would not permit reflection.

But there had not yet been unthinkable shock, and for him, no unthinkable violence nor catastrophic shift. Instead, it had been the slow gnawing of phenomena he had once safely ignored, or else considered metabolised. It was more than likely true, all things considered, that there really was no present anymore, that life kept on keeping on in the shadow of futures, indeed, possibly inside of them. No waking moment he experienced was actually, all things considered, lived at a remove from the future, because he lived inside of the future. If not strictly inside of tomorrow or the next day, then at least tragically subservient to their potentials.

I don't want to offend you, Lesley said next to him in bed, during the minutes before they arose to chop the clearing. I mean no offence, she said. But frankly, all this effort spent worrying is wasted energy, because even if you think you're going to die, you still need to live until the moment when you do.

So it makes sense to get them over to Sofala, Bon, don't you think? Because once we're there, none of us will have problems except for any new ones we create for ourselves. And the problems that drive us onward will be the stuff of simple survival, there will be no lingering evidence of here (she clawed theatrically at the ceiling), and there will be no reason to keep thinking about there (she flung her pillowed head eastbound). There's no such thing as a clean break, Bon, and you already know. But there can be a violent enforced break, and who's to say whether violence or force is wrong in the wide scheme of things. You just do what you can, don't you?

You just do whatever is possible, Bon replied.

One morning, as Bon and Lesley slouched down the decline from their clearing towards home, the air was smokier than usual. It was a typically misty spectral morning, but there was an atypical orange in the air, so rich that they veered off their path into nearby residential streets they'd never previously wandered. Whether for mild asphyxiation or the truth, Bon briefly thought himself stranded in dreams.

They got home in the nick of time – the smell outside was so pungent that even the boys were stirred from sleep. Steven and Jack did what they usually did: they lumbered into the lounge room, sculled water from plastic litre bottles, pressed tobacco into paper. But it didn't last for long.

Something's going on, Steven said.

Something's on fire, Lesley reckoned.

They poured onto the street, stood in the road. The sun couldn't puncture the smoke, it was a dull glowing orb. Steven started throwing rocks, like jabbing into the blear. When Jack walked they followed – they didn't want to lose him – down the curving cliff roads towards the main street into town.

The asphalt field around the Newnes Valley Plaza was swollen with stationary onlookers. Flames ravaged the building, and the signage had already toppled.

It was a beautiful scene, so Bon thought. It was not impossible for terrible things to be beautiful – that was a fact that he'd gathered to be a truism over the years. Supermarkets were useful and important, integral even, but somehow, dimly, they were also bad. And this collision pleased his senses; most truths were best left tangled in ambiguities.

No one dared talk. They stood there watching, shoulder-to-shoulder at the periphery as the building burned, its silhouette orange against the blackened air, purple oily streaks across the firmament. It was only Jack who stood a little behind, determined to neglect the scene. Most of the people on the asphalt were not of the town – they must have been people stranded by trains. At any rate none were recognisable, whether for the eerie lack of light or for the truth, Bon couldn't tell. And just like Bon and Lesley, they stood firmly without panic, awestruck by the flames, flinching occasionally for the pop of an explosion.

It wasn't fascinating for long – Bon soon wished the spectacle would end, and he couldn't imagine how flames could snuff from one moment to the next. It would no doubt be a slow, tedious process, and he anticipated his boredom morphing into agitation. Maybe if they had somewhere to sit – somewhere not dampened by mist – then he could gaze upon this crisis till its end. It would be enjoyable to do so while seated, ideally also nursing a beer, and he knew Steven felt the same: he was shifting his weight from leg to leg, looking around at the streets away from the fire. He should enjoy this momentous occasion. But he also knew that lived moments could never rival the potency of memories. He dusted his jeans and broke the reverent quiet.

I've seen enough, he said.

Steven agreed. The fire will just keep going like this until someone puts it out, he reckoned.

But we've got no food in the house, Lesley said.

We'll have to walk to the petrol station on the highway, Bon replied. They have sausage rolls and pies and things like that.

And our money is running out, she continued. All the money between us – she waved at his pocket – is almost spent. And pies are expensive at petrol stations.

Bon led them away, he wouldn't discuss these matters in the presence of biblical spectacle. He walked across the road and over the field towards the RSL, and then through some quiet residential streets. A lane at the end of a cul-de-sac connected to a footpath along the highway. By the time they'd reached the highway, where strip motels went to seed, and where the windows of old homes were boarded for the highway noise, Lesley seemed to have forgotten. The air was clearer though still apocalypse brown, but in the west lay evidence of a blue winter sky. The odd car passed lazily by, high beams through the smoke.

The petrol station had a mini-supermarket inside, and it shared a car park with the McDonalds. They bought a half-dozen packets of large chips, two loaves of Tip Top, a jar of Vegemite and a tub of Buttercup. They bought the boys a sausage roll each and they munched them along the blackened highway.

Steven's torpor had lifted. He was invigorated by the novelty of shopping somewhere else.

There's no doubt someone lit that fire on purpose, he said, brushing crumbs onto the pathway. Plazas don't just go up in flames, they're heavily regulated, you're not even allowed to flick a match in them.

Catastrophes happen, Lesley said.

You don't need to tell me that, Steven snapped. But we can't keep living here if there's no supermarket. What would be the point of it? We might as well live in the bush. Jack would agree.

Jack didn't look like he'd agreed with anything. Bon had forgotten he was there.

Why would Jack agree with that? Lesley asked.

Jack's not averse to shaking things up.

That's bullshit, she muttered under her breath. And then louder: He's normal like the rest of us, just quieter. He doesn't want to shake up anything.

Jack's an enigma, Steven teased. Aren't you, Jack?

The younger boy looked away.

There's nothing wrong with shutting the hell up, Lesley said, brisk but jovial. Do you think I got off the train to listen to you speak foul of Jack?

Steven demurred, and said: He's not an enigma. Just a nutcase.

He's smart so he doesn't run his mouth, she said. And you're smart because you do. Somewhere in between is stupidity. So we have two geniuses on our hands and aren't we lucky.

We are, Bon said.

Steven laughed. It was always funnier whenever Bon weighed in.

Keep looking for those portals, Steven, Lesley added, and maybe we'll end up in the bush some day.

Bon laughed, but he laughed alone.

They had carved all stumps in their clearing to ground level, and with the passing of days Lesley's circular ridge had come to resemble a natural phenomenon. Dawn light pooled through a tear in the canopy and flooded through branches like in ancient oil paintings. Theirs was a proper open clearing, arched like a church, laid with artificial rolls of turf torn from the lawns of nearby abandons.

Lesley had used a metal-toothed rake to rip up the bushes, to tear out their roots, to flatten as best she could the slightly sloped surface of the area. Her work culminated in neat ridges at the walls of the clearing, thick knee-high hills of sticks, leaves and dirt. Once this ridge was formed she lined it on the inside with stones collected at a nearby cliff face. She carried and placed them with seeming expertise.

That's what Bon reckoned anyway. He reckoned she was a natural world builder, an oasis artisan. Each of the trunk stumps had taken a whole four-hour session to remove, but it had ceased to matter to Bon how much effort it took, for it had always felt like wasted effort. But now that the clearing was finished, it was easily the most impressive thing he'd ever been a part of, even though it resembled vandalism more than creation.

Lesley had found solar-powered fairy lights in the front yard of an empty house. On a whim, Bon unwound them along the circular ridge. But once he'd laid them, Lesley announced that they'd need to be removed. The clearing should not be the site of a farewell party to their present world, it should not come with any festive bells and whistles, it should certainly not be memorable. It should be unreal *but there,* a passage lost in a dime-a-dozen forest. The world is thoroughly explored, Lesley reckoned, but is it explored scrap by scrap? There must be scraps, she reckoned – and now she was deviating from her point – there must be refuges. No way can there exist these vast stretches of land without untrodden refuges to be found. There are ways to be excluded from the world, she reckoned, it just takes some initiative.

Bon thought it was dumb, she really seemed to believe it was true.

She said: We will get them out, now's the time. We'll ply them with alcohol and take them away.

She gestured towards the west.

Say what you like, but what could be better than Sofala? Nothing ever happens there, and no one there knows anything. That's why we got off the train, isn't it? We can be simple there. Hand to mouth and nothing else. It'd be nice. I feel like there is far too much to know here.

He didn't pay attention because she was always idly theorising, and anyway, that's not why *he* got off the train. But he muttered that she was right, and that it was a good idea, only they hadn't the money to buy a car and besides who was selling them. It was a good idea, an excellent one, a truly well-meaning one. And yet: impossible. Reflective silence followed until Lesley shoved him with a plastic bottle of home-fermented alcoholic juice.

We can just take them to their mum's house, Bon said. She's gone to the desert. Sofala is a small town: they'll all want to bash us up. These boys are weirdos.

The point is that they'll have gone through the portal, Bon.

And then what?

They'll be changed – they'll be in a different version of the world. And we'll make sure they come up in it correctly. It'll work on Steven. Jack will come along for the ride.

He sculled. It didn't matter anyway because without a car it was impossible.

There's no use throwing sticks and straightening stones anymore, Lesley went on. Step one is done. And mind you, it's the easiest step.

Cold breeze pushed through their coats. Bon pressed his shoulder against Lesley's, and nestled his head in the cup between her chin and shoulder. Lesley patted his back firmly. She must have sensed the tension in Bon's body, his labouring to devise a series of words that might protract the occasion. What words could supplement his gesture? It wouldn't do to make a joke, because he was not a funny person. And it wouldn't do to launch into a description of his feelings, because the only feeling he felt with any clarity was the desire to touch her. Not just her, not especially Lesley, but any woman.

You're right that we're going to need a car, Lesley added.

As he swigged the juice, it was possible to imagine a certain kind of life with Lesley. During a certain era, barely two decades past, it might have been possible for them to meet in a halfway thriving club in the city. He might have encountered her, by chance, standing at the edge of a half-hearted dance floor, a dance floor crowded with people their age, all role-playing the abandon of their now-matured forebears. He would move towards this solemn woman, with her drink neglected on a wall-hung bench. Having noticed the cynicism with which his imagined version of Lesley monitored the room, he'd not be able to resist moving towards her. He wouldn't say anything to this speculated Lesley at first – he might just look at her – but he would place his drink next to hers and gesture in the most subtle, barely perceptible way, that he had grave reservations with regards to the proceedings. Lesley would also gesture gravely at the dance floor, to show that she had grave reservations too. The music playing would belong to a tradition of youth ostensibly belonging to them, the abandon on display would belong to this tradition...but he would communicate with his body that he believed these *of tradition* routines to be beneath him. He would demonstrate to Lesley that he believed all of their contemporaries to be pathetically indebted to antiquated traditions. Look at the way they dance, he'd point out. Look at how carefully they role-play their abandon. They do not understand *real* abandon, he'd eventually say, they do not understand the tension that would warrant it (and nor, frankly, do we, he might have chanced). The revellers did not understand then, like he did now, that for a fraction of history corresponding to their coming of age, there were no urgencies, they could only pantomime. Let's not pretend we don't have everything already, he might have said to Lesley, back then. Look at their neat clothes, listen to their cheerful music, look at how civilly they queue for their drinks. We should just move on, and grow up. It's all so undignified, he'd probably say.

Whether via a shrug, or a wary throw of the arm, or in some way even more subtle, his imagined youthful Lesley might have let it be known that she agreed that it was beneath them to masquerade as loose and abandoned and desperate, that it was no longer necessary or smart to be agitated, that all attempts to commune with the tradition of youthfulness were pathetic and subservient to the well-documented experiences of their parents. And that would be the basis for their love, and that would eventually be the basis for all the loves that would blossom on the dance floor. The realisation of the pantomime of their agitation would be their coming of age, they would soon surrender to the things that endured. They would marry, they would rear children, rent or buy houses, maybe aspire to invest, become ensconced, join community Facebook groups. And they would watch as eventually, reality was corrupted into alarming and shocking new forms. They might at first welcome these aberrations, for it would be about time, frankly, that things were shaken up. But at a certain threshold of severity they would veer into tastefully moral terror.

If by chance Bon and Lesley had met at the edge of a fraudulently agitated dance floor in the prime of their lives, then surely it would have been easy to build a love centred around camaraderie. They could have coped together, and it would have ceased to matter that they felt like the surfaced bacteria on a stale pond. They would have just gotten on with it. Maybe that very night, they might have discarded their pre-packaged youths. And they might have had two children, two boys, named Steven and Jack. And together they would ensure that these boys' lives would not carry out in the shadow of imagined futures, they would not cling like barnacles to the ship of imagined futures...they would make it clear as day to their boys that the future had arrived, that it had ceased to be a useful concept. And under these circumstances their boys might not have felt any corresponding urges, for Bon and Lesley would have made sure that they did not feel railroaded into performing them. And now Bon was confused, because his waking dream – it couldn't be called a fantasy – had become dull and familiar. Isn't this what he had fled? What would it take to derail this inevitability, even in his dreams? He couldn't untangle desire from fate.

He shouldn't have got off the train.

The colourful fairy lights sparkled to an erratic rhythm. Lesley swore, stood, and started to gather them into a ball. Bon watched as a swelling circle of flashing colour swallowed the ridge. He lay back and shut his eyes.

Minutes or hours later Lesley prodded him awake with the end of a stick.

There's another path over there, she pointed.

The clearing was dour for the clarity of daylight. Trash littered the earth and his head throbbed at the sight of it. Newly sober and disgusted, he picked up the cigarette he'd been smoking before, put it in his mouth and heaved. Lesley stood over him, but it hurt too much to look her in the eyes. He scowled and gurned at her jeans, and tried to inhale the smoke again.

She whispered it loudly: There's another path over there.

He shut his eyes. It felt like a mother's warm palm across his forehead. He cupped his hands across his chest and the world faded away. He was awash on the edge of dreams by the time she shook him. He sunk his chin into his chest, and tucked his fists between his legs.

There's another path, Bon.

The drowse lingered until suddenly, he was marching through a low canopy tunnel molten orange with morning. Lesley was hurrying ahead, her footfalls explosive, with the wound-up fairy lights slung over one shoulder. Traffic hummed on the highway. He didn't think for a very long time. His legs moved and there wasn't much to do about it, he found himself in unthinking motion. They climbed up mild inclines, down gullies and over narrow crevasses, and soon the path narrowed to a squeeze, bending between fern, stone and eucalyptus. Somewhere water trickled, and occasionally to their left, whenever clearings in the thickets permitted, the texture of Newnes was visible below, sentried by the BP sign on the highway. Under the circumstances, it was difficult not to remember the kind of things one should be doing during the sun's first show. Now was the time to tend to sleepless children in the hours before work; now was the time to rise from dreams rife with vague allusion. Now was the time to listen to the reverse gear siren of garbage trucks, to the shattering of recyclables into the mulch. Was that a strange kind of longing Bon felt, with the rising of the sun? Was it possible that he missed his dread of work and morning light?

When the tunnel widened into a sloped clearing, Bon thought they'd looped back onto their own. Lesley paused at the threshold of the widening, and when he caught up, he saw in the centre of the clearing – much larger than theirs, actually – a wooden hut. The hut's sole window was covered by a mouldy blanket, with a metal door beside. Ruined building materials lay splintered in a pile nearby, and next to it was a hatchback, its rear window barricaded with swollen plastic bags.

Bon wasn't surprised; Lesley expressed nothing. She walked in the hut's direction without first consulting him. The door rattled and reverberated when she knocked, and he shut his eyes to block eventualities.

Of course there was no answer.

You know who lives here? Bon asked.

He followed Lesley around the whole perimeter of the hut. Rubbish bags were piled against its wooden exterior. There was no other door or window, so Lesley knocked again.

No one lives here, Bon said hopefully.

She turned the handle and the door unlatched, but something

on the other side served as barricade. She shook violently until the obstruction toppled, and then forced her way inside.

The dark hut smelled of meals left on the sink to rot. There was a desk with a computer against the blanketed window, and on the floor, a waist-high filing cabinet lay toppled by the door. A small kitchenette was strewn with the remains of ready-made microwave meals. Empty plastic bottles breezed across the wilted linoleum. In the far corner was a double mattress with no base, and a tangle of sheet and blanket at its foot. Music played, a strange and serene tune, like the tapping of melodious rainfall, but the computer fan almost drowned it out. Lesley ripped the blanket from the window and cruel light flooded the room. It was exactly the room Steven's descriptions had evoked, the perfect likeness was nauseating. He held the computer desk for balance, disrupted the mouse, the screen came alive and he shuddered, turned his eyes away.

Lesley flinched too. She warned him away from the computer. It needs to be destroyed, he heard her say. Next thing he knew she was pulling cords from the rear of the tower, causing the pleasant music to pop and die out. She launched the tower onto the cement floor, but the result was unimpressive and she immediately lost interest. Then she picked soiled ceramics from the kitchen bench and dropped them on the ground with babyish mirth. Bon watched for a moment, then launched his own soiled plate. There wasn't much satisfaction in it. He stared at the meekly shattered plate, bloodied with pasta sauce. What a funny thing to do.

What was on the computer? Bon asked.

Lesley ignored him. She kicked a clearing in the trash, and lifted a mat laid carefully in the centre of the room. He watched as she did it, hoping there wouldn't be a trapdoor.

We'd better not, he slurred.

The trapdoor thudded open onto the cement, and inside, a ladder led down into complete darkness. Lesley unspooled the solar fairy lights into the mouth, and it was shocking how far they reached, the dimming lights barely coiled upon the surface.

I take it you know what's down there, Bon surrendered. Why get involved?

With her foot, Lesley pressed the computer tower to the precipice of the mouth, and with more force than necessary kicked it down. The smash was quiet and unsatisfactory. She retrieved the torch from her pants and shone down uselessly.

We'd better not, he repeated.

She mounted the ladder and disappeared inside.

Bon roamed, crooked and impotent, back and forth. There was no pulling her out by force, but what would they say if he lost her? Fear gave way to irritation – it was offensive that she had gone down there. It would have been better to discuss it first.

On the computer table, sitting right there, was what must have been the hatchback keys. His arms shook for the delicacy of picking them up: he dropped them, picked them up again. He couldn't get them into his pocket so he shoved them down his pants. The computer monitor, still plugged into the wall, shone a drab office-space blue. He was stricken by the screen, his eyes fit its bezel so neatly, his mood surrendered to the glove-like comfort of its shape.

He was shaken from reverie at the sound of hissing slide. The lights had been dragged and the whole length had collapsed into the hole. To follow her down wouldn't be the wisest thing to do.

He yelled down the hole: Get back here!

And then several minutes later: I'm standing guard!

The ball of light slowly uncoiled out of his line of sight. From what seemed a great distance he heard her grunt in the affirmative.

He stood hands-on-hips staring into the hole. Standing wasn't sustainable. He felt seasick. With great effort he lowered himself onto the ground, belly-down at the mouth of the hole, and rested his head across his forearm. He yelled down the hole and there was no response.

The stupid idiot had probably heard him. She probably didn't consider him important enough to respond to. He yelled again, this time on the verge of a scream. He wanted to berate her for not telling him Jack's secrets: if he knew them, he might already be down there too, or more likely, he might never have let her enter the hut at all. He pushed with one leg the toppled cupboard against the shuttered metal door, and with an abandon that impressed himself, knelt and descended the ladder.

The dark tunnel ran north towards town. He stood at the foot of the ladder, cupped his hands, whispered loudly. He trod with care, dimly believing it wise to take a stealthy approach. Then he plunged his foot into the ruin of the computer, which crushed and dragged coarsely across the ground. So he kicked it aside, pushed forward with fingers against both walls, and deciding his presence must be known anyway, shouted 'Lesley' every now and then. With the knowledge that she had trodden this path not long before, the darkness acquired a faintly exciting quality, it was almost titillating. It was at least interesting, to be wandering a secret tunnel during weekday breakfast time.

Right at that moment, had he not left the train at Newnes, he would be awash in his usual mild self-contempt, waiting for his egg-and-bacon roll. Every morning he had resolved to stop purchasing egg-and-bacon rolls on a daily basis. During the moments he disembarked the train, he'd sometimes feel confident that it wasn't going to be an egg-and-bacon morning. But then the drowse of the commute would lift, his pace would quicken, and the leadenness of his routine would sink in. It was $7.50 for an egg-and-bacon roll, which added up to $37.50 a week, $150 a month. But he'd only make these calculations on especially sour mornings, more often than not he'd purchase the egg-and-bacon roll with not a care in the world, callously, almost nihilistically.

His fingers trailed off into air on the left-hand side, then he collided with a wall. He turned a corner into another passage of unknown length, and in the distance sounded three reverberant thuds.

His daily egg-and-bacon rolls had always been a secret and the routine had an air of debauchery about it. He'd duck meekly into the café, making sure that his boss wasn't nearby, in front of whom it always seemed wise to role-play a man close to the subsistence line. Then there was the indignity of the transaction. It was impossible to hide from the café operator that he purchased egg-and-bacon rolls everyday. While she might have welcomed his patronage, the café operator no doubt judged him in the back of her mind – he'd seen waitresses express utter contempt for customers on social media. She must have thought: fancy indulging in a café-bought egg-and-bacon roll nearly every single day! He came to feel as if egg-and-bacon rolls were a sinister controlling force, designed to sap his agency, to sap his determination and his income, to keep him in his place. There he was, a panicked and anxious human, far from who he dreamed he'd be as a child, with the very same face of that child, decimated by stress and age...there he was, chowing egg-and-bacon rolls in back lanes, utterly weak of will. Meanwhile in some quarters – it didn't take much research to know – men were steeling themselves to cope with violent and unaccommodating inevitabilities, and they would be ready when he, half-crippled at a desk, was taken by surprise and mulched in the slaughter along with all he was tasked to protect. His was a putrid sponge-like life, he moved from one lowly gratification to the next, he harvested leftovers from the muck of servitude. Sometimes when the bacon was all crisp crunch with no layers of soft, and when the egg was stiff dry, a rubbery gelatin husk, it cast a shadow over his morning. He wasn't alone, of course. Pleasures ought to be scattered and foraged for, it couldn't be any other way... that is what he'd truly once believed. But it bothered him to not be remarkable in some way, to not be an exception. How could one live without being remarkable, even if only remarkable enough to truly enjoy – to wholly embrace, to find comfort inside, to never encounter friction within – one's own unremarkableness? To be trapped inside a self so faint, a self so deprived of transformative plot beats, how did other people cope? And if the orthodox plot beats proved sufficient – to be a child, to come of age, to have a family, to rear it correctly – doesn't one just die, and usually for illness at that? To grouse to oneself about egg-and-bacon rolls, and for their salty greasy satisfaction to be so tainted by remorse... it laid bare the cynicism of the world. He wasn't a man, he was a pot-bellied aberration, every muscle atrophied, a kind of mutant to be honest, narcoleptic for endless grease and inactivity. He was under the thumb of his work, under the thumb of the train, and under the thumb not least by forces that, even there in the dark, he refused to recall. To realise that every bite only seemed to invite the urge for ever more bites...to wipe one's lightly stubbled mouth with the complimentary napkin, to never feel sated, only urgently embittered, and then to work, to work, during every sunlit hour, for desperate egg-and-bacon rolls. Truth to power: it might bring some guarantee of self-worth, if he had to use his arms and his fists to survive. Beneath the glut of a tyrannised body must surely lay fallow a powerful weapon, one most effectively wielded when coated in lustrous bronze, clad at the very edge of tastefulness... this body, once liberated, would neither trip nor bluster. Whether reedy or bulbous, it would not shiver for cold nor confrontation. His wrists would not phase in and out of clarity, and he wouldn't need to catch his breath after a single flight of steps. He would slay the pig, nurture the hens, massage the dough, blow gently just so into the blue of the fire. And then, the orthodox plot beats might start to make more sense.

He had never seen quite so much nothing as he saw in the passage. It was so dark that his thoughts seemed to air as if through hectoring megaphone. And his self had a certain drab monotone quality that wore him out. It was not strictly himself, it droned with a weary practicality, like a detached arbitrator. During moments like this, when he could hear himself, he wanted as little to do with himself as possible, because it proved that under circumstances other than those he was used to, he could not survive. When another corner emerged again to the left, he had already acclimatised to it, had anyway become lost in routine anxieties unrelated to mysterious tunnels. He called out 'Lesley' and it sounded bored, faintly ironic.

Bon collided with a wall guarded by another ascending ladder. He mounted it unthinkingly, and only thought to look above after a half-dozen rungs climbed. A soft interior morning light seemed to emanate from above, but the climb was so long that he lost his bearings. He came to wonder whether he was crawling horizontally, or else vertically at a milder gradient. The featureless dark – it wasn't exactly black, more a fog of alluded colours – dulled the pain of his exertion as much as it blindfolded. Maybe he was climbing downward, skull pointed to the ground. He was going somewhere, and he would likely get there.

He reached the mouth of the same trapdoor he had descended. Lesley ripped his arms and he collapsed onto the hut linoleum. She was chewing her whole face with her bottom teeth, and when he went to grip her in his arms, she pushed him back. Then she demanded the keys. He wanted to lie that he didn't know anything about any keys, but chickened out, pulled them out of his jeans, lacerated the skin of his thigh, tossed them onto the mat, and lay prostrate for deathly exhaustion. He didn't know how long it was, but eventually he was awakened by a horn, and a dim awareness that something had too easily fallen into their laps...

They sped along an unsealed track between parched, stoic gums. The road climbed and dipped, puncturing forest right and left in illogical spirals. Their heads collided with the ceiling of the hatch, and even mild turns tossed them back and forth. Bon could only muster the question: What happened? But no way was he entitled to the answer, he supposed. It would likely take much coaxing and sensitive sleight of hand to dislodge it. She looked older, too, blotched, blued, reddened. He had always thought her to be young, just as he had thought himself to be young. But neither of them were young, nor were they particularly old, nor did they have the qualities of middle age.

Lesley

Lesley stumbled into the weatherboard at around midday. The boys were sitting in the lounge room ignoring each other.

I've just gone to pick up some rum from the highway bottle-o, she announced by way of excuse.

Then, in case her walking to the highway alone for rum sounded implausible – which it was – she added: Bon put me up to it. Then: It was a good idea.

It was true, albeit her idea. Bon had driven her to the bottle-o on the highway for crucial supplies. Then he'd gone into hiding with the vehicle, agreeing to meet up later when she had performed her portal sorcery. For the thrill of the approaching event, Lesley had supplied herself with quite a bit of the rum on the way, enough of it that by the time she had hit their street, she no longer cared how ridiculous she must look. Anyway, the rum had helped make it clear that she was right: that it was right to move to Sofala, that it was right to draw a line, that it didn't matter what they did to make it happen. Because in the event that they didn't, what else would they do?

We're going to go search for pathways, Lesley said, adopting Steven's way of saying it, all the better to persuade. She went on: Bon and I have decided that now's the time. We'll spend the whole afternoon on the job, and we'll hit the drink while doing so. There's no reason why we shouldn't: it's Saturday. Bon will meet us when we get there.

She wanted to raise her fist and cry, 'They've got to be out there somewhere!' but managed to refrain.

It took a while before Steven was convinced, especially in Bon's absence, but by mid-afternoon they all set off together. The smell of smoke had briefly subsided and there was the slightest evidence of blue in the sky. Lesley and Jack rarely got involved in the search, but whenever they did Steven would revel in his expertise, he reckoned he had a good strategy and a certain careful way of searching. He'd always said that it was important to pretend for the land that you didn't expect anything untoward. So he'd chastise them the whole way, he'd complain that they never had any success because Lesley or Jack were looking too hard. He would stop and bark: Stop looking so hard. But neither ever looked at all, especially Lesley. For her, Newnes had already become as monotonous and unmalleable as all undesirable homes. Now she dreamed of heavenly Sofala.

But on that day Steven didn't chastise Lesley for searching too hard, instead he argued against the hill. They stood outside the weatherboard for three-quarters of an hour. There was much complaining. Several times the older boy stormed back inside, collapsed onto the couch, had a smoke. Lesley would sit on the front steps and flick through an old catalogue, because she knew he'd come grovelling back: he couldn't stand to be alone. In the end she had to bribe him with a glassful of rum – might as well start sooner rather than later. He took fifteen minutes to drink the glassful of rum and once it was depleted, he wasn't inclined to move until he'd had another, because it was better to climb hills slightly toasted. So she poured another for him, a larger portion for Jack too. Then when he'd finished his second, he'd needed a much smaller third, so that he'd have something to finish his smoke with.

Up the hill they went, Lesley and Jack rearguard to a faint and weaving Steven. In motion and en route she let him handle the bottle himself. Steven tended towards where he had been commanded, to the top of the hill, and then around a mild bend into a cul-de-sac, where the mouth of Lesley's path was hidden only metres away from the threshold. He had searched there before and he announced as much, but Lesley reckoned if his previous reports were true, one day's confirmation couldn't guarantee the next, to believe so was to ignore a crucial characteristic of portals.

At the foot of the cul-de-sac, between two boarded and overgrown homes, Lesley swung at the foliage. Steven poked too, he was regaining his spirit but his body couldn't rise to the labour. Jack stood back like he always did, like Lesley usually did, because he wasn't allowed to search properly, he couldn't be trusted to search the right way. As she brushed the trees at the periphery with a stick, she'd sometimes issue a helpful remark, or point to a suspicious-looking shadow. She was herding him, gradually shrinking the boundaries. But Steven had no interest in her directions. After a while she stormed into it, stood at the mouth of the tunnel with her back to it, and nervously fondled a trunk. Then she rolled a smoke. Steven was always keen to stop and have a smoke, could sense from rooms away when someone was rolling. He ambled in her direction and sat down with his back to the tunnel and his arms crossed. He said his wrists were sore from the threshing, so Lesley had to roll him one.

Jack stood at the kerb of the cul-de-sac and waited for the search party to return in their casually defeated way. Steven sat and sipped from the bottle. Lesley called to the youngest: come and have a drink with us. She was normally the least interested in booze among them, but it served an important purpose now.

The smoke reprieve was almost over; the sky was brown-grey above the eucalyptus canopy.

Is this what you mean by a hidden road and pathway, Lesley said, glaring east.

Steven didn't look but said it definitely wasn't what he had in mind.

She repeated it, grabbed his skull and twisted it gently, to emphasise that it was something that really had to be seen.

The misty smoke had settled again but it only served to accentuate the shape of a tunnel. Steven lay flat on his back and it was possible to see how, from his point of view, the canopy spiraled clockwise and muddied. He was seasick, obliterated.

Lesley and Jack sat opposite sides of Steven near the centre of the clearing. The older brother was comatose, dead to the world, but Jack still needed some time – he was still too young.

A brown wind had arrived and distant bushfire ash sprinkled the clearing. Lesley had lit a fire all the same, because it had always been her plan to light a fire in the clearing, as close to the centre as she could tell, daylight and bans be damned.

You're still too young to drink yourself deliberately to sleep, Lesley chuckled to the boy.

And then she said, drunkenly: We've found a portal and you must know what that means. You might think you're not used to things changing from one day to the next, but listen – and she ashed her cigarette away from Steven's lumpen body – you're more used to it than I am.

Jack just glanced at her bemusedly. It was because she was drunk – but it was an unavoidable by-product of the plan.

Whether further into this tunnel or back the way we came, it's never going to be the same, she went on. Steven talks a lot of shit about hidden roads and pathways but he's right. Everything is true and the strangest things can happen. The wildfires create their own weather events, it's terrifying but you can't not be impressed. Anyway, you don't know how it feels to expect the world to always stay the same...we used to believe most of the things we were told. But now I know if you want something to be true you just say it, you just say it then it's true. And only the haters can tell you otherwise.

Jack shrugged, still bemusedly.

You're the hero anyway, she slurred. Look at us idiots ten years your senior having our crises, we can't cope. And all you hear is our bullshit not to mention the elderly. I wouldn't talk either if I were you, it's more dignified just to watch.

He still just sat there with one side of his mouth slightly raised. But she was too drunk to stop talking. She felt good and emboldened, and on the verge of something new.

That's why we've become friends, she slurred, because I just say whatever sounds sensible and then it's true. But I don't believe any of it. And you can tell I don't believe it. But some of us can't go around saying little to nothing, you've got to have things available to say, and if there's nothing available you improvise. And I know you'd hate me for it if you couldn't tell that *I knew* I was talking out of my arse.

She dragged herself around the fire and wrapped her arms around Jack. He let her fall into shape around him.

Drink up, she said, proffering the rest of the opened rum. I'm getting you out of here.

In the late afternoon, an hour after Jack had gone to sleep, Bon emerged through the smoke of their portal with his own bottle of rum. They carried the boys to the hatchback, one at a time, and bundled their bodies in.

2

The hatchback arrived at the outskirts of Sofala that night, via an old sandstone bridge across a wide riverbed.

From kilometres away it was obvious that the tiny town was engulfed in flames. Reddened black clouds like inflated garbage bags had dominated the horizon. The smoke scent, normally stale, was pungent with fresh burning, even through the sealed car windows. Nevertheless they had driven towards it, because it might not have been Sofala after all. Maybe it was a farmer burning off nearby.

Upon their arrival, even through the smoke and fire, and despite the total destruction of the buildings, it was possible to tell how beautiful Sofala had been.

Of course it must have been beautiful, Lesley thought. It couldn't not have been. It had taken a full two hours to get there, along a lonely narrow road so dark, quiet and mountainous that it had seemed to depart the world entirely. Any town that existed at the end of such a road must have been a secret worth keeping. Thanks to the bright light emitted by the blaze, it was possible to imagine how richly green the trees surrounding were, and it was possible to spot the fire's reflections on the surface of the nearby streaming river.

But now it was gone, or going: she watched as a powerline slowly toppled onto a two-storey corrugated-iron roof, triggering the total collapse of the fire-frayed building beneath. No onlookers mourned, no trucks nor fighters fought it.

Bon had pulled into a car park on the edge of town, near the old sandstone bridge, where a dirt path led north towards the riverbed below. Splintered park benches glowed for the nearby flames, and a red sign warned that camping was an offence. They sat in the car and said nothing.

Jack and Steven were passed out in the back, the latter's snoring audible over the wildfire.

Lesley felt inclined to give up, or else, to flee the hatchback and stay in Sofala, disaster or not. But her amazement was of a crippling kind, she couldn't move a muscle. Anyway, soon something exploded and it seemed to rock the world. A towering cloud of smoke rushed towards them. Bon started the car, they sped away, and through the rear-view mirror, Lesley watched as the car park was consumed by unfathomable hell.

After school Lesley had gone to work, and then worked. She had worked in the day and then worked in the night. Arriving in Newnes is when that had stopped.

Years ago she had left home and found work. It had been a privilege to do so, because working was how one survived, and without question she had wanted to live. She would work to live, and then work to sustain, and then live to work.

On one of her final commutes between her city rental and western regional hometown, during a summer awash in smoke, she had wondered if there was some mysterious cabal tasked with dabbing a believable foreground on the future. Of course the country was burning here, thirsting there. Between the dabs and the panic there were two distinct futures to bear in mind. Urban property was tipped to undergo profitable inflation, office spaces would become more flexible and liberal. Electricity prices and jobs would remain stable. Life-affirming film franchises promised instalments into the next decade and further, many billions of dollars were at stake. Her mother was getting older and closer to death, and frequent were loud panics about global wars, though the panics always trailed off the next day. Decline or decadence, it was never possible to tell.

But as the train had departed the heart of the city, on a hot December morning overcast for smoke, she doubted the resilience of streets and towers, and the shape of the world itself no longer seemed stoic and impermeable. The people on the concourse were no longer innocent by default. It wasn't for the expectation that the world might look dramatically different sometime soon. It was for the feeling that it might cease to exist, that it was gradually eroding, and that she and everyone else would soon feel the surface buckling, swaying gelatinous beneath their feet. Or more to the point, perhaps there would no longer be anywhere safe to stand.

Freshly laid roads weaved cul-de-sacs through once rolling plains in the western suburbs, and the early evening streetlights shone upon empty lots. The plains beyond the suburbs and mountains were grey and desiccated, and for miles around there was nothing to burn except arid grass. But fires weren't what troubled her. She knew the land was hungry for it, human and wildlife be damned, the fires spread with the rage of last resort. That's not what troubled her.

What troubled Lesley was that she could find no good reason to be troubled by it all. She knew the two futures would collide and that one would prevail, with the result that all of her work and all of her taxes would provide no comfort at all. And it was a pent-up kind of life she lived, bored one moment, furious the next, with this irrational and ever-present fear of *wasting one's time*, she had too much of some things and a terrified want for others. And there was no use in creating a family – she could not in good conscience raise a new family. The one certainty that had remained was that any day now, she would be left to her own devices, perfectly alone, to face all of this.

Bon was driving the unsealed road at an agonising low speed – he was spooked. And the spectacle of the fire had them in silent agreement that drinking on the road was acceptable.

We can just go and live in their old house, Bon said, swigging from a bottle of fermented juice. Their mum has gone to see the desert. She's old and nice, she won't mind.

A partially distorted power ballad enraptured Lesley for a while. Her shock had turned into a dumbfounded rage. But the sight of the figures in the back seat, slumped and shadowed in the rear-view mirror, called for a more sanguine approach.

Eventually she slurred: Yes.

And then improvised: What if we took them back to their childhood home? That's where the portal will have to lead. We can just pretend that was our plan all along.

We have no choice, Bon said.

Because that's kind of what we were going to do anyway, wasn't it, Bon? In Sofala? Well this will have to do: we'll take them to their childhood home and let them be children again. We can cut them to their trunk and let them grow again.

Lesley's head stopped spinning for her newfound lucidity – she felt like she had boarded a rostrum.

Where would we have lived in Sofala anyway? he said. The sign there said no camping.

As undeserving as they may be, Lesley went on, as ordinary as they are, as truly – let's face it, by certain standards of thinking – useless as they may be, their being double-crossed and disappointed *men* not boys...what if we just let them start again? Everything they've done or neglected to do, every failure big and small they've ever suffered: make them forget. All the frustrations and even the small victories, they were all dreams. Not exactly nightmares, just bad dreams.

Bon said: It took a trip to the mouth of hell for you to rule out vagrancy.

He had said it to himself, but was too drunk to say it quietly, and too drunk not to say it at all.

She too was very drunk, but also too inspired to rise to the bait, so continued: Whether they like it or not that's what's happening. That's where they're headed and that's what's going to be real, and anyway, they don't know any better, they've never properly lived before, and they don't know anything else. So they're well equipped to start again, in the best way available to us. And none of us will have to be alone.

An out-of-date advertisement for a Bathurst tyre company aired on the radio. Then there was an errant silence in the broadcast.

As if to deliberately belittle the silence, Bon just said: Well.

A minute or so later he added: Yeah.

And then when the silence threatened to become eerie, he added: Christ.

When Lesley had delivered this speech to Bon in the hatchback, on their way back from Sofala, back towards Newnes through the tinder-dry winter, on the night they thought themselves absconded forever, she had understood that her own ruse was over. She had hoped to convey a different kind of self to Bon and the boys. In Newnes it had been easy enough. In Newnes, it had been possible to adopt and then maintain a whole new version of herself, a rugged and wise version, a been-around-the-block version, a version that imparted carefully unfalsifiable wisdom. It wasn't exactly the best kind of person one could be: that of course would be impossible for her. Anyway, the whole point of it was to be vital and dependable, the whole point of it was to be liked. Just as importantly, the whole point of it was not to be meek. In Newnes they might not have noticed that she was trying. On the other hand, everyone she had ever known before she disembarked at Newnes, all those people in her actual life (it was still her actual life) faced with a similar role-play, would have seen clear as day she was *trying*, desperately and pathetically *trying* to be something else. To be caught trying to be someone other than who one was had always been undignified, indefensible. Life was a game of not being caught.

Clear as day Bon was confused about her, which was better than him knowing who she was. And he'd probably have learned her truth much faster in Sofala anyway, than he could have within the bounds of Newnes, where her efforts had seemed unusually successful. But how could she know? Bon's role-play of detachment was so very steadfast, so rock-hard, that she wanted nothing more than to wear it down.

So she said aloud in the hatchback, ecstatically drunk, still: Don't underestimate the comfort of Newnes, don't write it off as a hole. It's not even a town let's face it: a bunch of shops around a train station, and then some homes along some winding roads. I didn't even know it was there until I got off in it. Call it what you want but it's not really a town, that's why it's not on the timetable. It's not a place where people like us live. It's in some ways just as remote as the deepest country, you just have to look at it a certain way, you have to use initiative. We're not in the old world even in Newnes, Bon, the trains don't even go there anymore. It's ideal for us. We're protected there. It's a bit like a new frontier.

She wasn't sure whether she had said all this or thought it, and anyway, Bon was hunched over the wheel peering into the dangerously close foreground, for the road was drenched in a soupy brew of smoke and fog, it veered at random, even on the highway, and even when the lights of a town appeared in the distance. These lights – unmistakably Newnes: the McDonalds, the BP, the Shell – dipped in and out of the horizon, the road seemed to cower from the town, it resisted the town in wide arcs, until finally it gave in and did what it was supposed to: it reached somewhere. Reluctantly it joined with the highway which coursed between old bedroom windowpanes in once-warm homes fleeced by arterial growth.

You sound like Steven, you know, Bon said, with all this old-world new-world mysticism.

Don't mistake Newnes for a home, she railed (or did she really? She really couldn't tell), it's more of a depository, and you think you're better than to live in any mere depository, but here you are, Bon, you poured yourself deliberately into this jar, and so did I let's face it. It's a town for gazing point blank into a lightbulb blind drunk, it's a place for when you don't want to be anywhere, you've got to admit. No one else wants to be there, so it's right for just us.

I'm sorry about Sofala, she added.

And then, pointedly: You were right all along.

As they rolled the mild eastward descent into town she focused on the radio. There was no talk or ads, though a prerecorded pitch-shifted baritone announced that they listened to 2NW FM, 'The Best of Yesterday and Today'. Songs were left to fade in their completion, leaving moments of disquieting silence between. Whoever had scheduled these songs – all old and sentimental, buoyed by decades of relentless exposure – must have done so knowing they would air during an event of such magnitude that announcers could no longer announce. Maybe not all was lost. To keep broadcasting, to trigger a temporary loop, must mean the voices and the joviality expected to return.

But who was she to know the fate of the loop, whether it would abruptly stop with some flick of a button or whether it would continue unheard in the absence of listeners. Maybe music would remain in the air, an encrypted invisible weather phenomenon, afloat to be decoded in some far-distant future.

Whatever you or anyone else thinks about it, Bon said after a while, at least there's a house.

They pulled up in a street on the opposite side of town, the side closest to the old blast furnace, and the house – so Bon reported – didn't look much different from how it had looked when they took Jack away. She knocked on the door gently, because it was four o'clock in the morning. Then she knocked again violently, but there was no evidence of movement inside. Bon motioned at the driveway and noted the absence of a caravan.

She's gone to the desert, he said.

She banged her shoulder against the door as an invitation for Bon. He walked calmly around to the back of the house and opened it from the inside. From the front step the house smelled of cold lamb fat and old carpet. Leaving the boys in the car, they entered the bright blue-lit living room, which Mother Grady had left in a state: dirty coffee mugs and well-read shopping catalogues crowded the coffee table, and indeed, shopping catalogues were everywhere, on the couch and across the carpet, stacked atop the television cabinet, a thick dust coating them all. A chest of drawers with three framed photographs – two at either end, one in the centre – was crowded with various knick-knacks, balms, tubes of assorted creams, more coffee mugs, a stack of mint-condition phone directories, a couple of toppled aerosol cans, and a modem, its lights illuminated. The kitchen and adjoining dining room were similarly just as much of a mess. The fridge was clean and almost bare (some margarine, several spoiled jars of pickled vegetables, a Tupperware container of indeterminate sludge) and the benches were stacked with old women's magazines, lightly used tea towels and oven mitts, and an ashtray in the centre of the stove under the rangehood, with two tailor-made butts extinguished into balls.

Bon took a bottle of vodka from an overhead cabinet, turned to Lesley, and asked: I don't have to drive again, do I? She laughed at him, for he had wasted all this time, all the way along roads surely prowled by the meanest of highway patrols.

We're going to have to return that car, she answered.

He poured some of the vodka into a plastic tumbler, threw it back and winced. He seemed to struggle with the notion but eventually said: Yeah. And then: I'm not scared of that thing, that man. He poured some more of the vodka. He's fat, slow and pathetic, and I could beat him in a fight.

But it was a bit much to steal his car, Bon added. That could be gaol.

Bon and Lesley carried the boys one at a time into the house, and dropped them flat across their respective beds. Jack slept upstairs in a boyish room with a double bunk bed, Steven in a more reserved, spartan room with a single. She expected Bon to dust his hands in a cinematic way, to tip his hat, or at least pretend to, since he never wore a hat. She imagined that he'd then wander off, down the drive, onto the road, back towards the highway and then in one or the other direction. But he just kept standing there, because she was still standing there too. ·

It was only four-thirty so they drove into town, along the winding parade next to the elevated train track. Then across the overpass, which offered a fleeting view of the arrested predawn town centre. The dead of night didn't change the mood of Newnes, the mood was perfectly familiar. Lesley had always struggled to pinpoint this mood by day, but now she understood that it had always felt exactly like this: it had always carried the mood of the deepest predawn sleep, it had always felt vaguely twilit, even in the Newnes Valley Plaza, even at the train station, only by day the sky had shone a light orange glow rather than a nurturing somnambulant blue. She had often wondered what the scarce wanderers or shoppers of Newnes were actually doing, why they were out, why they were not at home or somewhere entirely else. Newnes at four a.m. – during actual four a.m. – was just as populated as it was by day, here and there men wandered footpaths and lone women cradled children, as if the usual rhythm of day and night and all the attendant routines had always eluded them.

Newnes is a town of four a.m., she said, isn't it, Bon? And even he agreed, the classically pent-up undemonstrative Bon, he had replied that actually she was right: that it was definitely a four a.m. kind of town, he said it like there might be others of its kind. She wanted to say that it was a good thing for them, and she wanted to explain why it was a good thing, and she even wanted to explain what it was about four a.m. that was so uniquely strange, except she really no longer wanted to be the kind of person to plainly explain a sensation that was already quietly shared, and it took some great restraint, but she managed to leave it at that.

Bon slowed to a crawl as they passed the weatherboard, because it was always interesting to see – even for Bon, Lesley supposed – what a house one used to live in later looks like. The front door was open and from a distance she spotted an item of clothing in the lawn. They must have dropped it in their rush to leave. But Lesley didn't insist they retrieve the item of clothing, because she was unusually certain that she had shut the door behind her.

It made the utmost rum-drunk sense to Lesley that they should leave the hatchback in the cul-de-sac near their passage, and leave the keys in the centre of the clearing. Bon didn't mind either way, because since the vodka he had adopted the attitude of a spectator.

Only it was impossible to leave the keys in the clearing, because the passage could not be found. Try as they did, first with urgency and then a morbid curiosity, they could not for the life of them find the mouth of the tunnel. They kicked the empty bottles at the mouth, found Steven's headless mop stick, but certainly – no doubt for near paralytic drunkenness – no evidence of a path could be found there.

We're out of our minds, off our tits, Lesley laughed. She tossed the keys into the dashboard and slammed the door shut. The sky was a burgeoning daylight brown and neither of them had a phone. We should run or jog at least some of the way back, she reckoned, who knows how long it's been. It wasn't for fear that the boys would wake at a reasonable hour, because she knew they wouldn't. It was because that part of town felt dangerously changed, newly unknowable, the air seemed to have some gruel-like virulence, even the houses along the cul-de-sac – those middling chests of drawers – appeared alive with contempt. She was scared, and she could sense that Bon was scared too.

So they jogged, at first arduously and then, from the crest of the hill downward, with a frightful lack of control, and then, in the vicinity of the old weatherboard, they each independently quickened their pace.

Then they stripped their filthy clothes, crawled into Mother Grady's bed, and passed out with no further discussion.

The next day she woke with a sense of victory, because it seemed, in that strange bed beside meat-like Bon, that she was the first to wake. That's what she had hoped would happen, because she had wanted to be the one to improvise the tone of their new life.

She had pictured something roughly like this: waking first, heating some baked beans, maybe with the radio on, or maybe with the TV playing morning shows in the background. She had pictured filling tumblers of water and setting the table. She had pictured saying, simply: Good morning. She would have said it in a fond, customary way, like her own mother used to. They would all have had breakfast together – all four of them – and during the meal she would undoubtedly be able to see the effect of the night, which would provide her with the tools to improvise onward.

But her body was battered and smoked, it felt like there was not a drop of life-giving moisture inside her. Her head felt explosive, her mouth sickly sour, and her bladder was full though tolerable when she kept still. The faint memory of her behaviour hit harder: she had acted appallingly. She had revealed her true unsavoury self, the one who could not read cues, no matter how much care she put into interpreting them. The rum had ruined her guise, and Sofala had burned down to boot.

Much later she woke again and felt no better. She was in the bed alone. A gentle brown light shone through dusty lace curtains.

At least Jack had been passed out for most of it, Lesley thought. Though she vaguely remembered ranting at him.

Emerging from the room a familiar hum relaxed her senses, it was the sound of a television. Down a short hall into the kitchen and then the lounge room, she found Bon and Steven, both lazed across the couch, watching some or other action film. The couch faced the television, so they didn't see her watching them. They appeared tranquil, as if in keeping with some regular routine, and there was not the slightest evidence of concern on the sliver of Steven's face she could see. Bon's body did not appear anxious, he might have been asleep. She stood over them behind the couch, but they didn't acknowledge her.

She greeted them good morning in a fond, customary way.

They ignored her, so she finally said: What are you watching?

Bon looked up, creased his mouth, winced and looked away. Steven looked at her for what felt like a meaningful half-minute before saying: *Iron Man*.

And then he added: On 4K Blu-ray.

Bon was balancing a cup of Coke on his gut for the several minutes Lesley stood there behind the couch, herself feebly transfixed by *Iron Man*, but he eventually made a scene of twisting his lumpen body sideways to place the drink on the carpet. As he struggled to remould the position he was formerly so comfortable in – shoulders rested against two cushions, feet pressed against Steven's lap, head turned almost painfully towards the screen –

he accidentally made eye contact with her, and she seized upon it, but he didn't move a muscle.

She knocked on the door belonging to Jack and there was no answer. When she knocked again and then a third time there was still no answer, so she went ahead and pressed the door open. He was asleep on the bottom of the double bunk. He did not snore, but his body seemed to exude a hum, small evidence he was alive. She prodded him to see what would happen. His body showed not the slightest sign of having felt it, he was well and truly gone.

Bon and Steven were still lazed in the lounge room, staring at the ceiling as a looped Blu-ray menu jingle played. As far as she could tell the sun was close to setting. But it wasn't enough to sense it, she looked through a window. The syrup-thick brown was hard to read, so she idly shouted across the room: What's the time?

How should I know, Steven shouted, insulted.

It's probably around four o'clock, Bon added temperately. It sounded like a wild guess.

She leaned against the side of the couch closest to Steven. She wanted to say that they might as well turn the television off or put something else on, but she cut to the heart of the matter and said: If it's Sunday it must be takeaway day.

Steven sat bolt upright, dusted his shirt, and said that if they're getting chips and a roast chicken, then he bags a leg, and for that matter, he bags not going to pick it up, and why don't they get some spring rolls too.

With cash from Mother Grady's bedside table, Lesley and Bon went to pick up the chips and roast chicken. The brown outside felt like shards collecting in her nose, if she could get away with picking her nose out there in public, then surely a shard-like kind of syrup would emerge.

She said: I can't remember the last time I saw a shop that just sold roast chicken and chips.

Bon stopped.

So you don't know where you're going?

We're going to the chicken shop.

There was a familiar winter mist across that part of town, though none of the homes offered porch lights or screen-radiant bay windows. In the northern part of Newnes there was one significant road – the one they were on – and then other minor roads running off it, usually into dirt and brambles. To their right the elevated train track reached higher and higher, and on the other side was the blast-furnace ruins, so much grander than she had ever imagined them, almost as grand as European castle ruins, its silhouette poised before the distant foggy mountains.

And because she was not comfortable with silence – albeit aware of her discomfort with silence and how it was wrong – she said: It's a local neighbourhood kind of chicken shop, it's not in town.

It better exist, Bon said, or there will be a tantrum.

They were then stood at a crossroads. To their left was a train line underpass leading to a remote and overgrown part of town. Ahead was the wall and more houses, and to their right were more houses leading into mist. Aside from the near subaudible hum of the highway it was silent, but not an outdoor silence, it sounded like the quiet of a chamber.

It's just down here, Bon said offhandedly. Ahead the supporting wall of the train line veered right, revealing a thicker kind of suburbia beyond, and on the corner of the veer was the familiar harsh blue glow of a takeaway interior, its exterior plastered with faded signage for Kirks and Chiko Rolls.

I told you so, Lesley said proudly. I have chicken-shop sixth sense.

Inside, plastic tables and chairs were arranged crookedly before a counter filled with uncooked battered food, a typical array of salad (sliced tomato, shredded lettuce, pickles) and a single roast chicken. Glowing menus above promised an array of burgers in order of price. At a table closest to the counter sat a young girl – six maybe seven – staring up at a television airing footage of a festival dedicated to exotic types of car. When Lesley and Bon entered, a loud buzz sounded and the girl disappeared off under the hinged section of the counter. A man emerged and just looked at them.

How's it going, Bon said.

Yep, the counter man said, a bit over middle age.

Just eight dollars of chips and that chicken, Bon added.

Without a word the counter man shuffled over to a split plastic bag of raw chips, shovelled them into a net, and dipped them into the deep fryer. Then he stood there for a moment with one hand on hip, looking up at the car documentary. He bagged their chicken in a foiled bag, put it back in the bain-marie, lifted the net of chips and shook before dropping it back in. Lesley wanted to say something, for example: How's business, or maybe: How about this dust. But she was still experimenting with what it was like to say nothing unnecessary. The majority of people did not say anything unless it was absolutely pertinent, and while this behaviour had often impressed her, it was actually a normal thing, a reasonable thing, to not say anything if nothing necessary to say came to mind. Bon, indeed, was exactly the kind of person to never speak unless necessary, and there in the chicken shop, he was almost proudly lacking in anything to mention, he had even taken a seat at one of the tables, not a table closest to the counter, but a table three rows down, in order to not impose on the counter man, in order to make it clear that there was no threat of superfluous exchanges. She remained standing, near but not too near the counter, just in case the counter man had something to say.

Then she gave up: Sofala burned down, she said.

Bon stood and took her gently by the shoulders. He invited her to take a seat away from the counter man, and she did, feeling angry but more so contrite. As for Bon, there radiated from his body a sense of solidarity with the counter man. As Bon and the counter man waited out the encounter, each staring at the car documentary, it seemed as if they weren't just watching the screen, but that they were doing so together, that some silent complicity had bonded them. Bon's face had a subtle air of confidence that she had rarely seen before, his gaze had the quality of self-assurance, of understanding situations.

Not too many people buying chickens at the moment, the counter man suddenly said, still with his arms crossed, making the odd brush of eye contact with Bon.

The latter replied: Oh yeah?

And the counter man said: Yeah.

On the way home Bon didn't speak. It was probably because he was angry that she'd said something in the chicken shop, which had forced him to say something.

They had lived together for some months now, but Bon remained a dreary mystery to Lesley. All she knew was that he had come from the city, and that he had travelled daily to the country for some reason – probably for some humdrum management work, given the business-casual clothes he hand-washed every weekend. Steven had mentioned Bon's origin in some of his monologues, as a means to emphasise some or other absurd wisdom that only Newnes people could understand. But he might have guessed, just as she had guessed the same. No other facts were available about Bon, except for those she intuited based on his responses to her theories. Bon never confirmed nor denied, save for the involuntary responses written on his face, and while he sometimes made an effort to understand her, he always asked the wrong questions. Together, in Lesley's view, their respective pathologies ensured that they only ever orbited a breakthrough that might have brought them closer.

Back at the house Jack had emerged from his room. He was seated on the floor at the foot of the couch, watching *Iron Man 2* with Steven. It was impossible to make any eye contact with him while the film was on. Bon grumbled that a movie had been started without him, but he let it go, dutifully spread the chips in their paper across the carpet, retrieved four plates and four knives, and said that everyone should just carve what they wanted for themselves. A great rush ensued, each taking their turn to carve as much of the chicken as possible onto plates, and to bundle as many fistfuls of chips besides. Everyone got their share. In the lambent light of the television they ate their fill – especially Bon and Steven who got the legs. For all the uncertainty of the day, Lesley couldn't focus on the movie and anyway she knew what would happen. As she sank into sleep, gently propped on a cushion in Mother Grady's recliner, she considered it not a big deal that they go one day without getting to the heart of the matter, that anyhow, they were behaving just like a normal family would on a lazy Sunday night.

It must have been a respectable time of morning when she woke on the recliner. The Blu-ray menu played a looped orchestral score. She stood, opened the venetians, looked out on the dust and brown, and then shut them again. She tried to turn the television off but found no button, so allowed the looping orchestral score to continue playing.

Steven and Bon were sitting at the old formica table in the kitchen, poring over a document.

It's about a job, Steven said when he noticed her.

Lesley had a gut feeling that no good had ever come from being offered any job sight unseen. She sat at the table and told them so. Bon and Steven had already showered; Bon was dressed just like the boys usually were, in loose blue jeans and a brand-emblazoned t-shirt. He looked younger for lack of his usual rigid middle-aged attire, the wet of his hair obscured signs of pattern baldness. It made his expressionless face seem less wise and more sullen.

When she said 'no good has ever come from being offered any job sight unseen', Bon had looked at her with expert doubt, doubt that she knew much at all let alone about the subject at hand. He looked at Steven, and Steven said:

All we have to do is empty houses. We just go in, drag everything into the backyard, if need be we sprinkle it with kindling, then we set it alight. And I know what you're thinking (how could he ever know?), but they're not just offering full-time with benefits willy-nilly, this isn't a scam it's a matter of urgency, because it needs to be done by the end of winter, because in the spring there's the risk of new fires. That's just what it says. They need us now – there was a deliberate militant crescendo in his tone – and there's no harm in having a job. We're just burning the contents of homes for cash in hand which can't be hard.

It's easy work, Bon added.

And people burn things for the fun of it, Steven rejoined, so fancy having a job just setting things alight.

Lesley was unconvinced. She looked at the job offer, which had been left in the mailbox. It had no letterhead, though it was typed in an elegant serif font, and it contained no spelling errors as far as she could tell. It offered a flat, tax-free rate of fifty dollars a house between them. In an obscure and roundabout way, it explained that old houses full of wasting furniture and appliances were a menace to public safety.

Steven reckoned they'd probably get through three maybe four houses on a regular nine-to-five, more if they worked longer – it wasn't just pocket money. Not just one chicken, he encouraged, but two. A leg for all of us. Scallops and Chikos on the side, get a salad too. It's definitely worth a try.

What's the credibility of this mob, Lesley asked, fuming at the letter.

We don't need credibility we need cash, Steven replied, looking at Bon, who nodded.

It's just some community initiative, the latter added, and she couldn't tell who he was trying to coddle. She wanted to stand in a theatrical way, like brazen matriarchs in films, and she wanted to say something cutting with regard to Bon's obliviousness to the township's community, alluding to the fact that actually, it didn't have one, for surely all he knew. But far be it from her to act the naysayer in front of Steven, or to scold one for who they worked for.

You could give it a trial, she said. But it sounds like a scam.

Her half-hearted endorsement of the project seemed to deflate them, more so than her initial resistance. Steven grabbed the page from her, studied it closely again, and then pushed it away. He stood up, performed a stretch of great exertion, and left. When only her and Bon remained he pursed his lips a bit, for him a grandiose confirmation of his lack of anything further to say.

Everyone thinks they'll just move to growing cabbages in their lawn but it's not viable and I understand, she said.

To which he replied: What do you mean?

He didn't get up and leave after saying it, he just kept sitting there, and there wasn't anything you could say in response – so it seemed to Lesley – because objections to hazy, mysterious benefactors...it wasn't the kind of thing she supposed would make sense to Bon. To keep the discussion going, she wended further towards approval.

If people are leaving homes forever, electricity on, all manner of fire hazards in their wake, then yes, you can see the logic in it. Not that I'm saying – and she almost rose like a brazen matriarch – that there should be a logic in it. It is what it is, isn't it, Bon?

It is what it is, he said gratefully.

In his boyhood room, Jack sat at a desk scattered with books and toppled ornaments, visible only for the light cast by two screens. He was immersed in a military shooter, and when Lesley tapped him on the shoulder he flinched.

She knelt close beside him, too meaningfully, she worried. But committed to the posture she said: What's going on?

He didn't cotton on to the broadness of the question, he just nodded at the screen. Lesley had no expectations that her pathway and clearing had worked its magic on Jack, but she wasn't going to puncture the illusion herself.

I can see that you're playing a game, she said. I meant: what's going on in general. Jack's face remained neutral as his rifle coursed through a world of courtyards and shipping containers. On the smaller screen, the laptop screen, text trailed down the browser page, but it was incomprehensible to her, a busy assemblage of thumbnail images and argot.

He finally said: Do you mean what's going on in the world?

So nothing has changed since last week, for example?

Half-concentrating, he answered: I don't read the news.

In the days just after his arrival in the weatherboard, Lesley had set about cracking Jack open. The conditions had been favourable. As ever-determined drinkers, Bon and Steven had always gone to bed first. It had felt like an honour when Jack lingered with her, and as the days and evenings had passed, she had come to feel some certainty that Jack didn't hate her – an honoured status compared to his obvious dislike of Bon.

She hadn't pushed him for answers to questions at first. Instead, she had offered her own uncensored commentary on the night's discussions, occasionally challenging Steven's assertions in his absence. Sometimes she had made a vague comment about Bon: nothing too critical or dismissive, but enough to show who her allegiance lay with. Often she had talked about her life, and it hadn't mattered whether Jack cared or not because it was impossible to tell either way. They would sit and smoke in the ember calm left by Steven's departure.

In the city I'd be watching shows right now, was the kind of thing she had said. I'd be watching episodes and dreading the morning. Sleep rushes you into the next day, so you're better off staying awake for as long as you can. You get in at a quarter to nine, eat a dry croissant at your desk – granted, a free breakfast was nice – and then you're on the phones, answerable to everyone all day until five. You can be confronted by a customer or manager at any moment. And you're always making small mistakes. If you're not making a mistake of some sort, someone else is unhappy with you, because it's their job to find your mistakes. Then you leave and the sun has gone down. That's why there are so many shows, with so many episodes.

He'd always nod his head just once.

Get a job in an office they say, Lesley might have added elliptically – these are the kinds of things she said – though she could no longer remember who said that to her, or if anyone had. In the same spirit of employment advice, she had regularly warned Jack that he should never get a job.

Back in those early weatherboard days Lesley had sensed a blossoming trust, so she tried not to push her luck with Jack. She had wanted to be the one he didn't mind. Knowing his reputed quiet, she had dared not ask questions at first.

Eventually she had started with: Do you like this beer?

He wasn't fussy.

When Bon had by mistake bought them minty pork sausages instead of plain beef, she had asked if he liked exotically flavoured sausages.

He didn't.

It took a handful of nights to bring the strange young man around to her way of just speaking.

Is there a better way to dispose of our bottles?

I think.

What happens when the shed is full to the ceiling?

We throw them over the fence.

And then, as a bulwark, she'd toss in a semi-related monologue, to fill the room and steady the pace.

Then light questions again.

When are they going to finish the roadworks?

Never.

Has Newnes ever had Subway?

For a couple of years it did.

Whose house is this anyway?

He didn't know.

Then one night she had abruptly made her move: What's the go with the stalker Steven's always ranting about?

Her asking the question in that moment had been un-premeditated. Lesley was always prepared to weather a silence, though by the time she had thrown the question, she had thought herself undeserving of severe punishment.

A silence did follow, though, and she hadn't known how to negotiate it.

Jack eventually said: Me and him didn't see eye-to-eye on politics.

Lesley had almost laughed, but adopting the way of speaking she associated with youth, she joked: You bickered over an election?

Jack's face was all ironic scorn for a moment.

Then he had said: I helped them make a book. We left them around town for people to find. People found the book, and thanks to the book, someone online said they figured out who I was in real life. They were right. Word got out but it couldn't be proved. But that was it for me, I told him I'd had enough. I cut the cord.

Jack must have been so stuck in his own reality that he couldn't imagine anyone lacking important context.

Enough of what?

Enough of the larping.

She had wanted to ask why Jack deserved an outing and why it could be undesirable, but Jack said first: *He's* not larping.

So he's for real? Lesley chanced.

Very, Jack answered.

And you're not?

I was just larping.

What does his realness mean?

You can tell by the way he isn't quite there anymore, Jack said. His face seems translucent. He's getting bigger but fading away. Aside from everything he says, that's the evidence. He's outsized. Bigger than you can imagine. He reaches far.

Do you mean that literally?

He thought for a moment, and then said: yes.

But what's your role in all this, she said lazily. She had been affecting idle interest the whole time. The smoking helped her do it, she could exhale in nonchalant ways.

I got involved.

In what?

He's not really mucking around, Jack said. Once he was just smart with broad interests. You could be smart and curious once. Now you can only mean it.

Mean what? She was pushing her luck.

He lifted his chin and pouted like a toothless man. Understanding the warning, she pretended for a while that the matter was brought to a close.

And then she pounced in ambush.

Is he a threat to you?

Jack said: He could make my life a misery with what he has on me. But I don't know if he will. It could happen any day; he's angry that I'm weak. He's unsentimental. But Steven's off his head and just as crazy, he cares more than I do. Steven's just a mess, he's not focused at all, he's a hysteric.

Cut the cord from what?

When she asked this last question Jack had looked at her with open suspicion. He had shaken his last sip of Tsingtao with an air of finality, imbibed the dreggy bubbles, and patted his tracksuit pants, as if checking for his phone and wallet, as if making to leave a pub.

But was it suspicion? Or a disappointed expectation of understanding?

No rush, Lesley said. I'm not going anywhere.

I can tell, he replied.

Because I got off the train?

She dared add: Do you think I should get back on?

Jack smiled in a way that approved of whatever answer she wanted.

Back in the weatherboard days, when it had been Lesley and Jack's turn to do the shopping, the hatchback had relentlessly followed them, up and down the hill, along every street and even into cul-de-sacs. It had idled on the car park tarmac while they browsed the Coles. It had stopped when they stopped and sped up when they ran. Jack would feign obliviousness, if he noticed at all. Lesley would shake her fist at the car, and once she even threw a rock at it, which seemed to make Jack angry.

Jack didn't care about the pursuit. He only insisted that Lesley never tell Steven about it, because it was Steven who couldn't cope.

He thinks he's a one-man think tank because he once had a job and made a habit of reading the news, Jack had said of Steven, one night in the weatherboard.

He thinks he has one over me, he wants to be my father, he thinks he's a philosopher. But he's a dumbarse and a vagrant, drinking and raving in a mountaintop squat while the world burns.

Jack didn't think 'the bastard up the hill' would hurt him anyway. He always said: It's what he's got on me that's the problem. He doesn't want me to forget he's got it.

Lesley had wondered why Jack couldn't confront the man in the hatchback. He could do it out in the open, out there in public, in the drowsy smoke-veiled car park of the Newnes Valley Plaza. But Jack had delivered some obscurity about how his adversary couldn't talk, how he was barely physically there at all, albeit colossal.

He couldn't physically hurt anyone, Jack had said one day as the hatchback followed them home. It'd be impossible, Jack said, because he'd probably collapse with any exertion. It's hard enough for him to get in and out of his car. But even if he was Superman, Jack assured, I wouldn't be worried.

She didn't know what kind of thing the man could possibly have on Jack, and he had never explained to her the nature of it. It was likely he thought she wouldn't understand, because she had hardly made the impression of a great intellect. Or else – and she was aware the theory was a kind of self-flattery – he might worry that knowing would sway her opinion of him. That was impossible, though. About as impossible, Lesley thought, as a mother hating her child.

Her theory wasn't entirely unfounded, because he had said one night, when she had guided the conversation towards his seeming plight, that she should never read any book she might find.

Any book, he said. Just to be safe, avoid all books in Newnes.

Jack guarded himself against Bon and Steven, seemed to deliberately adopt the posture of a spooked cat when they were around. The gentle decline of his shoulders would rear up, a tension would enter his whole body, and his eyes would wander across stimuli in the far distance or another dimension. But in their absence he was an intimate kind of sleepy. His head would loll, his face would become unreadable but soft. Sometimes, but rarely, his words would take flight, but strictly only on topics of his choosing. He usually talked about his music, the justifications for which Lesley could not grasp. Sometimes he would describe some or other impenetrable philosophical conundrum he had read about online. Lesley would try her hardest to keep track of these monologues, to find something of present significance in them, but eventually she would derail, having misunderstood or not comprehended some small but nevertheless crucial point, the importance of which, though impenetrable, seemed to culminate towards some unsettling, maybe even grotesque truth about their lives.

He lived in a way that Lesley quietly admired: as if there was nothing he had to achieve. He lived as if still awakening, or not yet awakened at all, to the greyscale mediocrity of an adult life in Newnes. He was, overall, so Lesley thought, not an adult at all, more of a teenager, and occasionally, when he didn't know she was watching, younger looking still. What was adulthood, except the final consequence of a persistent wearing-down? What did it really amount to, except the disavowal of principle, and a long-fended-off surrender to the order of things? What had her own adulthood been, except the sapping of her spirit, and the emergence of unforeseen barriers she lacked the wealth, discipline or misanthropy to wilfully demolish? What had her adulthood been, except the trained renunciation of any fight? Everyone got what they worked for, usually, chiefly: a wage. But Jack had not surrendered to anything. He operated independently, so far as his circumstances allowed. That is what she thought. And it was easier to love and admire him, for all this.

In his boyhood bedroom, Jack coursed repeatedly along the same paths towards enemies who, as far as she could tell, also emerged from their own neutral zones towards designed points of conflict. It was a matter of who saw who first, and which was the fastest to respond. The world of the game appeared at first true to life, but with the benefit of minutes spent watching it seemed comically unrealistic, almost deliberately so, for there was an abundance of shipping containers, all ensconced within narrow and impractical concrete environments with a vaguely Middle Eastern theme. The general impression was of a reconstructed reality, arranged to accommodate brisk and emotionless fights to the death, fine-tuned to unwavering fairness.

As she watched Jack play, Lesley hoped that her having entered the hut, smashed the computer, marched the tunnels, and stolen the car (only to return it), might have caused the pursuit to wane. Had the disruptive path not punctured her clearing, she might never have taken it upon herself to interfere. It was right that she had risen to his defence, though. Jack was her kin. She was sure of it. He had never moved away from her. He was always reliably there, and he didn't mind sitting in silence next to her. She knew him to be smart, so you couldn't blame stupidity for the way he would just sit there with her, often in silence. But his intelligence did not overlap with hers, because after all she was, she supposed, intelligent in her own way: she had made him speak. She had spoken to him, and he had not resisted. He had replied.

A zipping military figure emerged in the generic Arabian container-scape. The screen faded crimson red, a counter started, and Jack quit the game in a mild rage.

Steven and Bon were watching one of the old *Star Wars* movies. They had already established set seats on the L-shaped couch: Bon across the main area, on his side, slightly propped by cushions; Steven flat across the side designed for lying, chin rested on chest.

It's not so uncommon for lives to change dramatically from one day to the next, Lesley supposed. And it's not so strange for whole decades of so-called lived experience to have the quality of a half-remembered dream. Most periods predating that present seemed insubstantial to Lesley, to the extent that she had sometimes doubted the older iterations of her own existence. There were periods of her own existence – whole years – that she did not remember at all. Whole periods of her life were lost to going back and forth and doing the same thing every day, the same mundane acts performed, over and over, with a value mysterious even to her superiors. It would have been nice to feel allied to one's previous self, to transmit comforting affirmations back through time.

Instead she felt dumber and vaguely ashamed. Even her teenage self, even her child self, seemed ridiculous, though these tended to cast a more authoritative shadow than what she could remember of her adulthood. Now that she had disembarked at Newnes, and now that she had chiselled a portal, it was probably inevitable that a new monotony would be installed. And maybe this was it.

She sat on the armrest closest to Bon's head and pretended to be curious about the movie.

So are you going to take that job, she asked eventually. Bon screwed his neck around to look at her, then he looked at Steven, who after a whole minute said 'yes'.

But we've got no phone, Bon said. And Jack probably won't let us use his (like he knew Jack better than her). So we'll have to go to a payphone. There's one in the train station car park.

Well let's all go, she said. Let's go right now. It's boring watching movies all day.

It took about an hour-and-a-half for them to get ready. Steven was hungry first, so they heated some baked beans. Then he needed to sit for fifteen minutes to let the food digest. He wanted to perform this due diligence in front of the television, presumably horizontally, but Lesley put a stop to it. Then, when he went to his bedroom to get changed, he shut the door and didn't return for another half-hour. Lesley had to remind him with a knock, she had to tell him to stay focused. Then he came out wearing the same clothes as before, because after all he didn't need to get dressed up to make a phone call. Meanwhile Bon was dragging his own feet, and in the process of him doing so (sitting on the bed, rifling through a basket of clothes he'd inherited from Steven, deliberating, losing his shoes, wondering where his wallet was but not looking for it) she tried to have a discussion about their present situation, she wanted to know what he knew about what Steven knew. But he'd always deliver this exaggerated, contemptuous wince at her, like it just wasn't the right time, like she was demonstrating yet again how poor she was at knowing the right time for particular kinds of conversation. Then Steven lost his shoes, even though he'd only minutes ago put them on. He couldn't remember why he'd taken them off again.

And then Jack emerged from his room.

We're going to the payphone, Lesley said cheerfully. Do you want to come?

He most certainly didn't.

It's not going to be relaxing that's for sure, Steven moaned.

But it has to be done, Lesley said. Unless Jack wants to let us use his phone.

For her benefit, he let them use his phone.

Steven wanted to make the call but Lesley politely insisted Bon do it, which raised Steven's hackles, because if he was responsible enough to have a job then he was responsible enough to make the call. Bon went into their bedroom with Jack, because Jack didn't want his phone out of sight. They shut the door and Lesley and Steven eavesdropped from outside. It wasn't a long discussion, and when Bon came out he announced – proudly, she thought – that he, or was it better to say they, had got the job, that they could start whenever they wanted, even right that second, but probably for the best tomorrow.

And we can just start with the house next door and work along from there, Bon said.

The system worked like this: Bon or Steven would put a note in the letterbox every morning with addresses for the houses they had 'liquidated' the day before. Then in the evening, once the operators of this business had ensured the work had been done, the corresponding amount of cash would be put in the letterbox, no later than seven p.m.

For the rest of the afternoon Bon and Steven watched movies. Lesley walked a dozen or so circuits of the overgrown backyard and then, bored and pent-up, went back inside.

Jack was seated at his computer but he wasn't playing the video game anymore. He was arranging audio waves on a grid, and clicking icons to manipulate their qualities. The resulting sound emitted from a small desktop speaker. She wasn't sure whether it was deliberately quiet and cloudy, or if the speaker was broken.

She lay on his bed and folded her legs.

If I was harsher I'd try to forbid television in the day, she said.

Jack nodded, but he was too focused on his own screen.

Anyway, do you think you'll help me?

He nodded again, and then added: How?

Moral support. And when they're at their job, I suppose we'll need to walk to the petrol station on the highway for supplies.

After a while he said: Okay.

It wouldn't hurt to mow the lawn either, but we'll need some petrol.

They'll have it at the petrol station, Jack comforted.

She shut her eyes and listened. Jack's music was not a soiled absence, like she'd once heard Bon describe it. It was the sound of their house. There was no absence at all, there was actually too much in it, so many variations on a simple theme, copied over and over again, every layer uniquely transposed, so that it did indeed resemble a sickly silence. But to a careful listener, hairline cracks emerged in the drone, and familiar subtleties poured out of it, so that this vigilantly unsentimental music blossomed with full spectrum shades, shades lacking describable colourations. With every insinuation of a firm colour arrived an element poised to undermine it, so that binaries inevitably collapsed, opposites were not opposed but in balletic conspiracy, engaged in a resistant, anguished, questioning kind of dance, a dance that undermined decades of stoic oppositional reality, a dance that even seemed to cynically wed these oppositions.

Maybe we can get your music released on a CD, Lesley said.

It wasn't a suggestion she had intended to make; she had to say something to puncture the music. The otherworldly murk seemed capable of changing her, somehow.

It would be a shame if no one got to hear it, she added, except for me and these two idiots.

No one has to hear it, Jack said.

Far be it from her to ask why. Whenever he answered her questions, it only invited her interpretations, which she never trusted.

They won't suffer if they don't, she said. That's not what I meant.

It's meant to be discovered by accident, he said. The more people who hear it, the more suspicious it becomes. If one person hears it, it's just that one person, happening upon the sound that I made. It might make them feel strange and haunted, like you say it does to you. Or they might just hear a minute of it and close the tab in boredom. Either way is fine. But if a hundred people hear it, you could start to suspect me of wanting to control people's minds. Maybe I would be controlling those people's minds, accidentally, and then...what if my sound drives them mad? Or drives them to do bad things? It's not as hard to do as you probably think. I've seen madness provoked by the most stupid so-called art, and by the most pitiable, repellent people. But even that concern aside, having lots of people hear my sound just seems demeaning, both to the sound, and to those imagined listeners. All so-called art created to be experienced en masse is mind control. Artists are the puppets who subconsciously volunteer to spread messages that have been planted in their minds by mysterious forces. Powers we don't understand or even know about, try to control us through music and film and all so-called art. Even the most radical-seeming so-called art domesticates us. Especially so, actually. That's all art is for – mind control.

Lesley nodded in oblivious agreement. She sat upright to gratify the boy.

So you're saying you hide it deliberately?

I don't hide it, he said. I put it on the internet.

She lay back down.

You must know what you're doing, she surrendered. But you don't deliberately share it around, do you?

It's on there – he tapped his monitor – with the worst extremes and the lamest banalities you could imagine, and a whole lot more that you can't. That's what strikes me as poignant about it. It doesn't need to be shared to just *be* there. The sounds I upload are just my contributions to this gargantuan, sometimes amazing, but mostly stupid mortuary of human activity, over which humans have lost control. When most people go on there all they see is propaganda, but what you're invited to see and consume by the algorithms is just the tiniest part of the whole. You cannot begin to fathom what else is on there, Lesley. He pointed at the screen again.

I think I can, she said. Conspiracy theories (she almost dared pull a poker face). Websites for ordering drugs and hit men. Porn. Satanic fascists. Things like that.

Someone could find my sound, Jack said, in the spammy dregs of search results, among the Russian scams and malware sites. Odds are against it though. I don't make it easily searchable, and as soon as the analytics tell me a particular one of my sounds has been heard – or just accessed – I delete it. Most of what I've put up there hasn't ever been accessed, and I keep a close eye on it. It's interesting to imagine what someone might think when they hear it, I guess. It's interesting to imagine how that might change their mood, briefly or forever. But that's the thing: it's interesting to *imagine* that, but the *reality* of that ever happening would not be interesting at all. In reality, if they didn't close the tab straight away, the listener would interpret the sound and contaminate it with meaning – the worst possible outcome.

You've got a unique way of going about things, Lesley said. She didn't add that it seemed quite pointless.

Any artist who wants their work seen by more than one person, Jack went on, who designs it to be experienced en masse, and even worse, who wants it to be correctly interpreted...they were first against the wall. They're already properly dead, co-opted, sucked dry by platforms, conglomerates and services, all except the loudest moralisers and hack pedagogues, the grifters who understand the algorithm of shifting moralities and who pander to the gatekeepers. But each and all of their concerns last twelve months before those same concerns become intolerable to the pallbearers of the next twelve months. People get sick of it, or their suspicions are raised. The secret puppet masters have to be constantly updating their tactics. Building tension, providing release; finding new ways to make everyone feel unique and smart and empowered. But my sound – and he said *my sound* in a tone verging on pride – will outlast it all for not ever being heard, it will never be robbed of its possibly meaningless power. No one will see themselves in it, just something entirely else.

Jack had turned to face her by now. She watched his face articulate, his upper lip supping from his lower, expansive and vaguely undignified, like a child who cannot speak fast enough for their ideas, but who nevertheless manages to express them, with a cogency foreign to their addled parent.

The music had hit upon a tight, nauseating loop. It was a dissected crescendo, neither the climb nor its goal remained. She couldn't formulate a careful response while it was on. Anyway, she wasn't sure what he meant.

I get what you mean, she said. But it's dumb from a certain point of view. And how do you know the mind controllers haven't just come up with a clever way to target people like you?

Jack didn't flinch, only scowled ironically.

Anyway, she went on, when you make something as good and original as this music, you should be rewarded for it. That's all I was trying to say. Do what you want.

He grabbed the mouse and reduced the music program; a media player was hidden beneath. A few clicks later a looping video appeared, playing silently in a quarter-screen window. Lesley could not take it lying down. She sat bolt upright, leaned towards the unspeakable footage.

What are you doing? Lesley cried.

This is a video that I couldn't stop watching for a while, Jack said. There are a lot of details in it you probably won't notice until you've watched it a couple of dozen times. But you shouldn't watch it that many times; if you did you'd be changed, and you're fine the way you are. The sounds I make may sound unique and alien to you, and they might make you feel haunted. But that's because you don't know anything, Lesley. Not my opinion; you're always saying that yourself, and if it's true, I admire it. But I have seen everything that close to no one else has. You can see anything you want, and I've seen it all. You don't need to order VHSs from freakish European mailgroups anymore. I can watch real people being killed whenever I want, any kind of person, you name it: it's free and itemised. I watched in real time as a man mowed down dozens in a mosque. I don't need the world's realities benign or evil spelled out to me, or left hidden in the open in so-called art, to be gleaned by interpretation. Those are mind-control tactics. There is nothing of any substance for me to learn, do you understand? Nothing has the power of this.

He tapped the looping video, closed it, and went back to his work. It could have been a cue for Lesley to leave, but she could tell by the performative way he was working that he preferred her to stay. In a way she had never seen before, he even seemed to want her to interpret his silence and his posture.

It took another quarter-hour of Lesley not leaving for him to finally add, with the thinnest attempt at unconcern, that a part of him wished he'd never seen the video.

Not just that video, he said, but all of them. You wouldn't believe what's out there. Everything pales in comparison. But they're all real, unlike most of everything else I'm expected to take seriously.

Back in the old weatherboard, Bon had always been the one to gently fish for desired answers and sentiments from Lesley. But in bed that night and all that followed, both wearing shorts and shirts borrowed from the boys, in the wan light of an IKEA bedside lamp, she was the one desperate for answers. All of them save Jack had spent the evening watching the second and then the third *Star Wars* DVDs. Bon had taken some stealthy draughts from the vodka bottle, and figuring herself equally entitled, she had followed suit. So it wasn't for lack of alcohol that the dynamic had shifted. After a long time spent staring at the wall and listening to Bon's nervous breathing – for they had performed this ceremony of long-winded silence every night – she said: What have we done?

He didn't answer at first because he was pretending to be asleep. So she kicked his leg, asked again, and warned quite but not too firmly that it was about time. His body slowly bunched up, he was curling inward and away from her, but she knew it and he knew it: it was about time.

He said that they had done what she had wanted them to do. We've taken them through a portal into a new and better life, he said. It's not perfect, he added, it's not heavenly Sofala, but it's a house with a roof, and there's a shop on the highway. What would we have done in Sofala anyway? We'd probably have been bashed, and camping wasn't permitted.

But the boys, she replied, haven't mentioned anything about the change at all. And I'm not exactly going to ask them.

What are they meant to say? Bon snapped. Against all odds your portal worked. Steven doesn't go around neglecting to say things he thinks need to be said. Anyway, if it hadn't worked, they'd have surely said something, something like: Why did you ply us with rum in the forest and then drive us to fiery Woop Woop? You should be satisfied. It's for the best they don't talk about it.

The conversation was killed by a loud crash above their heads, and then another, closer to the front of the house. The sharp rattle of corrugated iron faded into a piercing silence, accompanied only by the hum of the kitchen refrigerator.

Kids rocking our roof, Bon eventually said, relieved, like he'd been rescued by it.

Anyway, Lesley continued, determined to stay on course: Is it really that easy? Should I just relax? Are we going to stay like this forever?

Bon, in a tone designed to be sage, but rife with numb hesitancy: We're all just going along with life.

It's because you woke up first, she complained. I shouldn't have gone back to sleep, I should have been the first one to greet them in the morning. I would have set a different tone.

Your portal magically worked, Bon said, nearly shouting now. It's a miracle, you have to admit. How can you be so picky about what is here on the other side? And anyway, I didn't greet them. I got up and Steven was watching *X-Men*, so I just did what was natural, because you've got to be natural. And we've mainly just talked about movies and burning household goods, he's given no revealing talks, and what's so strange about it anyway? As for Jack – he hates me, he's yours to deal with.

He rolled over and squeezed himself impenetrable. My holiday is over anyway, he soon added. Tomorrow I have to work.

The next morning they had nothing to eat. Steven opened the tub of sludge in the fridge and a foul stench permeated. He opened the back door and pegged it container and all into the yard.

We might as well go then, he said. We've got our lighter (Bon patted his pocket and nodded), and I've got this mallet (he wielded the mallet). Bon held a jerry can of lawnmower fuel too – they seemed ill-prepared.

You've done a good job preparing, she said, patting them both on the chest. But you need to be careful because fire is dangerous. You're not just going to pour the petrol and light it up by hand, are you?

Steven groaned and said no.

You've just got to stand back from it, he added. We've got all these old phone books – he patted his backpack. We'll rip the pages out, light them, toss them into the petrol. We're not simple.

When they left she went up to Jack's room and let herself in. He snapped the laptop shut, but a video game splash screen remained on the second monitor.

We've got to do some shopping, she said. And almost added: just like the old days.

Lesley and Jack wandered to the petrol station on the highway. There wasn't any substantial food in stock, nothing rapidly perishable, mostly vacuum-sealed microwavables, foods eaten with one hand on a steering wheel, a perfunctory selection of tinned lentils and spaghetti, and jars of mushy baby food. They bought some of each. When they got home in the early afternoon, Lesley peered over the backyard Colorbond. In the yard next door there was a great pile of splintered cupboards, upturned couches and whitegoods, bed frames and chests of drawers, dining tables and chairs. There was a wall piano too. Bon and Steven were stood at the edge looking perplexed.

What's the matter, she yelled.

We can't get it to light, Steven replied. At this rate we won't make a cent today.

She knew this would happen. She tossed over a packet of Jiffy firelighters bought at the petrol station. Bon picked it up doubtfully – he couldn't perform gratefulness – and started to snap the white biscuit into pieces. Then he lit each and tossed them into the most flammable looking areas. The yard was quickly overwhelmed by black putrid smoke, so much that she lost sight of them. A ripening flame burst loudly for contact with some buried payload.

Five bucks a packet at the servo, she yelled.

In the bare rectangular block of yard, perilously close to the washing line, the fire burned with assuring emphasis, and from within the smoke and flame there occasionally came the thump of collapse or explosion. It didn't seem that loud, though it must have been, because she didn't notice Jack join her. He had dragged an old lawnmower to the fence for her to stand on.

A brilliant fire, she yelled to Jack.

It's a job well done, Steven called out, thinking himself complimented. He was hunched roaming the perimeter with his shirt off, tracksuit pants rolled to the knees. Only we'd better go make a start on the next house.

With his mallet he smashed full force into the Colorbond fence on the other side of the yard. He knocked out two panels, providing easy access into the next property. Bon watched, he didn't look alarmed, he might have taken part if they had another mallet.

You're enjoying this aren't you, Lesley yelled out, and then quietly enough so only Jack could hear: *you piece of work*. Bon wandered over and made a sipping motion, but she flared her nose and nodded sideways at Jack.

It makes no difference to me, the boy said, and this made Bon smile, he even attempted a knowing glance at Jack. So she had no option but to go and retrieve the vodka bottle, which was close to empty, but not such an emergency, because there was a sealed bottle of Kahlua as well, two bottles of Jamesons, an untouched Pimms, and a rare licorice absinthe. When she handed the vodka to Bon – making sure, at least, that Steven couldn't see – he made to wander off with it, so she had to yell, almost scream, that he not even dare.

You wouldn't dare, she seethed.

So Bon stood there and sculled the rest in three heaving draughts.

You're an idiot, she said, as the thwack of mallet against wood sounded two doors down. Jack was still leaning over the fence, staring at the fire. She told him he should go and help. It'd do you some good, she said, to get out there and wave your limbs around, to lift and drag things.

But with evidence of a looming lecture Jack slid down the fence and went back inside, much to Lesley's relief.

Bon was hazardously drunk when they got home. He must have found some more liquor in the houses along the road. But she didn't say anything, and nor did he, because his drunkenness had never been expansive, it had always culminated in a stumbling torpor. Alcohol did not grease his wheels, it ushered him further into a benumbed silence.

A hundred, Steven said, a full hundred cash-in-hand tax-free dollars. And it wasn't even that hard. Though don't get me wrong: it was hard.

Lesley was arranging the semblance of a meal onto four floral plates. A small pile of heated tin spaghetti, another small pile of Burger Rings, a portion of microwavable alfredo pasta, and dried wasabi peas on the side.

And you think burning furniture is fun, I bet you do, Steven continued. But when it's your job it's a whole other thing. I'd prefer to be watching Blu-rays (a glance at her) or playing video games (a stare at Jack), or going on daily trips to the shops, then I might get some say in what we eat. But as hard as it is, it's satisfying to work, isn't it Bon?

Bon nodded.

You can't not do it, there is nothing else to do. Not having a job, it's verging on criminal. Because you're just seated there, you can really just be seated there doing nothing if you have no job, while the rest of the world toils around you. It's unfair. Not that I'm pointing any fingers – and he nodded at Lesley – because you've got enough on your plate as it is.

Do I? she said.

You don't need to measure up what you do against what I do, he replied. I'm not comparing. You've got Jack to look after.

Jack said nothing; Lesley rose to his defence. He doesn't need much looking after, she said. And he's just as capable of burning furniture as you lot are, aren't you, Jack? (He still said nothing.) And anyway, you don't want me walking alone to the petrol station, do you? Jack doesn't need to come. I ask him to, and he does, he doesn't refuse and he doesn't argue, and it's not exactly fun walking to the highway. You wouldn't be eating if it weren't for him coming with me, you never know what might happen out on those streets.

You might get bitten by a mozzie, Steven laughed. Though he added that he was just kidding – he was always making these jokes – and that indeed it was difficult out there, with the wild dogs and all, and now that she mentions it, his job wasn't exactly safe, entering houses and extracting their innards and burning it all into ash. Bon was invited to agree, and he did.

They watched the fourth *Star Wars* movie the following night. Lesley joined them because Jack's music put her at risk of falling asleep, and though she had no good reason to stay awake, she didn't want to waste any time. Watching the movie – which was reportedly not very good – she almost didn't notice when a headlight panned the lounge room curtains. She rose quickly and bent over the television to see. But there was no light outside, not even the streetlights anymore, nor any lights in any of the other houses, and it had been months since she had seen any stars. The night outside the window was not – all things considered – a night, not any more, it was something different, it did not appear traversable, it was the exterior of a map, the threshold of an illusion. She watched as a blur of human shape dropped something into their mailbox, returned to the car – it was too dark to see what kind of car – and then drove away, headlights carving featureless passage through placeholder space.

The money's come, she announced over a dramatic orchestral score. Neither Bon or Steven were especially eager to go and retrieve it, so she went upstairs to fetch Jack, and they went out there together, into the seeming nothingness, fingers carefully tracing the wild rosemary hedge – two fifty-dollar notes folded in an old shopping catalogue.

For a long time that was the pattern of their lives. It felt like a long time to Lesley. She had reached a hard barrier in her relations with Bon, there was no longer the sense that they were conspiring together. Instead, their bedtime discussions had become a ritual unpacking of the preceding day's routines, and there was no delicate nor overt way to breach it, in order to move on to topics with a broader view.

She would normally ask again (for she would also ask during dinner) how work had been. He would always say that it had been much the same as every previous day, namely, that they had done their job as effectively as they could, that they had occasionally met with obstacles, such as especially fire-resistant furniture, unusual abundances of it, or the odd starving cat resulting in distraction. Meanwhile rocks rained down on their roof every night with increasing force and duration, sometimes with long gaps between, at other times with staccato intensity, like the work of many hands.

They peered out windows front and back, but they never caught sight of the offenders. There was never any sign of movement, because the darkness outside was quite unlike any she had seen before, it was an almost pure black, there was seemingly nothing out there. And if it weren't for this, then maybe she could have gently insisted to Bon, or even Steven, that it was necessary to go out there to get a better view, maybe even to confront the bored children, for bored children they must surely be. But aside from the fact that no better view would likely be afforded out there – it was an astonishing form of black – there was an unreasonable fear, a childlike variety, the kind she had not known for years, even in the hut's tunnels, even in the old town Sofala. It was a fear that seemed dangerous to acknowledge aloud lest it spread, and it was easier to believe that the dark wasn't quite so dark or scary, that it was actually a problem with her eyes.

Jack was the first to speak aloud of it. One afternoon as they lumbered the railway parade towards home, weighed down by their petrol station groceries, he was even more remote and lethargic than usual. After a typically extended period spent trying to open him up, he finally spoke: he said it was hard to sleep for the rocks on the roof.

But that in itself isn't a big deal, he said. What makes it harder, is the feeling that the night has taken on an unusual quality, it is a clotted kind of night (he did say 'clotted'). Lesley wouldn't have described it that way, but it proved that they saw eye-to-eye on the matter of the night, that it was no longer what it used to be.

Because normally you see something, Jack said, even on overcast nights, even during blackouts – and there have always been frequent blackouts in Newnes, haven't there, with every storm and then sometimes without – but this darkness lacks shapes or the suggestion of them, there are no lines or shades in it, it isn't dark it's black. It's a black night, he said, though it doesn't even feel right to call it night, because even though night has always been dark, it has never been black, these are two separate things.

Bon agreed that it was especially dark outside, though he wouldn't have called it black. But he agreed it was a special kind of darkness, because when he peered into it he often saw the images inside his mind, or else, an indistinct – not exactly black – blur, almost like he had his eyes closed.

But that's what happens when you're not used to this kind of darkness, he added, like he'd read it in an article.

When Lesley stared out the window at night, with all interior lights off, in serene, perfect absence, it was possible to make connections she had never made before, associations that rattled her, complex connections between phenomena and numbers. She skimmed across the deepest mysteries of numbers. The world pivoted around a solved equation, coursed its rhythmic logic over and over. That's how it seemed in the perfect dark. Far be it from her to fathom this equation, because it was an immensely complicated kind, though also possibly stupid if it was born of her mind. No, she didn't understand or even quite see the equation – she couldn't have written it down – it was more a matter of finally knowing it was there, and detecting certain figures in it – not necessarily numbers, rather number-adjacent figures – and in some vague way everything could be associated with it, everything banal and everything profound and everything in between, *everything* could be torn apart just with the slightest brushing against this equation, but only for the briefest of moments. It seemed to Lesley, by night at least, that it was no longer true that nothing made sense, on the contrary everything made sense, even the most purely illogical things, ranging the whole gamut. Within everything coursed a metronome but its timing was incomprehensible in the presence of light. Anyway, it would take a life more wholly lived than hers so far to puncture this stultifying sense, she couldn't rule out that the lives of giant figures, true renegades, were lives that had simply derailed from the equation, maybe they were splits in reality itself. But then again, the equation did seem hungry for novelty, it loved to metabolise aberration, the equation seemed to generate its own playthings.

Bon and Steven cycled through the *Iron Man* and *Star Wars* DVDs. Sometimes when one sequence of films was completed they'd watch the series again, still too fatigued from the nightly binge of the other. Occasionally they browsed the special features, resentful of their self-importance but nevertheless engaged.

There were no other distractions. Sometimes they would watch a quarter or half of one film, before deciding on another. On rare occasions they would debate the finer points of the world inside the films, they would make oblique connections, theorise explanations for the errors in their design. They were more often than not in bed by nine. And once they had retired, Steven in his daytime clothes, Bon after two savouring swigs of the Kahlua, she would press Jack's door open. The door grazed across the carpet in such a way that he would have known she was coming. She would suggest that now was better than any other time to get some sleep, because no particular time nowadays seemed especially right. And then because he claimed it helped, and she had to agree, he would pair his computer with a small speaker, and a monotone wavering drone would fill the room. He would lay in his bed, still with the Pokémon cover – the one she always wanted to clean, the one that smelled too potently of him – and she would sit on the low bedside table, hand on the soft between his arm and rib, until he went to sleep. Then she would go and lie next to Bon, where she could still hear the drone from Jack's room, possibly only because she knew it was there. Maybe she didn't hear it, maybe it had become lodged in her mind.

But every morning seemed to dismiss the anxiety of their deepest nights. Because say what you want about families (and Lesley often pictured saying exactly this to Bon, or Jack) but for all their many benefits they do tend to make every day blend into the next, and that, she supposed, was what made them important. Because you're contending with a small handful of walking talking maths problems, and they're not particularly complex ones, but the solving of them taxes all available resources.

Most mornings they would wake together in the dull lace-shaded morning light, usually at sunrise. She always woke first. She'd untangle herself from Bon, who was unwittingly clingy in his sleep, and in the process wake him up. He'd rustle around indignantly and frown like a baby. He had a certain way of stretching his face in the morning, like it was an exercise routine, a process of reacquaintance. And if the boys took their time to stir, he'd sometimes hazard an arm across her chest, or else wrap one leg around hers languidly. He'd always pretend to be half-asleep, because his daylight self forbade any such contact. But she could tell for a certain reverberating warmth that he was eagerly alert.

One morning she just said as long as you're quick. She had licence to be brisk because she feared the boys. And her having said 'as long as you're quick' gave Bon permission for all kinds of exploration, in answer to which she could only say again – gently, she thought – 'quickly'. He was quick enough. And after all, it was only five minutes before their door was slammed open. Steven walked in and reckoned it was about time everyone got up. What's the point in staying in bed? It was morning. It was a new day.

Towards evening she would slouch to the kitchen, usually at around four o'clock, because it was a daily strife to ensure the petrol station food was served in just the right way. Some nights Jack had a natural aversion to wheat, and while he had never complained, Lesley had learned not to serve it to him. Bon had expressed an objection to obvious snack foods served on a dinner plate ('they are what they are') which had recently thrown her off her habit of arranging the paltry petrol station offerings into an illusion of a hearty family meal. Steven mirrored Bon in all of his objections, so she had taken to serving the most obvious snack foods – Burger Rings, Twisties, Kettle Chips – into discrete serving bowls, to present them as pleasant bonuses, *snackables*, designed to supplement the increasingly barren main dishes, which usually comprised off-brand miscellanies bought from the health-food snack section (herbed dried flatbread, jarred pickles, sun-dried tomatoes) and the reliable nightly dollop of microwavable packet alfredo pasta – which Bon couldn't eat, he said, because he was lactose intolerant. Sometimes they could only get macaroni, which Steven abhorred.

Then after dinner came supper, originally a simple serving of trail mix, which had proven popular enough that it was incorporated into the main dish to enthuse appetites. When Steven finally objected to trail mix as a component of the main – 'fruit and grains isn't dinner' – she had transferred it back to supper, only to find that Steven's objection hadn't been a matter of principle: he had simply grown tired of it. He didn't mind the banana – 'buy the banana by itself' – so supper for a matter of days was just the dried banana, manually picked out, because dried banana packets weren't available at the petrol station. Bon noted one night that he couldn't imagine eating the dried bananas just by themselves, and while Bon could happily forgo supper, Steven continued to insist on it. They'd probably go down better, Bon had said, if we had a cup of tea to go alongside. Bon could make his own goddamned tea, but someone – Lesley – had to make the tea for Steven, because he didn't like black tea – too bitter – and preferred chamomile, thankfully available at the petrol station, but inexplicably only as loose-leaf. He'd drink it only when shovelled with sugar (white, not brown, not raw), and usually alongside a dessert of some kind, for a while a Zooper Dooper, then a Paddle Pop, sometimes a jar of peach baby food, or occasionally, on colder nights, a line of Cadbury's Snack, melted into a cup in the microwave.

Lesley's dreams in Newnes were always accompanied by a specific version of Jack. Her dreams unfolded as a series of events, drowsy illogical narratives. Tranquillity segued into conundrum, conundrum into relief. Occasionally in her previous life, she'd sought out ways to direct her dreams, but the recipes and exercises had never worked.

But the version of Jack who inhabited her dreams eliminated her desire to control. Regardless of setting or period he was always there, a younger and more malleable version of the boy. He would ask questions and raise suspicions, and she quickly learned that the dream version of Jack was the unbeknown conductor of proceedings, events pivoted around his utterances. She had grown to love his waking version, but in dreams her love seemed rational.

There was compliance in his sleeping face. It resembled the face of a child, cosseted by playful and temporary limits. There was indignation too, you could detect a small trace of it, there was the arch of a scowl between his eyes. But it was overwhelmed by compliance, a babyish aversion to scolding or punishment. During these moments Lesley could picture how he must have looked as a baby. His face would have been smaller, and there would have been smooth skin beneath his button nose. It would have been rosier and chubbier. It would have shone, because the faces of even unhappy babies shine. It must surely be possible to reinstate that shine, to somehow dismantle and rebuild again. If it were possible to reinstate that shine, there would follow the desire to prolong it, to make it endure longer than seemingly possible. Lesley supposed, that if any of this were possible – it surely wasn't – then the only sensible thing to do would be to let the child roam like an animal, to teach it nothing, to follow at a far distance and then maybe, when required, to save it from the maw of danger. She'd refrain from the urge to make her rescues a learning experience. It wouldn't be the danger that drained his shine, it would be the coddling precautions. It wasn't fear that drained his shine, it wasn't anxiety that drained his shine, it was the monotonous powerlessness, the blossoming into servitude, the expectation of it. For lack of any of these, there would surely remain a shine, or else a natural ruthlessness.

As her train had passed the three or four stops before Newnes, she had imagined what it would be like to just get off it. A stubborn force had compelled her to stand. She had stood in the aisle, and there had been no onlookers to shame her into sitting back down. It had been a role-play at first, it was not possible that she'd get off the train. She had left her bag on the seat and there had been no reason to pick it up, because she wasn't getting off. As the lightly mountainous terrain outside had given way to houses, she had wandered up the aisle and then back to her seat. She had been pretending and it was enjoyable. Not living in Newnes, not having any reason to visit Newnes, not having any special interest in Newnes, but nevertheless experiencing the process of moving to disembark at Newnes, had been an invigorating sensation, also an eerie sensation. It was a moment she had seemed to have lived before, and countless times at that. Maybe, Lesley had thought, she was re-acquainting with some shadow version of herself, some portion that wandered neglected realities. Or else she had finally found her future. If that was the case, then she would no longer need to wonder about it for she had arrived.

She had always preferred the past, not just her own past, but the distant general past, the one she had never seen. She respected it more, she wanted to belong to it. But given the way things are and always have been, one must always face the future, so it was better to grab it by the throat than to cower in anticipation.

It was a strange compulsion that dragged her off the train, she thought, climbing into bed next to Jack, whose rod-tense body had loosened since they passed through her portal, and whose eyes when met with hers had gained a trace of shine. It had previously seemed impossible that her life could change.

The lounge room drawers were overstuffed with official documents, bills, shopping catalogues, the odd decades-old video game magazine, loose batteries, crossed-off calendars, and shrink-wrapped phone books.

In one drawer beneath all this debris was an old-fashioned photo album bound in dusty white linen. Lesley retrieved it from the mess, placed all of the debris back in the drawer and locked herself in the bathroom. She sat on the toilet and opened the album.

The first photo, alone beneath the plastic protective film, depicted a young woman with a baby – presumably Steven. The woman wore a downcast and ironic expression similar to Jack's in his lighter moments. She was undeniably pretty, she was in her early twenties. It was not a deliberately posed photograph: she was seated, curled on a single-person lounge chair. In a summer dress she nursed the baby, with half a flannel cloth laid over one shoulder, the other half draped across the baby's sleeping body. There was the faintest glow of photograph red in her tired serene eyes.

Over page, across the first double-page spread, eight more

photos were secured beneath the film. Four were professional shots of the baby against a velvet blue backdrop. He was a little older, now capable of lifting his upper body in a half-crawl, though his face was docile and ever-so-slightly alarmed, with the exception of the last photo, where his face was creased in a wary open-mouthed smile.

For Lesley, who had never had babies, except for those already raised in dreams, all babies looked the same – they were troll-like and ugly. And the photos over the page did not disabuse her of this prejudice. In less professional photos, the same baby (or so it seemed) was depicted in various unremarkable environments – laid across the cushions of a brown couch, held aloft in a dimly lit room with glowing light in the background, lifting himself on a rainbow mat, sleeping in a lace-shrouded bassinet.

And then, as if the album sensed her antipathy, it skipped forward several years, to a boy two or three years old, one able to stand. He appeared happy, though photographers had to be selective in the pre-digital age. His shining brown hair was trimmed to a functional crew cut, his whites were astonishing in their unblemished reflectivity, and present was that bizarre alchemy of a young child's face, every feature and every pore radiated peace and health, every expression was reliable. There he was, standing on a lawn, a Matchbox car in one fist, and in the next photo, he was seated at a dining table with cake on his chin. In the next he sat balanced on the shoulders of a male adult whose face was out of frame. In another, he was cross-legged on carpet, with coloured wooden blocks in the foreground.

But it wasn't Steven, and it wasn't Jack. When she realised this, Lesley flicked through the pages at speed. The child kept growing, its face grew incrementally less cherubic, more aware of the camera and its objective, more determined to undermine it with play. Soon the child learned a photo face, an on-demand caricature of its own happiness: eyes squinted, teeth bared, forehead slightly crumpled. There were other kids in the photos – cousins or neighbours – who performed awkwardly for the lens in roughly the same way, knowing the camera's presence was a cue for a certain kind of pose. By now, the album's starring child was five, six, seven...not shown was his growing knowledge and complicity with his world.

She fancied herself unusually capable of remembering what it was like to be a child, because those were her happiest years. But she had never been able to imagine what it would be like to be a parent. She vaguely knew that it was an arduous and transformative experience. Later on, in the weeks and months before she disembarked at Newnes, she knew it to be an experience that was increasingly hard to justify. It was true that some online articles made a good point when they reported that babies had been reared in chaos, poverty and war for the majority of recorded history. Other articles took the form of anonymous first-hand confessions, writers expressing fear for their newly created children, and these usually also involved grappling with the need to admit this fear to some significant other.

But it was mostly beside the point, because the child depicted, as pleasant as he seemed, was neither Jack or Steven. He was a mysterious eldest first.

Jack and Steven were men, you could smell it on them, naturally you could see it, but they were children, and she childless, all in a life surprising in its ambivalence, you could see it written in the brown of the sky. When they had met in the Newnes Valley Plaza, right after she had disembarked the train – when the replacement bus had proven not so – Steven had complained of hunger, anxiety, the so-called decline of his brother (and hence the world), and she had thought it a beggar's ruse at first. But even if Lesley fancied herself unusually capable of remembering what it was like to be a child, at the same time, she fancied herself quite hardened (for she had lived in the city), and while she had no taste for arguing, she had a great distaste for declarations no matter from where they came, any repeatedly shouted declaration triggered a lurch in the other direction, because all declarations nowadays seemed fermented in sanctimony. So she had been stubbornly drawn to this stupid drunk man, which was the very opposite of a good idea all things considered, he was just a mess of disappointment and conspiracy. She wanted him to be correct, to validate her own fears, but she also hoped he was wrong.

But she had disembarked alone, and had run the risk of staying alone, if it weren't for Steven. From a certain point of view she had gotten lucky. By the time she had reached the plaza, counter to what she had expected, it was obvious there weren't any hotels in Newnes, and it was obvious she wouldn't get back on the train.

When the actual, unmistakable figure of Steven appeared in the album, there was nothing particularly troll-like about him. It gave her pause. Weeks after arriving in the weatherboard, she had walked in on him masturbating in his bedroom. The door had been ajar; he too had been at fault. During the following weeks she had wanted to bring it up in private – in a jovial, humorous, conspiratorial way – but in all likelihood he would never gain that aspect of his pride back. *It's natural*, she had wanted to say. *I rub one out, too. Even famous people do, I promise you.* But insisting to Steven that she didn't care if he wanked wasn't a speech she had ever found the right time to deliver, and anyway she'd done her dash, it was off the table now, the mishap had defined them. It was no longer possible to imagine Steven as someone with any legitimate sexual urges. She could not help but to see him as a kind of rutting animal.

Jack wasn't in the album; it was difficult to imagine Jack in any album. The idea of Jack as a once-real child did not make sense. Even if a depiction of child Jack existed, she may have struggled to erase the version she'd encountered in her dreams. She knew what it meant to be the youngest of three. It was to have one's every behaviour reduced to developmental milestones, acclimatised as familiar phenomena.

There was not a single picture of Jack that she could find in the house. She guessed they might all be lost on antiquated digital storage devices, now incompatible with modern machines.

Bon and Steven allowed themselves the weekends off. They woke a little later than usual, normally well past ten o'clock. Then they would watch movies, or Steven would try to bicker with a staunchly unassertive Bon, because Bon harboured a bitter distaste towards certain films held in high esteem by Steven. Sometimes they'd go for little walks, but they never left the house via the front door, preferring to navigate through backyards, via holes pummelled through Colorbond fence. She followed them once, only a couple of blocks down – she hadn't wanted to leave Jack alone for long. You couldn't exactly call the mounds of wreckage ash, in fact most were very far from actually burned.

It's beside the point, Bon said with authority.

And Steven agreed: If you ask me they don't care as long as the houses are empty, he said. They probably want to knock them all down to build new ones. And it's sensible, you have to admit. Little wonder no one wants to live in this town: all the houses are old.

Lesley felt lonely again. Jack rarely emerged for long, and his airless, curtained room was unpleasant during the day. He was only in the mood to speak after sundown, and with the others, verbal exchanges only ever caught fire if Steven initiated them. He was no longer interested in finding hidden roads and pathways, hadn't said a word about them, and this was a good thing she supposed, it meant their improvised extraction had worked.

She might as well have been satisfied. If the world ended tomorrow, she wouldn't be alone. Someone other than her mother might care how she fared. There was a rhythm to her life that involved other people, four whirling components herself included, and each played their own mysterious role. Speech being rare was not a terrible sign. It was possibly a sign that these components were alive with responsibilities, resulting in a comfort she associated with her youth. Close to nothing had ever been said in her childhood home, and anyway – and despite how she respected that past – her childhood house had usually been engaged in a tactical war of silence, and speech was a tool for optimisation, it instructed and chastised.

As a distraction from anxiety there was the rest of the world. She left the house one Saturday at noon without telling anyone. She wandered the railway parade away from the highway and towards the chicken shop. She turned right through the suburban rail underpass, where the road widened towards a steep incline leading into the mountains. Along this road, between houses with front doors open and fly screens frayed, she eventually came to a clearing. Near the centre of the clearing was the old blast-furnace ruins, and a once-green park area beside it, with splintering picnic tables and a stretch of car park tarmac.

The old blast-furnace ruins were considered historical and were once open to sightseers. They had been fitted with safe metal walkways and informative plaques. Now every passage and every window in its tall facade had been boarded up, with flattened Coca-Cola cartons, warped chipboard, and thick draped coverless doonas. The ground-level barricades were the strongest, but Lesley didn't dare approach the structures to test, because she could sense life inside of them.

She stood there in the car park for a while, gazing at the ruins, stricken by a familiar tension. The day was passing, and all this useless walking was time better spent with her improvised family. Maybe in their company something important might be said, or something terrible might happen in her absence. It was impossible to spend time in any satisfactory way, and this awareness continued to trouble her, even off the train.

The chipboard across the closest doorway of the ruins started to wriggle, then it fell inward slightly, then a hidden someone picked it up to put aside. A woman came out, more or less a vagrant, with a spooling velvet winter dress and blackened feet in thongs.

What can we do for you, the woman said, politely confrontational. Lesley could smell cooking on her, a familiar boiled vegetable aroma. Her voice sounded frail though they were probably the same age. She just stood there in the doorway hands on hips, a little put out, like the vast clearing was hers and hers alone.

I'm just going for a walk, Lesley replied.

I can't imagine why you would, the woman shot back. There's nothing to see.

Well there's this – Lesley gestured at the blast-furnace ruins – and there's that – she gestured upward towards the mountains. And buildings are fairly interesting, though I'm not out to sightsee. To be honest I'm just passing time.

It's a dead town, the woman advised. There's no one in it now worth talking to.

Lesley wanted to rise to the defence of the people of the town, though she couldn't picture them as a broad phenomenon, could barely recall having seen them. And anyway, she loathed to point out others' insensitivities.

You look like you got off the train too, the woman went on. Can you believe we had the audacity?

It wasn't daring for me, Lesley said.

I regret not packing up, the vagrant woman said hastily, clearly famished for interaction. Because that's the objective. That's actually what we're meant to be doing, you know. Packing up, putting our things away, everything back where it belongs. I left a great big mess, and I tell you what: it annoys me when others do the same thing. I always say 'did you clean up your mess?' But only because I wish I'd done so myself, I shouldn't have left in such a rush.

My mess, Lesley said, was just a single room above a conveyancer in a suburb near the airport, so it doesn't play on my mind. But I get what you're saying.

The woman didn't seem to agree that Lesley got what she was saying. She said: If we could somehow broadcast to everyone – and I know it's impossible – the message that we should pack up as much as heavenly possible…it's advice that wouldn't go astray. I imagine some kind of announcement, from someone far more influential than myself, some kind of celebrity or CEO. It might come over the television or internet, it would warn everyone to clean up, put things back where they belong, just tidy the place up, and I don't mean the world, I'm not being political and don't get me started, I don't mean the environment or anything impossible. I just mean: put your stuff away or else in the bin. Vacuum your carpet one last time, declutter your balcony and sweep it, things like that. Ideally we'd dismantle everything. We'd take buildings down and slot their materials away, we'd rip up the roads and plant native trees, all very civilly, I imagine it as a worldwide working bee, a final act of solidarity. Imagine if everyone agreed to just pack up, like kids before bedtime.

But once they've packed up where would they go? Lesley asked.

Maybe the vagrant woman hadn't thought that far ahead, but she improvised anyway.

To bed, she replied sagaciously. Or else to a place like this. You'd be surprised how many places elude maps, you can fairly easily stray from the known world entirely. And you're not paying attention if you think it's untrue, but you must know it anyway, because you got off the train. You always thought these stops – and she waved west across the field towards the station – belonged to the half-asleep daydreams you had in transit, you must have thought these places were phantasmal, a result of motion and routine blending with the vivid mysteries of sleep. But that doesn't account for how real they always appeared and how material they've proven to be. There's not actually – she pressed a finger to one nostril, blew a font of yellow fluid from the other – any meaningful difference, because absolutely everything is true. You can't say to me anything wild enough that I won't believe it, and you can't describe for me anywhere that doesn't actually exist.

Lesley said: A village built in a giant marshmallow.

The vagrant woman flared her blown nostril and replied: You're not taking me seriously.

Then she sat cross-legged in the dirt at the doorway. Lesley sat too, careful not to close their distance.

Well it exists now if it didn't already, the woman conceded eventually. But you're still missing my point.

Lesley was sorry but the woman said not to be sorry. This lot – and she pointed at the blast furnace, where Lesley guessed others must have lived – think I talk too much and complicate every matter. We've all become a kind of family in there, always bitching at one another. But you've got to admit that before we got off the train, the places where we lived, the things we were forced to do, all the problems we were forced to solve, the habits, decorums, stresses...all those things and more...all of it was improvised from the ground up. Our behaviours and attitudes towards it all: similarly improvised. The right thing to do is someone else's dream, the right way to think is the same. Before I got off the train I felt angry and resigned, now I just feel philosophical about it all. It's actually very funny, she said, the world is a riot.

But there are innocents, Lesley argued.

The woman ran her fingers lightly through the dirt in wide butterfly arcs, and her prolonged silence felt scolding, pedagogical.

To be honest I've found no good conversation among them, she said.

At home the boys had splintered. Steven was snoozing on the couch; Bon was at the kitchen table smoking a cigarette, sipping from a mug of Kahlua, and browsing a road atlas he'd kept from the hatchback. They had lived together for some time, mostly in a state of hungover languor, but lately a familiar apathy had descended, an apathy towards the other, like those friendships she'd briefly flirted with in the city, desperate friendships with decent people she had no interest in speaking to or being with, with whom there had never been anything to share. These friendships – and she'd had a handful of them – had always been initiated after a long period of denial, driven by a last-ditch determination to do *something*, to leave the house, to be in a pub or a restaurant rather than one's home.

I can't find us in this book anywhere, Bon said, holding up the atlas for her benefit, so she could see what it was.

Isn't that the point, she replied.

Well you can't say Newnes doesn't exist, he said. Because we're in it. Unless we've got the name wrong, or unless I'm dreaming.

She was half-disappointed that Steven wasn't there boozing with him. Not much gratification could be squeezed out of Bon alone, even as he nursed his mug of milky grog, even as he directed the discussion. He barely looked at her anymore, and was more reluctant than ever to speak unless he'd had a shot. She wasn't going to have a bar of his pretending she hadn't noticed.

Roadmaps are for places people want to go, she said. They're just advertisements for places to go. What makes you think the places you've been have to be on maps? What makes you think they deserve to be in a book? It's the height of arrogance. And that's okay, she continued, more gently: it's only perfectly natural. But it's the height of common human arrogance to expect to find oneself on a map. Is every tree a dot, is every rabbit warren a loop?

She panned her arms around the room: Do you want all this detail on a page? It's better not to be on maps, she said, because events occur wherever land is carefully mapped. And wherever it's not mapped, it's reasonable to expect that you've been let off the hook. The world is mapped and look at it. It's for the best we're not on maps, that's why we got off the train.

The rocks on the roof came to resemble stretches of harsh white noise, loud enough the whole world felt awash in it. In the silence of their bed they'd wait for it, and for the nightly hope that maybe it wouldn't happen again, they'd each adopt a proper sleeping posture.

Then the noise would come, like the heaviest and thickest of hailstorms, seemingly on every part of the corrugated iron roof, a din that might have woken the whole of Newnes had there been many (or any) people to wake. Bon as usual would act surprised, scramble to put on jeans and jumper, and then he'd grab from an accumulation of blunt weapons taxed from properties surrounding: bats, planks of wood, heavy-duty curtain rods, a plastic toy shotgun. He'd dash into the lounge room, raise the venetians and stand there, poised, animal alert, one fist raised and weapon wielded, but only after the storm had moved on.

Steven would sleep through it, but Lesley always found Jack awake, so that it eventually seemed wiser to spend every night with him. The boy put up no argument because she did it secretly: she'd get in after coaxing him back to sleep. She would always wake several times in the night, nearly every hour, and occasionally their bodies met, whether a hand on a shoulder, or an arm over a stomach. Jack's body did not exude stale age like Bon's did, even though Bon wasn't that old. But Jack's body, despite everything he apparently knew, was alert and thriving. Bon's body, while far less sedentary than Jack's, resembled a heap, it did not sleep delicately, it slept greedily, it absorbed the air and pushed it out again, loudly, with a slightly sickly smell. But during an hourly awakening, she'd always return to her normal bed.

One night the din was so powerful that when Bon and Lesley emerged, as was their custom, into the lounge room to taunt the offenders with their silhouettes, the front door of their home was wide open, fly screentoo. They stared at the door statuesque and stunned. To approach that dark was a feat akin to trapping an oversize and dangerous spider. Eventually Bon fetched a broom and levered the door shut from a safe difference.

Sometimes, while knelt on the floor beside the window in Jack's room, Lesley would fade away, only to wake minutes or hours later, head rested across the windowsill, with shuttered venetian blinds crushed beneath her arms. At other times she would end up in Jack's bed or her own without remembering how she had gotten there. These habits worsened over several days until, within the space of a week, she found it hard to fall asleep at all. It wasn't because the attacks became more frequent and more ferocious, though they did – some nights the house felt close to collapsing. No, it was because night no longer felt the most suitable time to sleep, the world was no longer resting at night, the night had transformed into something else entirely. Of course it was terrifying, but the night was also newly fascinating, for the night appeared to have imposed its qualities onto the day time, it had transferred its responsibilities, and now it was – in Lesley's addled reasoning – a whole new thing.

Because at the weekends when she walked alone in increasingly wide and audacious arcs, the few people she encountered – always from a safe distance – appeared unutterably tired, stumbling crookedly along cement paths through the shallow smoky mist. On darker days when the sky seemed at the verge of storm, piddling trails of blacker smoke ascended from the yards around their home.

The woman at the blast furnace, whose name was one time Ebony, another time Elizabeth, reckoned it wasn't so unusual that the people of Newnes walked the way they did.

No one gets any sleep, she said. Being in this town is a big novelty for them. They're exhaustingly alert to it.

She was eating from a packet of Burger Rings Lesley had given her.

Try speaking to them, Ebony or Elizabeth said, or maybe it's best if you don't. None of them are from around here, they're not the people of the town, the people of the town have gone...they took their cars and kids and drove away. Now it's just all of us stranded by the trains – and she waved angrily at the train station – which, just in case you've not been paying attention, aren't going to start moving again.

One Saturday she walked north of the corner pub, a couple of blocks up, to where the brown yards of an old Catholic school backed onto ascending mountain scrub. This had been the school attended by Jack, and presumably Steven, though Lesley struggled to imagine Newnes as a place one might go to school.

She herself had gone to a Catholic school. Her family had been irreligious, she hadn't even been baptised. But she was bullied in her zoned public school, and the Catholic school despite its fees had been the only alternative. Her mother had wrongly supposed that religious children would be friendly, tranquil, austere.

She dreaded the school masses, which occurred only once a term. At the first one she attended, she had risen to queue for the sacramental bread. She had been aware that only true Catholics were entitled to it, and that non-Catholics should abstain, but she had not wanted to be among the few outcasts left in the pews; at any cost she needed to blend in. So she had taken the chalky foam-like bread on her tongue and had vaguely gestured her Hail Mary, all the while feeling sacrilegious, demonic.

It had taken weeks of pent-up fear before she told her mother about having taken the sacrament. At first she had decided not to tell her at all, but the regret boiled over, and she could not handle it by herself. At best she might be yelled at, but at worst she might be punished – and not necessarily at the hand of her mother.

But her mother had not even scolded her, she'd laughed. And then, because Lesley had become angry, her mother had adopted a consoling and vaguely patronising tone. She had said that it didn't matter either way, that she could eat whole kilos of the foamy bread if she wanted, that no god nor father would strike her down, that anyway, all the teachers knew she wasn't Catholic, and if her taking the bread had bothered them she would have copped it already.

As Lesley hopped the fence into the school and crossed the overgrown lawn, she was reacquainted with an old resentment. Her mother's arrogant, run-of-the-mill godlessness implied an attunement with the world's actual logic, it implied familiarity with some elevated modern truth. Far be it from Lesley to say with any authority that the world was stupider than it had ever been.

But just quietly, it *was* stupider than ever, albeit more complex, it was far stupider than anyone ever let on, and far more arrogant in its stupidity.

The nightly white noise gradually stretched into long quarter hours, and after a while into longer half-hours, to the extent that one had to ask – where did all of these rocks come from, and how many dozens of hands tossed them? No flashlight in their possession had the power to shine through glass let alone into the black.

Jack didn't know anything about it, said that it was all a new frontier for him. They had made a habit of not bothering to go to bed until it was over; normally she'd laze on his bed while he played video games or fiddled with audio files. They'd have conversations punctuated by long stretches of lazy silence. When the noise arrived, Jack would turn in his chair, and she would sit up, and they would each raise their brows. They would peer askance at the ceiling in case it collapsed. Within the din, some rocks would land more harshly than others, and whenever this happened she would flare a nostril and make very deliberate eye contact with Jack, who in turn would raise his brows even further, until by the end, despite how strange and terrifying the rockings actually were, both became animated. It did not seem wise to perform an objection to the rockings in front of Jack, it felt smarter to act bemused by them, deserving of them. Now Bon usually slept through the noise, and as far as she could tell, Steven didn't even know about it. Then she'd fall asleep, and for a few cycles of her hourly awakenings, Jack would still be seated at the screen, but eventually came the time when he had crawled into bed.

Of a morning while Bon and Steven were still at home, it was her routine to open the front door and to rip open the windows, to expunge the musk of the house. The brown air outside wasn't healthy, but it was preferable to the damp staleness inside. But on one of these mornings, the perfectly intact corpse of a large German shepherd was left across the front footpath, seemingly placed there before a rocking, because there were pebbles laced in its hair, and bricks resting on its gut. It did not at first appear to be real. She found Bon eating baby food at the formica table, and he reluctantly followed her to take a look.

He agreed that it was probably real. He approached it, cautioned backwards, and stood for a while. Then he retrieved a broom from the kitchen and prodded the gut. Bricks slowly slid and then rolled onto the concrete. There was no way to prove that it wasn't actually there.

I can't drag this thing right now, he said. I've got to be at work.

His body told her everything she needed to know: that it was an unsolvable problem. They discussed what might be done about it for a while. Bon reckoned they should just leave it there, because anyway, no part of town was inaccessible from their backyard anymore, because they had smashed routes through Colorbond fence in any direction you could want. The back door is our front door now, he said. There's no good reason to come out here anymore. The old roads no longer matter.

When Bon and Steven had left for work and long before Jack had awoken, she tied the dog's hind legs together, and with great effort dragged the fallen beast three doors down. On the median strip in front of two semi-detached townhouses, she piled old books and kindling from broken furniture onto and under the dog. She dropped a full packet of blazing firelighters in, stood jabbing for a while, and the corpse eventually came alight.

That night the dog's cinders seemed to disappear with the arrival of the dark, and the rockers hit with more force than ever before. It might have been an army. So torrential was the rocking that some of the roof rafters audibly splintered, and two corrugated iron panels collapsed onto the insulation.

The next day Lesley retrieved the tangled ball of colourful fairy lights from under the bed, dragged it into the backyard, and stuck the small solar charging panel in clear view of the sun. Minutes later the lights appeared to glow, and while they garnered power, she carefully unknotted the spangled length of the cable. There in the backyard just before lunch, it was possible to hear in the far distance furniture being smashed into manageable portions.

Before dinner she plunged the solar panel into the yard across the road, and ran the flashing fairy lights across the asphalt into their yard.

At dinner, Steven told her off for using the front door.

Granted you might not know yet, he said, but it's now forbidden to use the front door. We might as well board it up, just in case someone comes to liquidate us.

No one's coming to liquidate us, Lesley replied in a huff.

Well you never know what's going to happen, he said. Just today, we were going into the house next door to the chicken shop, and what would you know it (he performed a magician's kind of wonder) there was someone in there. The chicken man himself. He didn't want to have a bar of us going in and burning his things.

Little wonder, Bon murmured.

Lesley almost laughed.

Well we're just following instructions, Steven shot back. He shot back so aggressively, it was little wonder Bon almost never spoke.

We're just following instructions and I told him that, Steven went on. We're going to have to write a letter to the boss, to ask what we do in cases like that.

You'd absolutely not burn his things one which way or the other, Lesley shouted.

You'd think so, Steven said, but who knows. We'd better confirm. Only we can't go through the front door anymore to get our pay.

We – she pointed at Bon and herself – are not included in the rule. We're the adults. We know what we're doing. We make the rules.

Steven was relieved, and Bon was relieved too, because the issue seemed resolved. Lesley said she'd write the letter herself.

She didn't bother sitting briefly at the TV that night. She went straight up to Jack's bedroom, where the window provided a view out over the street. The sun was still setting, and it was an uncommonly spectacular sunset, the brown air was thin enough that an orange glow permeated it, she felt awash in some idyllic remembrance of teenage suburbia.

Jack sat at the window too, he'd drawn his gaming chair up to it. She knelt and rested her chin against the sill. From that point of view the line of flashing coloured lights resembled a festive tripwire.

She had expected Jack to at least make a comment. She had explained her strategy to him, in unnecessary detail given the simplicity of the matter, but he had only shown vague interest in watching. He had not held forth on the pros and cons of her tactics, and it had not turned into a discussion.

When she eventually said to him: It's actually quite a clever way to test the dark and the rockers, he had only nodded.

But his enthusiasm would have been wasted anyway, because as night began to fall, she remembered their mysterious employers might drive straight through and destroy the lights. She panicked, ran down the stairs – Jack didn't move to stop her – and once in the hall, she tiptoed and opened the front door as quietly as she could. They had lately left the money in the mailbox until morning because the rockers never took it, and even if they had, it wouldn't have been a disaster. They were rolling in cash. There wasn't much to spend it on. Most of it went towards tobacco – the cost of which raised by the week, even in Newnes – and a small fraction towards the dwindling chip packets and canned foods available at the petrol station.

It was by now quite dark, but not dark enough. She grabbed the loose end of the fairy lights, crossed the road onto the opposite lawn and hurriedly wound them up. All the while – maybe it was her blood rushing – she felt certain that a car approached. In her eagerness to dislodge the solar panel from the grass she tugged too hard, and the lights came unstuck from their power source. The flashing colour died, and everything fell black.

The noise she made was instinctual. She had not deliberately made it, it was not born of exertion nor want for help...she had just made a purely animal kind of noise, and she herself was surprised by it. It was unmistakably hers but it was as remote as an echo. It aired inside a variety of space she had never existed within.

In the far distance, seeming kilometres away, there briefly occurred a light phenomenon. An approach, a pause, and a departure. No vague glow framed it, no shapes attended it, there was no shape of a house or evening bedroom window. In truth, she might not have experienced that light at all. And for the realisation that she might not have experienced that light, even though she had seen it, any sense of clarity – a rare currency at the best of times – dissipated, the firmness of objects and surfaces, the assurance of one's physical area, disappeared, so that she felt intimately close to everywhere. It felt as if there was no where she couldn't go, though this was neither a comforting or liberating sensation. She did not stand, nor lay, nor squat, nor float or wade. She could feel her body – she still inhabited it – only there was no knowing its posture. She could hear herself occasionally hum, and this hum seemed to belong to another part of her, a co-existing and fearful kind, a version that wanted to demonstrate to itself that it was still there. There were a number of urgencies to keep in mind, but the overwhelming urgency was a longing for her humming version, the one that wanted to emphasise its ongoing existence. There was no moving towards this humming version, for two reasons: chiefly that the humming version was her, and secondly, that there was no moving towards anywhere, because she was everywhere.

Through all this emerged the sensation that she might actually be on the ground, though she felt no texture let alone grass, and anyway, she could have been facedown in it, or looking at the sky, or anywhere else around...she could have been poised vertically across a cliff face, safely suspended by ropes. And the humming version of her soon quieted, it now just breathed. This was the merest existence one could lead.

She went to her mother's house, in her old childhood home in the suburban country town of New South Wales, where a fraying trampoline stood mouldy in the yard. It was a twilit, four a.m. version of that existence, and for all she could tell there was no one inside – not her mother, and especially not her brothers. Then, with no sense of passing time, she was outside her city home, above a conveyancer's office on a four-lane main road leading to the airport, in the drab urban fringes. No traffic coursed under the streetlights, though lone walkers dotted the footpaths, all with indistinct faces. Then, urgently, she was back near her mother's home again (her real own home, still), where no evidence of her having been there remained, though of course the trampoline was still there, and her room must have been inside still. But there was nothing familiar about it, everything had changed, it was a four a.m. world, everyone – even the objects – wracked by anxiety dreams. It was so unutterably changed, so foreign, that the endurance of its shape angered her, it was simply *unfair*, it was not right for this semblance to endure. And its materiality seemed so abbreviated, so drained of its former essence, that it seemed all too possible to take it apart piece by piece, like building blocks, to put them away.

Back when Lesley had visited each weekend, death had lurked in her mother's eyes. Her yellows had trembled and teared up, every single Saturday afternoon, and then every single Sunday afternoon upon departure. Her mother's was the most powerful, verging on pathetic, most unconditional love, every Saturday night they'd eat supermarket brie and drink shiraz, they'd not even turn on the TV, and eventually Lesley would arrive at the topic of her decisions. She harboured a bitterness towards her mother, she often scolded her, told her off at the end of the second bottle, because how could she have not warned her about the nature of the world? Usually her mother would say that she didn't know the nature of the world at all, none of it made sense to her anymore, and believe you me it used to make sense, in a way. There had been confusion but broadly speaking it had made *some* sense, she'd say, but now none of it makes sense, not even a tiny crumb of it, virtually no sense has been left behind, and believe you me it would've pleased me to better equip you, but (and then she'd become philosophical, and thus impotent) I can't tell the future, better mothers couldn't either. I could have been a better mother, of that I have no doubt.

And for the feeling that she'd wrung her mother for as much as she deserved, Lesley would admit that every mother could be better with the power of clairvoyance, and since no one really had this power, neither mothers nor qualified clairvoyants, there was no use beating yourself up about it. Objectively speaking mothers are getting worse and worse in quality, Lesley would say, not for lack of love but for their function. To be a good mother is to anticipate and bridge junctures, except that their – her – particular juncture was quite possibly the most mysterious, the most treacherous juncture there ever had been, and there's no smooth sailing through it, especially now when the fires burn in winter. And then Lesley would become a bit foul again, because it seemed impossible to her that her mother, despite everything, despite her placidness and her role, and despite the loud ubiquity of soothsayers...it seemed impossible to Lesley that she should not have at least, on a bone-deep level, on a *motherly* level, anticipated that things weren't always going to stay the same. Lesley wouldn't say this aloud, because her mother would already be dangerously contrite. Instead she'd marvel aloud at how irrational a mother's love is, that it just keeps on keeping on, that it does so beyond necessity, that it does so in the face of slights and even deliberate undermining, it endures even if that child *hates* you (I've seen it, Lesley would add). If I punched you in the face, Lesley would tell her mother, I'm fairly confident you'd get over it, and maybe you'd love me more (and she'd say this to compliment her mother). When you think about it like this, when you think of how radically irrational this love is – because it's not a given among mammals, not a given among any animals, it's not categorically natural – it just goes to show, when you think about it – and it doesn't require much imagination – that the most commonly guaranteed emotional experience among humankind is just utterly irrational, this most fundamental and formative bond…it's perfectly irrational by the measure of the world, so-called reality is the antithesis of a mother, and so when you think about it, if things made more sense – if any single decision made by anyone, powerful or small, made the utmost sense – then it could only be made under circumstances deprived of mothers, or the disavowal of mothers.

At which point Lesley's mother would arc up, because they often had this conversation, nearly every single weekend. Lesley's mother would say that she had never made a major decision that hadn't seemed to her the most rational one. Then the balance of power would shift, and suddenly Lesley would be the scolded one, and relief would ensue, because it didn't exactly please her to be sitting at the kitchen bench in her childhood home at ten o'clock on a Saturday night, in her early thirties, with nothing to her name, telling her mother off. So her mother would mildly tell her off instead, or at least defend herself. She'd insist that for all the things that could be reported about her motherhood, all of the shortcomings and all of the devastating failures, there could be no question that she had always selected the most rational decisions, these decisions always being the ones that tended closer to a guarantee of safety and stability for children. Lesley would hear her out, because her mother would always articulate this very point in a half-dozen ways – and there was no stopping her – before falling silent. She'd provide examples and espouse the meticulous logic of them. And on especially drunken nights, Lesley's mother would admit that, overall, she didn't exactly care if she died, that for lack of any pain associated with the ceremony of dying, she might even enjoy the peace. But she didn't ever do anything that might lead her to die, barely even had a drink, hadn't smoked for twenty-five years, because even though it had sometimes seemed wise to do so (to die) it was of the utmost importance that she didn't. Then, maybe to gratify Lesley, she would circle back to the irrationality of it all, she would say that it was actually very unusual and strange by certain measures of logic, that birthing and rearing three children – Lesley and her two brothers – didn't entitle her to just die in a very peaceful way at the very moment of the last child's fleeing of the nest (because you've done the right thing, haven't you). And it's not that I want to die, she'd add. But you have to admit that it's irrational, all things considered I don't want to experience the worst of you, but then again, I must, mustn't I. When children depart the search for another meaning commences, maybe if you had a father we'd nowadays travel the country in a campervan...but there is no other meaning, none that seems substantial, surrendering to a late life of mild elderly hedonism would only fuel the meaninglessness. Because drunk as I am I'll admit – and she really was admitting – that in the purest terms of survival, I am as indebted to you as you are to me, it doesn't make sense to admit it – it is irrational to do so – but you showed me the most gleeful, most uninhibited smiles, they were electrifying, they tricked me into believing that nothing could happen to you except happiness, whether the merely sufficient kind or maybe even more. Even when you wailed relentlessly, it could only be measured against the power of your smiles; the crying was babyhood, but the smiles...they were a resource, more powerful to me than they were to you. Drunk as I am – Lesley's mother was always saying 'drunk as I am' – that smile and its gradual erosion into measure and performance, makes me think that, drunk as I am, we all should die at the advent of adulthood, at the height of our recklessness. That's when you should reasonably die. Right then, maybe eighteen or nineteen or twenty: take your draught from the world, imbibe its strange power, wonder at it for a time, make a mess for trying to sort it out, and before every logic poisons: die. I know it's impractical, Lesley's mother would say. Life is hilariously long, it's a bit of a joke, you have to laugh at how it just keeps on going.

And then Jack's music. Not versions of it she had heard before, for there was nothing inside of that sound to remember, it did not arrive in the form of a memorable trace. She did not hear it, though its mood overcame her. And her teenage brother with his recorder blew as hard as he could in accompaniment, and if she still had a reliable voice she might have laughed. And then the looped grandiosity of the *Star Wars* Blu-ray menu music seemed to harmonise with it all. Then, very quietly, the bass line from Nelly's 'Hot in Herre' weaved in. All of these sounds had in some way or another embedded themselves in her mind, but they served as entree to all kinds of other sounds, some familiar and others less so, until everything she had ever heard – every arranged or else cacophonous sound – seemed to join the morass, some giving rise to horrible sentimental troughs, others giving rise to fear or anxiety, the majority simply annoying. So that eventually she was able to see, in a way she'd often grasped at (usually while drunk), that the life she had led was remarkably lived, it had never been wanting for sensation, it was exceedingly well-fed. And amid the imagined din she did not hear, but experienced, Bon say (again): That's what happens when you're not used to this kind of darkness.

Her adrenaline was banking in a choke point, she longed to explode. She was unable to imagine swelling, and then exploding, without evoking the birth of her dream children, who were, it made sense, likely swirling in that discord of sensation. She was close to them, and could simply have visited them. But it did not seem wise to do so, it was of the utmost importance that she did not, for visiting them under those circumstances might have acquainted them with the living world, and it was not what was best for them.

But she was dragged towards them anyway, it was not her choice. Her son and her daughter, she could smell them, she could feel them latch at her. All the gratifications, and all the dismal failures pummelled her at once. This sensation of speculated motherhood did not penetrate the noise. Actually, it was significantly quieter. It was both gentler and louder, but also arrhythmic. It bobbed as a separate phenomenon alongside. She did not approach the children, because within the seeming terms of agreement of that darkness, they were simply on display. They lacked particular faces and mannerisms, but they were unmistakably real.

And then the humming other started humming again, and she understood why. She was trying to burrow upwards and out. The humming became louder, and then it became a series of briskly ascending roars, and then it became a kind of scream. And it was easier when it became a scream. You had to wonder why people didn't scream all the time.

It could have been any time of day when she woke up, because the morning and the afternoon had always looked the same in Newnes. The unfamiliar street was a blend of indistinct houses closely pressed, the road chipped and narrow, gutterless, and in the distance, the churn of the highway. She had no recollection of getting there. It seemed possible she had been levitated and thrown.

Supernatural encounter or not, Bon and the boys might think her drunk and absconded, or at least unreliable. Or maybe they had chased her into the dark and become similarly lost. If they woke from a strange dream in an indistinct Newnes street, could she rely on their wanting to find their way home?

It took less than a half-block crossed to see the blast-furnace ruins between the tiled roofs of townhouses. Reaching that landmark would provide a sense of direction, except none of the roads she wandered – and soon jogged – actually permitted access to the ruins, they always had the appearance of doing so, before veering away into yet another piddling narrow street, lined with pathetic houses, or else a tedious sheer cliff to the train line, or worse still, a wire fence she could not surmount. She jogged and slowed, jogged and slowed, in obedience to her wretched lungs and ankles, through endless residential blocks she had never seen nor imagined existing. Sometimes the blast furnace appeared in the west, other times it towered in the north. Worse was that she found herself returning to the same streets, it would hit her that she had been *right there* before, only it didn't make sense to go back, just as much as it increasingly made no sense to go forth, until eventually the going forth stunned her. After a rare long decline in a rarer unfamiliar street, she hit upon an operating shopping plaza.

It lacked the scale of the Newnes Valley Plaza; it was more a long line of attached red brick shops fronted by a yard of car park tarmac. There was a kebab shop, a fish-and-chip takeaway, a tax agent, a solicitor, and a Vietnamese bakery. Between all these, pride of place, was a miniature supermarket, with trays of vibrant waxed apples, brilliant oranges, verdant pastoral lettuces and sun yellow bananas, all laid across mats of plastic grass by its front door. The tarmac was lightly dotted with parked cars, and a small handful of figures browsed the fresh produce.

Lesley was spellbound; she wasn't confident it was real. The plaza looked ethereal, belonging to a fantasy. Had there always been this vast hidden region? And if so, how had they remained oblivious to it? Her awe didn't last. Whether real or not it didn't matter, because beyond the plaza there was no view of the blast furnace, but instead further lines of houses, along ever more chipped and gutterless roads, leading towards the near-distant mountains charred here and there by recently extinguished fires. She turned away from the plaza, and where she then looked, clearer than ever in the distance, rose with utmost clarity the blast furnace, and a seeming natural map towards its yard. With rare tactical forethought she traced the roads along the incline with her eyes, and for doing so noticed the chicken-shop intersection only two blocks in the distance. Once reached, the region of the humble plaza seemed to disappear. On the thin median strip outside lay a dozen or so plastic chairs, slightly charred and melted.

Along the road beside the train line and towards their house, Lesley's relief soured into apprehension, then curdled for dread, because she was definitely still there in the so-called town of Newnes, and whatever time of day it happened to be, no one had found her, which allowed for the possibility that no one had searched. The house was there – she had repressed questions concerning its reality – though her fairy-light trap was gone and the front door was discouragingly open, with two shifts worth of pay in the mailbox.

The lounge room furniture was gone. In the kitchen, the fridge and formica table were both gone. In the room she shared with Bon, only a wall-mounted mirror remained. In Jack's room even the posters had been ripped from the walls, and in the backyard, the home's interior smouldered.

Her first instinct was to run to the train line, and to follow it west all the way to her mother's. Only it seemed unlikely she could get there by foot. She quickly wrote it off as a shameful instinct, because her family was here in Newnes, though evidently no longer in this house.

Through the backyard holes in Colorbond she went, sheepish for how loudly she yelled Jack and Bon and Steven's names. Not that they'd be in the liquidated homes anyway, whether inside with the cats or among the burnt-out furniture in the yards – there were only two places they would likely have gone.

Over a fence she emerged onto the railway. She gazed westerly along it for a while, through the distant train station tunnel leading into the calm countryside beyond. Past that tunnel, further into the country, over tens of dozens of hills and through a couple or so towns, was where her own mother lived. There was just no way she could get there by foot. So she mounted a crest and paced a lonely railway parade towards the centre of town. From there, she followed the route to the Newnes Valley Plaza husk, where dust-caked cars still littered the ashy bitumen.

Up the hill she went, along streets unchanged by however many weeks or months had passed. When she entered the old weatherboard its layout surprised her and its dimensions felt skewed: it wasn't quite right. The house had been liquidated, quite possibly by Steven and Bon themselves, quite possibly they had done so without recognising it. Out of a mounting sense of futility she dared take a precious moment to sit there on the front steps. It had not been brilliant there in the weatherboard – it could have been much better – but it had been a period of plotting, with a mood of alertness, she had felt poised at the threshold of mysterious change.

Her boys wouldn't have escaped the town even if they could, though very likely they had fallen apart; worst of all they might have abandoned what she had made for them. If they were not carrying out in the same manner as they had before she crossed the road in the dark, then – in all likelihood – they had probably strayed, back up the hill, maybe even towards the forest, maybe even back through her portal. There wasn't anywhere else she could imagine them going, in which case, they had certainly happened upon the path to the hut.

Up the hill the hatchback was no longer where they had left it, but in the light of day the path or portal they had improvised was appallingly obvious – they thought they'd shrouded it well. No: it was the most terribly obvious thing, the route was strewn with empty plastic soft-drink bottles and cigarette butts. A bottle of their fermented juice remained in the clearing – she unscrewed it and sculled. Then she moved towards the other pathway, the one she hadn't made.

Roughly a year earlier, on her unfolded sofa bed, in her studio flat above the conveyancer under the flight path, she had been seated against pillows with her laptop, eating packet rice with soy sauce, ostensibly watching a television drama but also browsing the internet news, while also monitoring a feed. It was in the late winter, that's how she knew it was the year before. She had taken herself to emergency that night because she had fallen dizzy, suddenly incapable of making sense of the video she watched, likewise any of the articles she scanned, likewise any of the announcements she bore witness to. From one moment to the next it had all ceased to make sense, and at first she had taken it as evidence of exhaustion, because she had rarely slept deeply there under the flight path over the conveyancer. It wasn't that she had struggled to follow any thread long enough to trace it until its conclusion, it was that she had not been able to grasp the thread to begin with. Everything was suddenly, completely impenetrable; all knowledge, all context, her understanding: gone. She could read, but none of the collected words held meaning, and the television drama was a series of baffling non sequiturs. The announcements in her feed seemed profoundly, almost poetically inane. As she wandered the disruptive path towards the hut, she remembered how she had finally rushed from her couch, and how she had very emphatically stood, how she had jumped – as if banging a gadget to make it work – and finding that jumping had not the desired effect, she had jumped again, on the spot, on the tiles, and then again, repeatedly until she had lost her breath. She had thought she might be having a stroke, but in triage they said it was exhaustion. They had suggested she take some time off, though little did they know that her job was not arduous, did not challenge her, that she was not driven to work extremely hard towards some gratifying end. The problem wasn't the job, not in the sense that the triage nurse must have guessed.

In Newnes she had taken her time off and much more besides, and she could imagine herself telling someone – admittedly just her mother – that you could say whatever you liked about Newnes and her circumstances, but neither had permitted her to lose that thread.

The week following she had gone for a beer with Ben, Ben from the company, who did something or the other for the company, something that paid better than what she did. It was out of a sense of responsibility to herself. She never had any desire to speak to anyone at the company, but you meet people that way – you meet them via companies. Nevertheless she had been horrified in the city wine bar, by her inability to parse a single thing the man had said, which had anyway been all to do with the company – how it was good in some ways and bad in others. Everything he had said was spoken with clarity – the sentences were crisp and illustrative. But she did not understand why those sentences were being spoken in place of other more pertinent ones, and the dizziness had returned.

She had longed to escape to a location where every sentence and every deriving sentiment, everything, was expressed with utmost purpose and conviction. Maybe in a place like that, people would live not unlike she had in her adult life – alone and mostly silent –

only each would at least feel the responsibility to ensure that every interaction was freighted by the desire to lurch directly at the heart of the matter. Maybe too much to ask anywhere – maybe especially in Newnes – but at least the dizziness had not returned.

Towards the end of the disruptive path it occurred to her that, after all, here was not a place they would likely have decamped to. It was not at all likely that, upon her exit, they had convened in the lounge room and decided: *without her we're hopeless, to our terrifying brother we must go.* For this realisation, a following realisation occurred: possibly they were gone, not from one place to another but truly gone, subsumed by Newnes, metabolised by an abyss, as liable to disappear as unnoticed streets were liable to suddenly be.

The clearing was still there, though, and so was the hut. The hatchback had been retrieved. This time, there was also a caravan. Outside the caravan, near its steps, was a table with retractable legs. On the table was a stack of enamel plates, two enamel tea mugs, piles of sorted cutlery, and a single cast-iron pan upside down on a drip tray. A woman emerged from the caravan, rubbing a pot with a tea towel as she descended the steps. She was old but not appallingly so, not to the extent that Lesley had always imagined – she had imagined a withering crone. And actually, jarringly, Steven had aged into the spitting image of Mother Grady.

Lesley had sometimes imagined conversations with this woman, or more to the point, polite interrogations. But sighting Mother Grady only revived her conviction that her boys had retreated to the hut; what had previously seemed a last-ditch possibility now appeared a dead certainty. Lesley wasn't inclined to offer pleasantries to the strangely composed woman.

First came the accusation she could not contain: Aren't you meant to be in the desert?

And the reply: Any day now.

Then as brisk as she could manage, came the heart of the matter: Where are Jack and Steven?

To which she replied, almost theatrically: You would know better than me.

Having expected the encounter to weigh in her favour, Lesley was inflamed by the woman's composure, though she didn't look like a serious adversary.

You're lying, Lesley said.

They're grown-ups, you know, Mother Grady replied. They're independent to a point. It'd be cruel for me to keep a close eye on them. That would be belittling.

Then she waved at the hut, and said: But this one I have to.

Lesley wanted to punch the woman. Down the hill was a bizarrely sprawling town, one she had thought she knew. But any search undertaken in it now could not be successful, because what she had lost there, had existed before it had changed.

I've got to check in there, Lesley said. I can't leave until I rule it out.

You're out of luck, she replied. No way he'd let them in there anymore. *I* wouldn't let them in there anymore, if I was him.

You'll have to let me see, Lesley insisted, cop-like, but Mother Grady was not going to have a bar of it.

You've smashed his computer once and so have they, she laughed. I've got no money to buy him another. And you stole his car. If you hadn't given it back it'd be gaol for you, I promise. Mother Grady lifted the pot in her hand.

Are you going to hit me? Lesley asked.

For a while it looked certain that Mother Grady would hit her with the pot. But soon the animal drained from her eyes, was replaced with an acerbic irony, a kind Lesley recognised from her own mother, a kind that silently admitted: *I'm joking but don't push me.* Mother Grady lowered the pot and lightly beat its base in her other hand. The irony remained but had turned conspiratorial, with a trace of hopeful camaraderie.

These boys didn't have thoughts of their own ten years ago, Mother Grady finally said. Jack was at primary school, Steven was working at the car wash and playing in a band, and this one – again, at the hut – was as sedentary as always, but lazy rather than wicked. You couldn't even get them to vote. And Newnes wasn't the best place to be young but everyone we knew was here, and anyway, I'm at fault, I told them to move to the city, but I didn't make it easy for them. It used to be normal to come of age in a town like this, but now they either wilt (she waved down the hill) or grow thorns (she pointed at the hut). I should have made them work for warmth, I should have let them know it was rare. I should have made them move to the city.

But I just wanted them to live, she said. People have been doing that for a very long time. But you sense that it's drawing to a close, you've got to admit. They say 'you can't go back you can't go back'. And I suppose it's true, but it also seems impossible that you can't just arrest it. The past remains inside me, but it's an existence I've come unstuck from. Every new day feels insubstantial measured up against it, every day is a new limbo, like a chunk of surplus time. It's not for nostalgia or longing that I'd like to go back, she said, it's not for wanting to return, it's not for peace of mind. It's for the sense of rhythm and logic, do you understand? It's for the passage of time to be stabilised again. It's for the want of a past, present and future again, all three side-by-side in their correct place. Do you know that we're living in the future, Lesley? And do you know that's why everything has this insubstantial quality, do you know that's why it's all come unstabilised? There's a period between then and now that we never got to see, don't you agree?

Lesley wasn't going to indulge any monologue. She grabbed the cast-iron pan from the drip tray and sprinted to the hut.

She collapsed through the door and into the room, which smelled of sweaty sheets and multi-purpose spray. A great crash sounded and a figure descended the trapdoor. On the monitor a rifle hovered in the foreground of a video game ruinscape, then the screen flooded red.

By the time Mother Grady's howls blared, Lesley had boarded the ladder and started her descent. Soon she was in the tunnels, but she wasn't put out. She had experienced perfect dark and this could not rival it, even for lack of fairy lights. The tunnels could not slow her now, and actually, she was newly capable of seeing in them – the absence of sun and artificial light were the most trivial obstacles, because the materiality of the tunnels was indisputable, she was able to touch their walls and ceiling with her hands, and what she was able to feel with her hands was the only reliable sensation, because her eyes, ears and mind had earned her distrust. When grasped from behind, Lesley smashed the older woman in the chest with her pan, and the latter collapsed.

She yelled out: Jack!

(And in case they were there too: Bon! Steven!)

Lesley stood ashamed next to the fallen woman. A heavy

squealing wheeze aired and faded in the distance. She yelled something at the fading wheeze, something about how all she wanted was to check.

They're not here, the woman on the ground moaned.

Lesley pushed on. She would likely encounter the oldest brother, and so tried to formulate the things she could say to him. She would likely try to funnel these inexplicable animosities into a lesson, because what else could she say? There would need to be a lesson, and there would require the teaching of that lesson, bridges would need to join warring lands, and it should no longer seem wise to fight in the presence of such sweet and very well-meaning sentiment...and it was appalling to Lesley that even under duress, her imagination could only extend this far.

What exactly could Lesley say to the Colossal Man, now that the opportunity had arrived? Right there, nearing the solution to a particularly taxing puzzle, the questions she might have wanted to ask him eluded her.

It was not impossible that she might see eye to eye with the Colossal Man, if she dared ask him to explain himself. Maybe she could be conspiratorial, sympathetic to his supposed charge towards repulsiveness, admiring of his urge to upend. She could even admonish him – 'your efforts have been substandard at best' ('do better') – but maybe his efforts had been more consequential than she would ever know. Maybe she was jogging into the maw of a fearsome intellect, maybe she would just cower and try to escape. Maybe he was too angry, too smart, too primordial, for his attitude to be diluted by her well-meaning effort. He had exited after all. He had only done what she and Bon had clumsily done, but maybe his grievances had mutated into something powerful.

As she stumbled through the tunnels it occurred to her that there was every chance that he was correct, and there was a chance that she could be convinced.

She yelled again, meeker than before: Jack! Steven!

...Bon!

But maybe she could touch him, and that simple conciliatory touch would change everything. She was not concerned about the truth of any matter, but for extending this olive branch, she might eradicate the need to ever address it. Except she found it impossible to express anything that didn't rail towards filmic banality, her intellect was clotted with ready-made solutions.

Maybe she could approach the Colossal Man and simply ask: Where are my boys?

Or she could go in with her fists.

She yelled out: Jack! And the tunnel kept winding.

Who could win any real fight? Probably not a sole life phenomenon in the mountain bush of Newnes, especially one that she herself wasn't scared of. Though surely it depended on the rules of the fight, the rules of engagement (it seemed such a delicate, euphonious phrase), and out in the world, the rules of engagement (what a soft-sounding euphemism) were actually rules of tolerance and submission, strategies to exist more prosperously in the melt. Only in darkness of the utmost remoteness, was it possible to feel the future's haunt with clarity, and to negotiate some alliance with it on one's own terms. Or, with whatever strange powers one had at hand, lay plans to expedite its arrival.

Would she lurch directly at the heart of the matter when she encountered the Colossal Man? As far as she had known, great intellects – she had decided he was one, now – spoke in cryptic allusion, or else with words so pointed and specific she'd never heard them. The likes of him would not be interested in explaining anything to her, anyway it was not their job to do so, it really ultimately came down to her, she should not have wasted her time.

This gave her pause.

A hand on her shoulder disrupted her thoughts. She thrashed her elbows defensively. Then she felt embarrassed for doing so, because it was not *her* being chased: she was the antagonist.

But it was only Mother Grady.

It would be easier for me if they were here for you to find, she muttered.

Lesley unlatched the woman and carried on. The older woman was *really* averse to reaching the heart of the matter, that now being the question of her eldest. Granted, she might not know how the heart of the matter had shifted, but Lesley wasn't going to give a speech about it.

From a nearby bend in the corner, a third figure emerged with the waft of spoiled meat. The figure grunted and dragged Lesley by the wrist, and for the fear and thrill of the drag, Mother Grady's protests sounded like noise.

And then, not gradually, but immediately and completely, Mother Grady seemed to disappear.

The thumb and index finger around her wrist slowly relaxed as they both plodded through the dark. Lesley couldn't control her tongue – it kept pressing harshly against the inside of her chin. Eventually she placed her free hand on top of the flesh handcuff. She pressed her tongue into her teeth until the chrome taste arrived.

Lesley asked: What is your name?

The voice emitted an animation of moans, they did not culminate in anything like a name.

Your brothers are arseholes, Lesley muttered. Fancy just nicking off.

And then: Where could they have gone?

Again the voice, and this time some evidence of words. But the words did not collaborate towards any sense, to the extent that Lesley, upon hearing them, immediately forgot their sequence, and couldn't have quoted them, even there on the spot.

She chuckled stupidly and said: Yeah.

Then she added, that it was very little wonder that it was all like this for him – she brushed her fingers against the wall. Your mum's an idiot, she said.

There wasn't anything she could think to say immediately after this, nor in the many minutes after. But after those many minutes – long enough to regret having said anything at all – the figure stopped and wheezed more heavily, and she mistook it for a laugh.

Don't fuck around, she said.

Then more strange vocalisations as the figure continued on.

They came upon a narrow dimly lit avenue in the tunnels. The figure tugged her gently through, and in the eventual room was another mattress, several fluorescent battery lights, and a great pile of identical books, stacked perfectly, as if dragged shrink-wrapped from a pallet, and with the smell of fresh plastic.

Now she could see the face, but only for a moment because it vigilantly avoided eye contact. Anyway, it barely resembled a face, it bore closer resemblance to a swollen drawn caricature, one created by an especially cruel artist. Stranger was that his eyes were the least gripping feature, you could say that they were impassive. But actually, they were gaping portals, joints in a colostomy bag, avenues into barrens.

The figure tugged her by the wrist as it bent to pick up a tobacco pouch next to the mattress. She had no access to the figure's face during these moments, only to the glacial keeling of its body, and there was something about this graceless motion that endeared the body to her.

Instead of smoking the cigarette, he ate it.

I've got a light, she said.

So he bent over again and retrieved the pouch. She rolled it herself, lit it in her own mouth and passed it.

Feeling lifted – tenderly pedagogical – she told him that you can't just eat tobacco. It seemed like the right thing to say.

Then she added: But I'm not offended if you do.

The face faced her for a very brief moment. He wore his jaws open in what she interpreted to be a defensive expression before turning away. He puffed on the smoke she'd lit and looked at the ground, then he let go of her wrist.

She picked a book from the stack. The cover bore a white Germanic font on coal-black cardboard, with lethal barbed wire in the foreground and a ruined tower behind.

Is this some kind of horror? she asked.

The voice strung together a series of ill-fitting words. She was unable to connect even two of these words, though all the words together seemed to form sentences. Meaning or the evidence of it thrusted in incomprehensible directions, while the tone of the voice likewise wavered between a monotone and a yelp.

What does it say? she asked, waving the book.

The Colossal Man collapsed onto the mattress. He could have been staring at her, though it was hard to tell whether his eyes were peering at her body, or beyond or past her body, or into it, or at something else it could see in her place.

She opened the book and flicked to the text.

I was warned not to read this, she said.

The body didn't move, so she opened the book again. She had always dimly believed that reading was virtuous, that one only ever learned virtuous lessons from reading. The correct way of seeing and interpreting the world...you learned those things by living, and then those learnings were articulated by books, which provided the raw material to espouse wisdom to others.

But the Colossal Man's book made her retch.

The body below could have been asleep for all she could tell, so she brushed it with her foot and it pulsed awake. But then it pulsed back into stillness.

She flicked to the middle of the book. Her eyes rested on a sentence that trivialised any extreme she was able to imagine.

I'm not going to be able to forget that, she accused.

The figure remained inert.

Less to him than to the listening mother, she asked aloud: Is there anything to drink down here?

She pottered around the room for a while. It was a better furnished room than the one above, albeit lacking a computer. It was also better decorated, with an array of seemingly printed images so shorn of their context that they failed to move her. Some inclined towards perverse, but were cropped just so, so that any sense of form or performance was missing.

I'm not going to just sit here and read your book, she said after a while. She said it as dismissively as possible, to cultivate a mood she was familiar with.

She pillaged a frayed ALDI bag in the far corner of the room, where two bottles of Tsingtao beer were lukewarm and seemingly forgotten, dusty like artefacts.

At least have a beer, she said after a couple of her own sips. It tasted like frothy water. She cracked the lid on the second bottle, knelt before the figure, poked at its girth.

Have a beer and let's chat, she said.

But he didn't respond.

So she stood and kicked his shoulder gently, and he emitted his usual guttural perplex, though the sound was no sure indication of either wakefulness or rest.

She set the beer aside and thumbed the foul book. The font was an ugly sans serif and the margins at both sides of the text were unprofessionally thin. For the noticing of this defect she happened to catch the theme of several sentences, and the beer bubbled back up her throat.

After the things Jack had shown her, it was troubling that words could hurt her. She swallowed hard.

What's the go? she shouted it so the mother could hear.

But was every sentence in the book as bracing? She flicked towards the end, and of course, not every sentence was quite as lethal as those she had already read...though each sentence implied its culmination, which was as unimaginable as it was terrifying to speculate about. It would take reading all the sentences in order. And it was tempting to do so, because at the other end, through the other side, there might exist a new kind of Lesley not wracked by the most vapid varieties of despair, a better armoured kind. She started the book from the beginning – with no intention of reading until the end – and was both pleased and disappointed that the writing seemed childish when read from the start. Maybe it was actually stupid, and she could write it off.

It's good stuff, she muttered.

Whatever the figure said in response sounded matter-of-fact, though as always the words together were indecipherable.

But it didn't take too many more sentences for her to snap the flimsy paperback shut. She was not strong enough to absorb it.

This is a masterpiece, she said.

And in response, unmistakable condescension.

You sell these? she asked.

He gives them away, Mother Grady interjected. She was standing at the entry point.

Plenty have read it – he could have made a fortune.

Lesley bristled, told the old nag she'd had a gutful of her.

Give us some space, she hollered.

Who would take this seriously? she thought to herself. It doesn't resemble any real book.

The figure was suddenly on his feet marching towards his mother, who panicked and fled back down the entry tunnel. Then he hobbled back to his mattress, collapsed onto his knees, heaped onto the sheets.

It's a masterpiece, Lesley continued. It makes me feel strongly.

The Colossal Man's response seemed dismissive of whatever feelings she might have felt due to the book.

But based on what I've read, it's not particularly interesting as a broader concept, she said.

She thought the figure seemed contrite.

You're a true artist, Lesley said, encouragingly.

You've got to read the whole bloody thing, Mother Grady yelled down the avenue. Otherwise you'll piss him off.

You can't read the book, Lesley replied, as much to the figure as to the mother – that's the thing about it.

You can, the mother said, and I have.

This prompted the figure to start raising from its dead again. Lesley heard the mother's rapid retreat.

Every time the figure moved a muscle, a new regime of shallow laboured breathing commenced. She set her bottle down, and the book next to the bottle, and she knelt before the man's body and patted his rubbery arm. She patted, and patted, then slowed the patting, until her hand rested on its pillowy surface.

She edged up the mattress and lay down. She removed her hand for a brief moment, then let it collapse across the figure's upper chest, and turned her body inward, to hold the figure in its entirety.

Should I read it from start to finish? Lesley asked him gently.

A little while later, she added softly: Would little old me get much out of it?

The brother and child had wasted all his energy tracing the tunnel, holding her wrist, dragging her here. It was unmistakably bedtime, visitors be damned.

Maybe you need a nap, she cooed.

In response came a short, exhausted utterance that suggested nothing readily interpretable. She chose to receive it as an approval.

But before you nap, she started, patting his gut: reflect on what you've done. And let it sit for a while.

Mother Grady was muttering barely audibly down the avenue. Lesley raised her non-patting hand violently, demanded silence, as if to say *don't wake the child*.

And then it was so quiet she heard the phantom sirens in her mind.

She nestled her mouth against his head. Who would have thought? she whispered to the figure. She had always imagined saying that to her children, just as her own mother had said it to her: *Who would have thought?* She was unusually capable of remembering what it was like to be a child, and so prone to callow disbelief. She whispered the words not as salve but in the spirit of their apparent meaning, for the hope that circumstances might shear their platitudinal moss. In the strange mountain tunnels, surely once plundered of its resources – surely not dug by this figure alone – there was nothing that could touch her, especially not this figure, and save for hunger and thirst she need not ever emerge...the notion had the appeal of a weighted blanket. Just like the one she'd had in the flat above the conveyancer, the one that had not covered her so much as it had pressed her into another realm, and under that blanket she had even sometimes been able to sleep, with the aid of certain imaginary stimulus, such as *adrift at sea*, or *cemented in a forgotten chamber*. Who would have thought, she thought, that this was how one escaped the draft, or escaped it to prepare or role-play for another one. She was adrift enough to shut her eyes, and the ensuing blankness immediately conjured the figure's writing...but the evocations had blunted already, enough so that they were fascinating to behold now warped by interpretation. The sentences she had read, upon reflection, narrowed existence rather than expanded or further confused it, the intolerable sensations made sense as a cardinal direction. Maybe a mysterious fifth, or a simple fourth belonging to a foreign kind of wayfinding, maybe past and through all barriers she had known.

It was impossible to tell for sure, but when Lesley felt that the figure had fallen properly to sleep, she stood and gazed over it for a while. Mother Grady eventually cautioned into the room, stood next to her, and gazed at the figure too.

He's dead to the world, Lesley said, with faint pride.

You've done well, the older woman said, dangling a set of keys.

In Newnes the powerlines sagged, all windows were browned, there was no sound save the highway, and there was nothing left to discard.

At the station, metal roller doors had been ripped from the platform stairs. On the city-bound platform Lesley found the three of them seated against a glowing vending machine. From a distance she could see Jack's eyes squinting at her; Steven and Bon were fast asleep. Jack yawned when she squatted to speak.

Enough of this, she said, pulling at his arm.

Jack grunted and made no effort to move.

She climbed over both of their bodies to get closer to sleeping Bon. She rocked his body and pulled at his cheeks. Then she levered his eyelids open with her thumbs, which had no effect. She moved to Steven, who she did not bother rocking and pulling, she levered his eyes and held them open until the body animated and started to thrash.

We're not having a conversation about it right now, she warned the boy. She even pressed a palm against his lips. When she was confident he understood, she removed her palm and stood, and Jack did too. Steven remained against the vending machine, red-eyed and indignant.

He's not dead, he said.

Pointing at a nearby stick, he added: He's not dead, but we've beaten him black and blue – gently – and he still won't wake up. He told me not to follow, but what else was I going to do?

She picked the branch up and jabbed Bon in the arse, and then in the shoulder, and then briskly at the back of the skull. He breathed shallowly in his sleep; his body barely registered the attacks.

He's wasted, Steven said. And you're wasted too. Fancy going on a bender in little old Newnes.

He waited for her to respond.

She didn't respond.

After a while Jack said: It's getting dark.

I've slept in the dark before, Steven replied.

(Lesley's head spun until he added: Outside.)

And then: In Iceland it's daylight half of the year. They go to sleep in brightness. One way or another it makes no difference whether you sleep by day or by night, there's no point being uptight about it. You just do whatever you want.

It's time to go, she said, dropping the stick next to the body. She took Jack's hand, held her other out to Steven, who made an act of taking it begrudgingly.

Are we seriously going to leave him here? Steven asked.

If he won't wake up, Lesley whispered, what choice do we have?

I don't think he's actually drunk, Steven confessed.

Jack laughed, which prompted Steven to ask: what's so funny about that?

There's nothing funny about it, Lesley said, but he wouldn't want us to be out here freezing in the dark. He'd want us safe indoors. His primary concern would be safety, you have to admit.

Steven agreed with this assessment. He wouldn't want anything to happen, he added.

He's not an advocate for things happening, Lesley replied. She turned towards the platform steps, and Jack did too. Steven didn't.

Couldn't we just drag him? That'd wake him up.

And break every bone in his body? He's not a healthy man, he might have a stroke or something. We'll get him tomorrow if he doesn't come home in the night.

Then it occurred to her to ask: What are you doing here, anyway?

Jack laughed again.

We were looking for you, Steven replied. Pointing at Bon, he added: He said he was going to leave forever unless you came back. He reckoned you must have been waiting for a train.

And you reckoned that too?

I don't know. Steven was growing impatient and confused.

He was drunk, she announced. Without a doubt. The stress must have taken its toll. Because there's no such thing as trains, he must have been obliterated.

He must have been.

Jack sat back down again.

So what's all this for then, Steven asked, waving at the track and the platforms, at the station.

Trains used to stop here. They went along these tracks, stopped at stations, let people on, let them off. But they haven't worked for a long time. There's no such thing as them now.

So why hasn't it been removed?

It has, Lesley said. At least, the trains have been. They've probably been packed away into train sheds. Everything is being packed away in Newnes.

The wild dogs might eat him, Steven muttered.

Lesley said that she had yet to see a single wild dog during her life in Newnes.

We'll come back for him, she assured. Anyway he'll probably get home before we even wake up.

For emphasis, she unzipped her jumper and wrapped it tightly around Bon's torso.

It's pretty dark, Jack observed.

It was true. The sky was a deep crimson, bilious for smoke.

I reckon just because you haven't seen wild dogs, it doesn't mean they don't exist, Steven replied. And that's not the only thing that could hurt him.

What else could?

Steven's expression was barely legible in the dimming light. Other people, he said.

She arced up: You can't say we didn't try, she yelled at the man. She kicked Bon in his exposed shoulder, then bent over, held his eyelids open again. She couldn't see the whites. As loudly as she could without distressing the boys, she implored him to wake up. All she got in response was the draft of his breathing.

What are you doing sleeping on the platform anyway?

Well you've been gone for days, Steven said. Jack reckoned you'd left but we thought you'd come back. Eventually we went looking. Bon had a few drinks – he pointed at Bon – and I did too, to help us with the search. He gave it to me. Anyway, he said the trains would start again eventually, and that we might as well just wait.

You haven't been back home, have you, Lesley?

Lesley swore.

It's too late to go home, Jack said, pointing at the sky.

Lesley ripped her jumper back off Bon and grabbed both boys by their necks.

Let's all hold onto one another and not let go, she said. Take me as seriously as you want, it's your choice.

Giving Steven the choice seemed to appease him. He lay down next to Bon, Jack lay next to Steven, and she took the edge. The vending machine ceased to glow.

You have to not let go, she said. Shout if you can't feel each other anymore. And under no circumstances go to sleep. If you think you're falling to sleep just talk.

Steven laughed and Jack laughed at Steven; Lesley kicked them both. It was all a bit exciting.

Then there was nothing. And then came that peculiar light-headedness, and that bizarre absence of physical orientation. But she knew her arms were wrapped tightly, maybe excessively so, around Jack's. When she tried to tell him never to let go of his brother, her speech didn't sound. All she could do was wait for the morning. Then they'd get into the hatchback and leave.

3

Photographs of Lesley and her two older brothers gathered dust on the ornamental mantelpiece. There were three photographs. In each of them, Lesley the youngest sat front and centre, and her girl smile from left to right became more complex. Her brothers from left to right looked more and more like the fathers they became. In between, carefully positioned, were two clear oil vases with scent sticks, and two elaborately carved miniature wooden chests. Beneath the mantelpiece a low coffee table held a tissue box, a basket of dried flowers and a packet of wet wipes. The carpet in the lounge room was mottled light brown and the sun through the window shone the routes of a vacuum cleaner.

Jack and Steven sat on the couch watching her brothers' *Star Wars* DVDs. In the open-plan living space, Lesley and her mother sat at a distant kitchen bench and smoked while they watched the boys.

Daily for lunch Lesley and the boys followed the winding cul-de-sac streets to the light industrial area. This area was littered with blocks of disused land, sprouting wildly among dirt quarter-acre paddocks prepared for development. They'd march the curved tarmac between the sun-blanched lawns of giant modern homes, and then they'd march the rugged industrial road, between workaday facades with roller doors up and business conducted inside. Between a mechanical repair shop and an upholsterer was a hole-in-the-wall takeaway designed to service workers in the workshops surrounding. The man at the chip shop had grunted at them for a while but as weeks passed started to greet them warmly. They'd order a medium tray of chips with money owing to Grandma's stash. And with every day the tray would bulge fatter and greasier inside its protective paper bag. They'd march home and eat most on the way, leaving the rest for Grandma.

Otherwise they'd sit on the front lawn or in the backyard. In the afternoons they'd watch *Star Wars*. Then they'd have dinner and then it was time for bed: Jack on the bottom bunk and Steven on top, though sometimes Steven wanted to be on the bottom but Jack didn't really care.

Lesley slept in her old bedroom. The posters were removed and the stickers were razored from the dressing-table mirror. Plastic storage boxes were stacked in one corner and she cowered from them. It was no longer her oasis, and long gone were expectations of space of her own. She could no longer imagine what it was like to desire to mark one's own territory. To wear a costume and to inhabit a semblance of something other than oneself, to imagine becoming some other, to be dazzled by the image of a different kind of self, to diverge radically away, to shed one's skin, to live one's best life knowing even one's best life would be laden with strife, in all honesty to anticipate and gesture arrogantly at that strife, to welcome it as a variety of exercise almost...to do all this, to disavow the condition and to usher or catalyse another, to do so perhaps violently (only in one's dreams) and to then grow out of it...the desire for all this lingered in her old bedroom.

She'd sit at the kitchen counter and smoke with her mother. They'd always be drinking coffee or tea, sometimes just a glass of water. Her mother would always want to hear about the circumstances that gave rise to her having these two boys – men, really – and that surely time hadn't become this dislodged, this disarranged. And when she promised her mother they were hers she didn't expect to be believed. Time was different and the world was different, and the things permitted to be true and the things denied the quality of truth now swung in all directions, loose on an axle, not even dependent on circumstances or prejudices.

When her mother said something like: do you intend to send the boys to school, Lesley would say they had already gone to school.' They've been to school, she would say, they're schooled.

Her mother, their grandma, was not overbearing or instructive; she lacked a strong short-term memory. Whenever the semblance of a lecture arose it would be dispelled by her inability to arrive at its point, so that the moral of any lecture was annulled by Lesley's sympathy. Understanding her own limitations, Grandma usually made do with immediate concerns, such as the postures of the boys: the way Jack always sat tense with his knees against his chest, the way Steven stretched his jaws when in deep concentration. These things bothered her. She spoke about the neighbourhood dogs and the fact Lesley was home once and for all and for always.

Grandma would yell at the boys playfully that they should at least make her a cup of tea every now and then. Jack seemed to agree, he would sometimes make her a cup of tea. But Steven couldn't have cared less about Grandma's cups of tea. Steven didn't talk much to Lesley and he never spoke to Grandma, they weren't on his wavelength. He'd splay himself long across the couch with his jeans unbuttoned, and occasionally in the yard you'd hear him speaking his truth to Jack, but he rarely spoke a word inside except for the functional things.

We're not on his wavelength, Lesley whispered knowingly to Grandma.

Jack spoke to Grandma about whatever needed to be spoken about. He would sometimes sit there on one of the kitchen stools and meet her in the eyes. The skin on his face was plush despite his diet of chips and chops and Vegemite toast, and he seemed interested in whatever adults had to say. Sometimes when Grandma lit a cigarette Lesley would order him away, but he wouldn't leave, and she never insisted (blow it over there, she'd order, pointing at the rangehood). He'd sit there, with the palm of a hand cupping an elbow, hunched according to whatever course the conversation took. He'd look at Lesley no matter who was talking. Other times he'd gently ambush Lesley from behind, to wrap his arms reflexive around her shoulders and merge his skull with hers. And then he'd move off just as abruptly, to walk narrow lazy circles from one wall to the other, dragging his fingers across surfaces. And then he'd collapse again onto the lounge room floor.

For long stretches the two women would sit there on the kitchen stools and comment on the minor details of however the boys were holding themselves. The boys liked being spoken about, they'd throw glances at the women. Grandma thought Steven needed a good kick in the arse and Lesley reckoned he ought to be left alone. He's a smart kid and very imaginative, she would say.

He's lovely, Grandma would agree.

And then bedtime and then morning, everyone laboriously fed. And then an hour-or-so lull as the boys languished in the still freshly minted gutter of the suburb, sitting there to be seen and perhaps interacted with. Lesley would go out with water and make them drink and she'd say, as if it were a treat every day: Let's get hot chips. And the boys would rise and follow her along the winding streets and onto the main road and then down several kilometres to the lonely strip of businesses at the outskirts of the town proper. And it must have only been months that their routine remained like this, though it felt much longer.

Your brothers were much different to these ones, Grandma would sometimes say.

Over the course of weeks or months of Grandma saying this, Lesley had fine-tuned her response. It was not strictly wrong the way the boys lived, she said, though she had hoped and still hoped for better. The boys were seated in a waiting room between one world and the next, so they don't quite know what to do with their bodies – look at what they do with their bodies. They lay unthinkingly prostrate (she waved at Steven) or else they never let a single muscle loosen (she waved at Jack), they're always one way or the other. The world doesn't see them in particular, they're both enslaved and oppressor. The powers that be might soon send them to war but not quite yet and mind you, there will be no warning. They're pawns spoiled by decadence, seated too long on the bench, Steven's getting fat around the waist and his teeth are yellowing (she whispered it). He's a gear ground and rusted for inactivity. Anything worth fighting for can't be fought against and besides it's got him on its side, he's on its side, even if he thought himself opposed he'd be embedded in lock step, just like everyone, you and me included, even his father, even more reluctant parties and even the agitators. Everyone with good or better intentions is on side they can't help but to be. He's worn down by an insidious modern slavery, he begs the acceptance of slave drivers and their cheerleaders. He's got no choice and anyway the world agrees that it's his fault. History will abhor him, it does so already, and so he wilts. He seeks solace in fantasy and remove, it no longer matters whether dreams can be real because dreams unreal are quite enough. Under better circumstances he would slave in the day and dream screen-side by night, space operas and superheroes, and these slave drivers would mould his dreams and impart their wisdom and sometimes concede that yes, you're a slave, and isn't it clever that you noticed. But he will be dragged into war I know. And Jack already knows. And it won't be with the military and there won't be admirers waving their hankies – there will be no bystanders.

Grandma would always say that no matter what one or both should go to TAFE.

Jack would crawl into her bed in the hours before dawn. He'd lift the doona and edge close against Lesley's side. Most nights Lesley repositioned herself around him, or else let him entwine with her. He'd sink his face into the narrow of her neck or against the soft beneath her shoulder. And then a silent battle would be waged, and whoever fell asleep first lost. She always lost, exhausted wondering what lingered in the boy's mind and what had been expunged. In the morning Steven would leap onto the foot of the bed and tear the blankets away and coax them out, because he was hungry and it was a new day.

She'd take Steven's jaw in her hands when she scrubbed his teeth. She'd place a thumb on one cheek and her middle finger on the other. He'd eventually open his mouth but only just.

When she coursed the brush in circles across his front teeth he'd always leave his tongue slightly hanging. He'd stare at his mirror reflection with vacant eyes. It was neither a reflective or imprisoned expression, it was the vacancy of bored surrender. Try though she did, he never embraced the associated routines, he only buckled to commands. He slightly loosened certain muscles according to the pressures she applied. When his mouth was safely malleable, she would rest the jaw hand across one of his shoulders.

Lesley lovely Lesley, Grandma would sometimes say. Quiet and timid as a girl, undercover monster as a teen, now a beautiful woman. She had always said it, every weekend when she visited. Now she said it all the time.

Steven scowled whenever he heard Grandma talk like this; Jack ignored her. There were times when Grandma was newly overwhelmed by emotion, it seemed to hit her with immense force at times. She was getting old and she was going to die. She would take her knowledge with her, and the rest of them would need to keep learning from scratch. Except the lessons would keep reconfiguring, and they would all be left feeling hopelessly sentimental, or else benighted and embittered, having learned nothing with enduring application.

Lesley would warn her that the boys didn't need to hear about her as a girl.

Whenever Grandma asked about the father, Lesley replied that he'd left them on the platform. Grandma thought she was being metaphorical at first, but eventually asked what they were doing on a platform.

But she didn't know. She had to tell her mother that she didn't really know what she was doing nor what she had done, that every choice had always chosen her, even the ones she had considered over months. You have to realise, Mum, that I don't really make choices, she said. And it's not for lack of opportunities to make choices, it's nothing like that. He never made choices either, we didn't choose where we went or where we ended up. I'm not saying others made the choices for us. What I'm saying is that choices were provided but we didn't make any of them. We've got legs and wheels and minds but I'm not sure any of those have much input into where you end up, and I don't believe in predetermination. What I mean is that there was no motive or impetus, that choices were available but we moved towards none of them, and so we allowed the tide to carry us wherever it saw fit. I don't believe in predetermination, I don't believe in narratives, but I do believe the right choices won't grant us much leniency. We don't move towards fate but towards our reckoning. As for him, I know when he left us it wasn't for having made the choice. The only choice he had was to stay.

Steven started digging a hole in the backyard. Grandma didn't care. There was nothing out there except a cement path to the washing line, bordered on three sides by green Colorbond fence. It was good exercise, better than watching movies. Jack didn't like to watch movies alone so he'd stand around watching Steven as he dug. Occasionally Steven managed to convince Jack to have a turn, and he'd stand at the edge, instructing on the best ways to dig. Then he'd hop in to measure its depth. He'd crawl out orange dirt smeared across his shirt, and Grandma would shout out the flyscreen 'bloody hell!'

The women stared out the kitchen window beholding the boys like they were ornamental plants. You just didn't know what was going on in their minds or why they moved their bodies the way they did.

It's hard to tell what kind of men they'll grow up to be, Grandma said.

Very different kinds of men, Lesley reckoned.

On Thursdays Lesley shopped in town with money from Grandma's stash. From the underground car park she'd mount a cement ramp into the plaza. Music played from hidden speakers in the ceiling, just like it always had, and the songs hadn't changed since she was young.

The plaza had come to resemble a tunnel. It was a warren lined with shuttering on the way to the Woolworths. Along certain stretches of tunnel the lights had blown out, and for the absence of opened shops, it seemed to wind harshly left and right in illogical spirals. These warrens, striped with shutters and lined with bygone signage, eventually led to a food court dotted with tables cemented in place. Despite the lack of chairs around cemented tables, a lone Baker's Delight held its ground, just across from the supermarket checkouts.

Her first job was in this plaza, selling clothes at a teen boutique. Her friends had incessantly dropped in, with pink bags of donuts and frozen Cokes. They'd stealth the aisles to talk to her out of earshot of her manager. Nineties pop would billow through the store, blending with the music of the plaza and all the shops surrounding. The plaza used to be a cacophony of intermingling music, and it had felt like a sample of a city.

It was not changed, it was different. There were no familiar faces, scarcely any at all. Along the main street outside, cars wore drought dust in the late spring heat. Here and there shopfronts held desperate sales for cheap shoes, shrink-wrapped party plates, connect-the-dot colouring books, and fluoro plastic sun visors.

A worthwhile wilderness might blossom there some day. Despite the baking sun her old town appeared vaguely twilit. A corner pub remained open at the juncture of the main street and the highway, and inside men and women drank themselves to stupors. She'd gone in there one day to see if there was anyone she knew. None were recognisable, and none were ever seated, they were not drowsy and resigned like common drunks. They wandered to-and-fro with a bizarre urgency, beer froth in their stubble and lashes, taking one another by the shirt to speak. A half-dozen or so drinkers roamed the soiled carpet with a flagrant lusty air. All the same she'd had a beer, it had been a very long time since she'd had a normal tap beer. She sat at the bar, away from the stamping action of the drunks, and the man behind the bar had said to her: You need somewhere private.

Lesley had replied that she didn't need one thing or another, that she was just going to have this middy because as far as she could tell why not. But the man behind the bar replied placidly that there were several pubs in town where one could go to drink alone. And they're not even secret, he said. You can just walk into them and have the whole place to yourself. You can get bone-deep drunk and not answer to anyone. It's possible to just sit there and drink, he said. This pub, by dint of it being adjacent to the highway, is a magnet for wild transients. Far be it from me to turn you away from this pub, he said. You're welcome to stay if you want. But if it's what you need, there are pubs where you can get drunk alone, and the bar people are trained to not utter a peep. And you can decide what's on the television. You can even smoke inside, in some of them. They won't even care if you sleep.

By night kids rocked the roofs of neighbourhood houses, they landed as bracing and crisp as gunfire. And the dogs were trained to kill when off their leashes. On a lawn at the nearest corner, men and women sat all night drinking bourbon and Coke from cans; sometimes they'd light a fire. And they'd play music that made the dead of night feel like drive time. Some men sidled shirtless and tattooed with half-scrunched tins in their fists, others wore loose shirts over bulbous guts and all looked the same. Lesley half-wished they all believed in god. She'd monitor them from the lounge room window, their liquor scent present even at that distance.

But the street was serene by day, and the home belonging to the corner revellers lay quiet as if unoccupied. She always had the boys fed by seven and in bed by eight.

They've got a lot of learning to do, Grandma reckoned. If they think they can just sit out there and get obliterated every night, they've got another thing coming.

Most of their evenings were spent discussing whatever sounds emitted from the end of the street. Occasionally they'd fall into rumination. Grandma would turn the TV on but then switch it back off, she'd return to the kitchen counter for another smoke. Lesley poured them small servings of white cask wine. They'd talk about the boys even though by the end of the day they were both fed up with them. Grandma always alluded to her experience as a mother of boys but Lesley didn't think she knew much about hers.

I'd like to tell their father what for, Grandma often said. They'll end up at the end of the street with the rest of them drunks, celebrating for no reason.

My boys aren't like that, Lesley would reply.

No one's boys are like that, the older woman would say.

The children of the corner revellers played up and down the street until the early hours. Sometimes late at night she'd look them in the eyes through the lounge room window. They'd sit astride scooters or pushbikes and peer at her with no inhibition. They roamed in large packs. Some of the boys tried to grind their scooters against gutters, others climbed the nearby telephone booth and leapt off, collapsing into awkward military rolls. Grandma said if she'd ever caught Lesley's brothers doing that she'd have sent them to boarding school.

Sometimes smaller groups of corner revellers would splinter off all down the street. One night three women sat huddled in a circle on Grandma's lawn – a love affair was being discussed. Lesley could tell by the way they hushed their voices and touched between gesticulations. Far be it from her to chastise the women, but she didn't like them being there. She watched discreetly through Grandma's drawn hessian-coloured curtains, but not discreetly enough, because one of them waved at her. Lesley waved back petrified. The young woman waved more urgently so she opened the window.

Come and have a drink with us love, she said. She must have been in her early twenties, she was all sympathy and understanding but who knows why. Lesley said she couldn't come out because her boys were fast asleep.

If they wake and I'm not there shit will hit the fan, she added.

You're a good mum, the young woman said.

Lesley groaned. She went through the front door and across

the lawn, stood over the women, who were all much younger than they'd appeared from afar.

We were just saying it's time to get out of this neighbourhood, the woman said. The other two nodded, one of them had been crying.

Rebecca wants to move to the city – the woman pointed to the girl with mottled wet cheeks. You seem like you've come from the city.

Lesley hadn't 'come' from the city, she'd briefly become lost there. I've lived here all my life, she said. I grew up on this street and I remember when the likes of you were in nappies.

The girls all laughed. Lesley laughed.

That's cute, Rebecca said. The other two girls were Tina and Jessica. Tina, the one who had beckoned her, said those were the days.

It feels like a long time ago, Jessica said.

It was a long time ago.

A young boy of maybe four crashed his scooter at the edge of the circle, dived onto Tina's lap and latched onto her breast. Three other children stood around the circle too, lazing on handlebars limbs ajitter. They'd come to see the stranger Lesley and to make an impression on her. They stared unblinking.

Sit down, darl, you'll hear the boys, Tina said.

Jessica passed a Coke bottle mixed generously with bourbon.

That's a good mumma, Jessica said as Lesley swigged, and all of them had a laugh.

Lesley pointed up the street. That house you're staying in used to be where a friend of mine lived, she said. She had a massive trampoline in her backyard, we'd listen to the Top 40 while jumping. We'd jump all day or else lay flat getting suntans. And her mum used to bake us frozen pastizzis for lunch. It was better than what Mum would give me, always a cheese-and-tomato sandwich. On Saturday morning she'd come to my house to watch the Top 40 on television, my place was better because we had speakers hooked up. My brothers would tease us for liking RnB music. I'd tape the film clips I liked onto video, and when the video was full I'd start again at the beginning, so that over time traces of older clips were softly visible under the new ones. We liked it that way, it was dreamy.

Do you still keep in touch, one of the girls asked idly. Lesley said they didn't, that she couldn't even remember where her friend had gone.

That's so typical, Rebecca reckoned.

It's all so typical, Lesley agreed. You must remember how the streets used to be. My house was so busy and loud that it would grate. But I miss that loudness and I miss the feeling that everything will stay the same forever. I miss waking and being exhausted by the dullness of it all. It was dull but you were intensely loved and aggressively looked after. I miss wanting to grow up.

I'm five, one of the boys announced.

You're all grown up, Jessica told him.

I will be when I'm ten, he advised.

These ones own the street now, Tina said, waving at the children. It's a busy playground for them, we're just getting old.

True, Lesley said.

Rebecca reckons the city but I reckon the countryside, Tina added. Make a little farm, grow vegetables, maybe get a cow. The kids would love that.

You'd be bored, Rebecca reckoned.

It's nice to be bored, Lesley interjected.

That's what I reckon too, Tina said. Maybe I'd start knitting, or pickling, or reading books. And all I need is kids anyway.

They'll nick off when they're older, Jessica supposed. Rebecca nodded.

But not far, Tina said. They love their mum. She squeezed the boy in her arms, and he restlessly changed position on her breast.

Then sounded an overwhelming roar. One of the men on the corner was revving his engine again. A couple of other men stood drinks in hand watching. The women just sat there, and Jessica said he was a dumb cunt.

That's going to wake my boys up, Lesley shouted over the noise.

Sorry darl, Tina mouthed.

The shaved exhaust popped, and the motor shrieked between soprano and baritone. And then it stopped entirely, and you could hear the men sharing observations. She heard the flyscreen open, and when she looked, Jack was standing on the landing with Grandma. Lesley sprinted over and hugged him, and Grandma shook her head and went inside.

Calling it a night, she told the girls. They waved and she went inside. Grandma gave her a filthy look.

Jack got straight into bed with her. He didn't ask what she'd been doing outside. He lay facing her, forehead pressed against hers, his breath smelling of toothpaste and sour. She watched his eyelids occasionally part. After a while he nodded off, his mouth parted, and his face adopted the expression of a curious child. She laid a leg over him and fell asleep.

Grandma reckoned they still did Carols by Candlelight at Christmas.

The Christmas carols are techno now, she said. The kids and their children sing along to robot voices and you can barely understand the words. The music plays through giant speakers, and the beats are loud enough to stir the desert. Occasionally the beats stop and there's a calm section, but then the beats gradually come back, tapping away in the background, increasing in speed, tap-tap-tap louder and louder towards a horrible climax. Then there's silence again but only for a second, because shortly after a chorus arrives and it's even louder than before. The bass is so heavy that you can barely hear the melody, and the kids dance like druggos, their children do too. There's a frenzy of violent limb-thrashing. It's very ungodly.

Grandma chuckled. Far be it from me to care whether something is godly or not, she said. But the Christmas carols make you want to be rich. They make you want to own a yacht. And you're not supposed to drink but everyone does anyway. They scull spirits in the shrubs near the car park, then they sprint manically when the music gets intense. No one can just relax and celebrate, everything needs to work towards a climax, there's no pleasure in just being there.

Lesley puffed her smoke indignantly. Good luck putting on anything without a climax, she said. Everything needs to culminate, doesn't it? Maybe your culminations – and she pointed at Grandma – were more tasteful back in the olden days. But don't lie, they were climaxes, even if they seem pathetic now, even if they were classical or whatever...they culminated. No way did you not anticipate climaxes – don't lie. You wanted them, you were hot for them. That's what you were there for, that's what gave you purpose. Who made it so? Ancient musicians and storytellers? Don't ask me. It's a generational arms race towards ever more overpowering climaxes, isn't it? Your climax is the starting point for others, and then these others, their climaxes are the starting point for ever greater ones. Maybe it's not healthy but it is what it is. Whoever invented climaxes...they invented something worse than tobacco or booze, that's just my opinion. Everyone is addicted to climaxes now, hopelessly so, they want to see everything that has ever happened culminate in a supernova thematic explosion. What else are all their efforts for? It's a good question you have to admit.

Lesley butted her cigarette and started to roll another. Climaxes have come to a head, she said. They've reached the ceiling, there isn't anything more climactic than what's in store and you'd want to hope there isn't. But people still want it, I know they do. People are pushing and pressing outsize climaxes through narrow holes and they're making it through, just for sheer desperation and desire. They want it, and who are we to argue that it's not right? The world is yours for a tiny window. They don't want quaint piano music, or just the cicadas. Its unimaginable what might come after this climax, better to relish its ascent, better to befriend it.

Grandma laughed and Lesley arced up. We know the world is here and there populated by unspeakable evil, Lesley said. Only death will save us from having to learn about it every day. The best way not to rejoice in it is to care for children. That's why you hate modern climaxes, you see? For lack of filthy wealth or abject poverty, having people in your care is the only reason to abstain. You cannot be a revolutionary with children in your care, no matter how sick the world, no matter your anger...you cannot want change too drastic. Maybe in the past it was different...but they've been careful to create the best world for just making children, even if you can't look after them. To not have people in your care is to surrender to misanthropy. I'd gas myself for lack of the boys, the gas is supposed to be painless. If it came to dying painfully, I'd go ahead with it, but there's always the lingering anxiety, you might misjudge the leap, you might botch the poison cup, and then be incapacitated and stuck.

Lesley bought the boys new clothes for Christmas because it was what they needed. And she bought them *X-Men* on DVD to share. Steven had wishes for Christmas but none that were feasible; Jack couldn't have cared less. Steven wanted a cubby house ('of his own'), but Lesley had to warn him that no one ever got exactly what they wanted, that it was Santa's decision, and that he always got them what was best.

Steven wasn't cheered by clothes on Christmas morning. He said he already had clothes. But he added in a fateful way that Santa decides what's best. The boys watched *X-Men* as Lesley and Grandma carved ham and set snacks on a platter. They all sat at the table near the kitchen, the boys in their crisp new clothes, and Lesley savoured the sourness of chalky supermarket cheeses. Jack didn't like the apple sauce. Steven reckoned ham didn't taste that much different to chops. They dug in the backyard in their new clothes and Grandma scolded them out of earshot.

Tina came around in the afternoon, reckoned they should all have Christmas drinks. Lesley wasn't sure, because her sons got ratty in the hours before bed. But Tina said it was Christmas Day and it was worth not giving a damn for once. Bring a chair up to the corner, she said. The boys are welcome, they can sit around or play or whatever.

Lesley wanted to drink with the other women; Grandma said it was a slippery slope. You'll be on meth before you know it, she said. And you'll no longer have the boys inside before dark, they'll start tossing rocks and setting Otto bins alight.

She went anyway, partially in defiance of her mother. But she waited until the boys were asleep and instructed Grandma to shout with any sign of waking.

A dozen or so men and women sat in a circle around a gallon drum stacked with kindling and wood but not yet alight. Tina and Rebecca made space for Lesley's seat, but no grand introductions were made. Four young boys fought theatrically with sticks in the centre next to the drum while the men commentated and laughed.

How was Christmas, Mum? Tina asked.

Lesley adopted a stoic pose. The boys didn't get much but we had a decent time, she said. Then she pulled a cask of wine from a shopping bag and poured some into a cup.

The girls nodded at her. She'd arrived halfway through their conversation and they returned to it, speaking over her lap. One of the young men, tattooed and rake-thin, smiled at her as he scrunched old shopping catalogues into the drum. He applied a packet of firelighters, and the drum glowed then soared in the orange summer night. The children waved their swords in the flame and flung baby embers around. Lesley waited for them to be reined in but no one cared. Down the street her home lay calm and for all she could tell no eyes peered through curtains, neither lounge room nor boys' bedroom.

The girls spoke about tension between people she knew nothing about, but Lesley raised her brows all the same, to show she could sense the gravity of the matter. Gradually the subject changed and she was drawn in, though the conversation orbited any pressing concern of her own. They spoke about the street and they spoke about the men. Rebecca wanted to move to the city but Tina had to warn her that it wasn't a good idea.

We'll all move to the country and start our own town, Tina said. We'll become savages.

And they laughed.

My boys would fit right in, Lesley said.

Tina said they looked pretty good to her. I've seen them on the street, she said. They look fairly peaceful if you ask me.

Lesley said it was true that they looked that way.

You're strong for keeping them like you do, Rebecca said. Props to you for keeping them inside and making them sleep.

They've got a lot to sleep off, she said.

Kaitlyn should be in school now, Tina sighed, gesturing at a girl seated on the verandah with a crowd of others. But I'm not going to send her.

You shouldn't, Rebecca snarled.

Lesley drifted off, nodded from time to time. She watched the other men and women at the far side of the drum, all so at home they bickered rather than conversed. Some just stared into the fire, now obscenely bright for the absence of sun. She drank her wine and stared into the flame and wondered how they dared let it rage albeit contained. Many if not most lived their lives flirting with disaster, poking at it provoking it. And yet it was rare that anything ever spilled over. The world was rife with examples not events, her circumstances were silt rings in the glass. She felt out of place, like some sage elderly enigma. But she didn't leave, she kept on sitting, wending a brown piece of grass around her index finger.

The town used to go hard, she heard the tattooed man say. There were nightclubs when we were kids, all types. Even the pubs would put on dance music, and in the '90s, raves and drugs and everything you'd want. Not just old cunts gambling and bickering: actual rough-as-guts shenanigans.

Back in the day, he said. And then someone else aped: Back in the day. They all looked into the fire.

Back in the day there was a nightclub in town so rough it was famous even in the city, another man said. No more depraved nightclub has ever existed. It was near the train station, but not on the commercial side. You exited the station, went west along a quiet street of brick houses, and then followed north as the houses petered out into a cul-de-sac of warehouses. You know where I mean. At the foot of that cul-de-sac, between two disused warehouses – you know the street I mean – was a doorway with a sign above. The paint had worn off the sign so you didn't even know it was a club. And you couldn't hear it because the door, when you entered, led downwards for a long time, into a deep basement area. Getting out was a nightmare apparently, you'd need to take a carry-out for the journey, assuming you could walk.

This club was known statewide, he said, but only among a certain kind. It was pre-internet. Apparently you can still find stunted men in the pokie corners of the deepest New South Wales pubs who know the club existed, stunted more so those who went. Later there was a thread about it on an internet forum, he said, that's how I know about it. The thread was populated by hundreds who wanted to go, wished they had gone, and a half-dozen or so who either did or reckon they did. The place was legendary among online wack jobs. They talk about clubs in Europe where you've got full-on orgies going on in the rafters, but at this club, everyone wanted to fight. You'd leave the final flight of steps into this place – a long and narrow unventilated room, stools and tables on the left and right, standing room in the centre, bar at the far end of the room – with your fists out. If you didn't get hit on the way to the bar then you were in huge trouble: it meant people thought you were a challenge. They'd come for you later. But most people would get decked the moment they entered the standing space, just a casual cheerful decking, and if you couldn't handle it everyone would laugh at you. If you were lucky, you could sit on a stool if someone got up. Dead set, the first vision when entering the club – if your first vision wasn't a fist colliding with your face – was a flurry of men getting decimated by one another. They didn't roar and cheer like men usually do during an all-out brawl, because the brawling was the business of the club, it was just what happened: no need to make a big deal of it. It wasn't a fight club, it wasn't organised, you'd just go to hit and be hit. They'd just play the usual Top 40 music. You'd be getting decked to the tune of Peter Andre. The only time the game was off was if you were ordering a beer, but once you'd ordered your beer it didn't matter if you were holding it: if you can't hold a beer and get punched in the face you needed to practice or else you weren't good enough to be in the club. One of the club's biggest no-nos was standing at the bar pretending you were ordering a beer: if you were caught doing this you'd get knocked over and stomped relentlessly. Standing there at the bar, pretending to order a beer, was what people did if they had bitten off more than they could chew. The men's bathroom (there was a women's bathroom too) wasn't any different: you could be standing at the trough and someone would coward punch you from behind, you could pass out with your face in piss. So you just didn't piss or else you pissed in your pants, because it didn't really matter how you smelled. The club smelled like an ashtray muddied by the worst beer, it smelled like piss and shit and body odour. The people on the internet forum reckon the smell had become so pungent that it was alluring, they reckoned they felt nostalgic for that smell, it was the smell of war. All the most disgusting smells. According to the internet experts, if someone died the local police hushed it because they were in cahoots with the owners of club. There's a story online about how, one night, the most vicious circle pit occurred during 'Go West' by Pet Shop Boys. Men were naked and not just punching but clawing, everywhere, below and above the waist, above the neck, just a bloodbath, everyone was utterly slaughtered, not from drink but literally. All these men who you vaguely recognised. Several fatalities. Apparently you'd always see people you knew, that was one of the tricks of the club. You'd notice a man who was familiar but you might wonder if you'd only dreamed about him earlier in life, because you didn't know him, you only recognised his face, and you were punching and scratching and tearing at him without restraint, and he was doing so too, probably to a third person, that third to a fourth: it was an abattoir. Apparently you'd leave with skin under your nails, between your teeth, hair-matted flesh in your clothes. That feeling of bashing a man you vaguely know was embedded in the club, you were always bashing or being bashed by a man you vaguely remembered, and then later during a break at the bar you would think: he served me a pie last week, or: he fixed my carburettor last Monday, or: he's the teacher of my eight-year-old child. You'd always be wondering, they reckon, who you were beating, and that made it more exciting: what was at stake and how can it be more at stake? That was the beauty of it, according to the internet experts. You were always wondering what veins of effect you were sending out into the world. It was emotional: it wasn't like regional football where everyone has a beer afterwards. You'd feel hatred the moment you entered, it would be so unbelievably real that you'd lose inhibition. Like in war, the man said, the club was a war. Did you know you can go to war, that you're a contender? Many people who don't think they should go to war, many people who have felt themselves unfit, have been forced to go to war. Joe eating poached eggs and cucumber at the Black Stump café on Saturday morning with his young family: he's a war machine. Just punch him in the face like it means nothing to you, and you'll see. What if one day, you were walking to the park with your kid and someone simply punched them? You would be a war machine, right then and there. It's a delicate balance, it's kind of amazing that we're not going at it all the time.

But no way could a club like that exist nowadays, the tattooed man said. Now we have to drink at home, or else with the old punishers at the highway pub.

The other men laughed. Tina reckoned it was all bullshit.

You're making this crap up, she said.

They'll get their chance soon enough, Lesley said. She dropped the empty cask between her legs.

The party sprawled in all directions, and eventually Tina and Rebecca joined with other crowds. Lesley wandered amped up, no longer caring if she looked strange or out of place. She wanted to speak her mind but no one asked her questions. Occasionally someone shoved a tin of something into her fist and she'd talk but they'd duck away. Women danced on the corner lawn to the sound of unfamiliar music, bass-heavy, synthetic and cocky. Lesley thought they looked like professional dancers. The fire from the drum cast their silken silhouettes over the street, they brushed their arms into the air and twirled downward in brief respite. They'd volley in concert from one leg to the other and combine in open arms, and the children mirrored clumsily at their hips, swaying and dizzy but utterly serene. A young boy dragged a line of fairy lights into the group and other children picked up its slack, running in circles around the dancing women, giggling ecstatic, as the colours strobed. The women inside the lights joined hands in a circle and glided counter to the direction of the lights; children jumped around inside. Lesley's joy gave way to an itch, she could not ignore tomorrow and the day after, and the sun was faintly evident north.

Jack waited in the hall half-asleep. Steven leapt onto the bed an hour later.

The corner erupted more fervently on New Year's Eve but Lesley didn't want to have a bar of it. She drew the curtains and lit some candles and she and the boys watched *X-Men* until just before midnight. Then she set a tray of leftover exotic cheese and biscuits, and a small bowl of coloured lolly snakes. They each drank Coke from tall glasses. Steven stood beneath Grandma's clock counting down the minutes, and Jack sat at the kitchen bench and gazed.

Minutes before midnight loud explosions sounded from outside. Steven dashed to the curtains and flung them wide. On the corner a group of men launched fireworks from plastic buckets, and coloured bursts blossomed in the night. Steven swore, and sprinted to the door and out. They joined him on the overgrown lawn. At the end of the street a hundred-odd figures stood in the flickering shadow of the drum fire, each peering up at the criss-crossed fluorescent blooms. The projectiles whistled in their ascent and crackled at their apex, the crowd screamed with every salvo. Then they commenced the countdown, from ten until Happy New Year, and Steven mouthed the chant under his breath.

The street lit up daylight purple bright. Corner-reveller children poured onto the street with hands cupped to catch the fading sparks, and Steven did too. He leapt around the tarmac like a playing kitten. Some of the adults jogged or marched into the street and scruffed their children. Jessica approached Steven and wrapped her arms around him tight. She rubbed his shoulder blades, brushed her face against his, and pulled his body closer. Everyone but Lesley and Jack was in some form of embrace but it was only Steven who resisted. He broke away, jogged to Lesley, and grabbed her by the arm. They stood there side-by-side as the spectacle gradually diminished, and Steven's panic-stricken silence only lifted once indoors again.

She was just wishing you a happy new year, Lesley said later.

He shrugged. The boys were lazed in the lounge room. They refused to go to bed. They peered out the window whenever they thought she wasn't watching.

She's pretty, Lesley said. Isn't she Jack?

Jack shrugged too, but not in support of his brother. He didn't care. And she couldn't quite believe how placid the two of them looked, Steven splayed on the couch and Jack leaned against cushions on the floor, half-watching TV between trailing-off exchanges about fireworks and spectacle. They were exempt, they had found their way out. Only, what if she ever died?

Bon

When Bon left the train station the eastern sun had come alight, and it hadn't been a dream or a misunderstanding that the line had ceased to operate.

So lacking the confidence to seek help he walked. Back to the highway and then along, beside old houses once serene now devalued by the traffic. At the eastern edge of town he longed to go back, but all things considered and entirely against his will, he knew he couldn't return to the weatherboard alone.

He struggled up and down the mountains, and his body whipped inward on the freeway for passage of high-speed traffic, but he didn't put his hand out.

And when the chance availed itself he left the freeway and entered an obscure suburb at the edge of the city. The way would be labyrinthine and long, but he wanted to be seen and taken into account. More as a test than anything else. He would never put his hand out.

Arteries bled into main streets, which bled into long stretches of houses and apartment blocks. Then another artery, then more streets lined with shopfronts, then more houses and apartments. Whenever a road sign listed his target it beckoned him onto the freeway, but there were other ways more circuitous and less expedient.

He lost track of days, and he lost track of the number of times he circled around and back onto a path he'd walked before. Roads were for deliberate passage, they were not for path finding; roads were not for human figures improvising on foot. Neighbourhoods varied mildly in their formations, tethered by the connective tissue of boundless road and warehouse. Neighbourhoods were sites of foreign-yet-familiar comfort, and it was possible to mistake most for certain regions he'd once known. But once convinced he did not know them, neighbourhoods were revealed for what they were: labyrinthine obstacles in the way of due east, formidable barriers with a logic reliant on precious means and technologies that he, at least, had no confidence would exist for much longer.

Compared to the speed of the train, his feet were slower than he wanted. Back when he'd first taken the job outside of the city, the slightly better paying one, when he was still determined not to let the city expunge them, he had wanted the trains to go faster. Then came the days when he had wanted them to go slower. On foot was a tedious in-between. His destination might no longer exist if he dawdled, but if he moved too fast he might eventually get there.

He ate discards from bakeries, and he grazed fruit and vegetables wherever they laid open in buckets or trays. He drank from playground taps, or else sculled squat in aisles from bottled water or soft drink.

But he couldn't tell for sure whether life was business as usual. Since he'd disembarked the train it had never been clear. Films and TV taught of frenzied rushes for resources and bloody wars in undead-harried apocalypses and yet, maybe his and everyone else's apocalypse would continue to just be: going to the shops.

He knew he wasn't mad but he knew how he appeared. It was uncomfortable to sleep in the rough, it was also dumb and pathetic, but it was early summer warm and he'd usually sleep barely dressed. He unfailingly woke at dawn and then he'd keep on walking.

His was not a form of self-assured sanity that precluded others being wiser. It was obvious that most people in homes and shops were smarter than him. His actions were not prodded by the belief that he was capable of understanding the shape of the future better than anyone else in homes and shops. It was possible, in all seriousness, that many of the people inhabiting homes and shops had pictured the shape of the future long before he had. No doubt many, if not most, had already metabolised it. Maybe they hugged closer or got more angry but otherwise their shops stayed open and their venetians still tilted open to sun. Maybe they did it more deliberately, maybe they lived more deliberately, but not in a demonstrative kind of way. Maybe mothers and fathers fought tooth and nail after bedtime in screen-lit lounge rooms for undefinable fears. Or maybe they spoke in tones of lenience, quiet tacit avoidances for something verging love. Or maybe they met it headlong and shouted and felt all the better for it. But there was just no way none of them knew. None were smarter for knowing, anymore.

One night the tarmac of a minor road morphed old grey into new black, then in freshly razed plains it weaved inward and outward and then inward again, left and right at random and often into cul-de-sacs. The surrounding horizon was a mesh of newly raised streetlights illuminating plots of levelled earth all bordered by freshly laid gutter. Cranes brushed against moonlit cloud and all was silent except for the purr of distant artery traffic.

Fed up with roads, he made a decision. He marched pure east across the plots and towards a Colorbond threshold. He had no phone, map nor compass but his body understood east. He climbed through backyards and front yards and through the premises of businesses. At first it felt daring, but after a while he understood that rare were the times when another person inhabited a space he needed to cross. It wasn't for impossibility that he'd never traversed due directions, it was only for the tyranny of roads.

Sometimes he'd hit an impenetrable barrier, such as a barb-wired storm drain or an insurmountable wall. He'd make his way around even if around was for kilometres.

Other times, at least three times maybe more, the barrier was the well-fortified train track. He couldn't help himself: at the fences of train tracks he'd spend a moment comparing the view from the street with the view he'd always seen from the train. He sought the uncanny thrill of foreign vantage points on familiar settings. But it was never particularly satisfying. These vantage points each belonged to separate worlds. The in-transit and the ensconced existed inside different albeit parallel lives and he'd never quite figured out which one was preferable.

He'd sleep by day in parks or else on the wider roadside strips among trees. Occasionally he'd be jabbed by a council man wielding jabbing stick. Or else he'd awaken to the giggles of children or the grunting of men. Although he moved in due direction he'd still encounter the same kinds of space: lines of shops and interminable roads and most common of all, vaulting gauntlets of backyard the likes of which could have existed anywhere, above-ground pools and trampolines, rectangle plots of greyed lawn strewn with feeble summer gardens and children's bikes. Only twice did his drop into a yard prompt a shriek, and since he lumbered rather than marched he never lacked the reserve to sprint in circumstances when it was required. It was never lost on him, how powerful his appearances could be. For those who believed that nothing could ever penetrate the fences around their homes, he had rudely distended their boundaries forever.

In Newnes it had felt as if the world had crossed a threshold, a no-questions-asked, one-way kind of threshold. The land had seemed alarmingly broken.

It had been a relief to rip himself away from the regions that landlocked Newnes. It had not been without sadness – that followed him everywhere, often for the stupidest of reasons.

He had not resigned himself, he had extricated himself, and it was the bravest thing he'd ever done. But this notion of himself as *brave* quickly soured – as all notions concerning himself, every single one, had always been liable to do. There was no consolation in the seeming reliability of this old world. That it remained much the same was devastating, despicable.

The landscape continued unchanging until one evening, when passing through, without noticing, a series of tree-lined townhouse blocks, he saw fireworks explode in the east. His surrounds clarified, and suddenly he was in familiar territory. He'd walked there several hundreds of times before, but for lack of the world-famous New Year's fireworks spectacle he may not have noticed. He might have walked in wide-arc circles for the rest of his life.

In any case, regrettably, he was home.

The windows were illuminated. The night lights shone inside. Bon moved towards the light and stood on the path outside.

Pamphlets hung from the mouth of the rental mailbox, scoured pastel by the sun. It was definitely past bedtime, and the children would be in bed. Had the children learned to sleep yet? Had the process changed? It surely had. The bedtime process had always changed, and no solution had ever lasted for weeks at a time. The children had yet to surrender to routine.

If the children had fallen asleep, and if they were asleep, what was she doing, right now? Was she sitting doing her work, at the fragile table inherited from his family, the one they'd wanted to replace, the table with one loose leg? Was she working with presence of mind, or did his absence endure? Surely not: it was New Year. But his absence endured, he was certain of that. Whether as a point of despair or inconvenience, he could never know. Would his absence endure in a way that was palatable to him? It angered him that it surely did not. What of the duties he'd once handled? The routines and the duties had always changed. What would be his routine and duties now, if he'd never disembarked at Newnes?

His children were inside and so was she. Through the partially drawn venetian slats he detected familiar furniture and a bed. The bed contained a body wrapped in blanket. His daughter had always struggled for hours towards sleep, but once there, she would lay statuesque until dawn.

Many times he had watched her while she slept. Her face had appeared alert even in sleep. Her face had always remained taut with mouth slightly open, and her eyelids, ever reluctant to close, would be arched and stubbornly disapproving. She objected to sleep, even in her sleep. And because she was alert even during sleep, he had always wondered about her dreams. Whenever he had asked her about dreams, she had not understood. In all likelihood, her dreams were a phenomenon she had not yet distinguished from waking life.

Her baby life was a dreamlike collage and nothing was impossible. Her concept of the passage of time and the gaps between events had yet to blossom, so that within routine, there still lay the possibility and the acceptance of unutterably strange aberrations. But, so he thought, it was impossible to rationalise the words and behaviours of children.

And his son would be in his bed, next to his wife. He would be stretched across the mattress, though whether she had yet dared to cover him in blankets – for she feared suffocating babies – he did not know. He had loved the baby boy, though he had long grown to fear men.

They were inside, and he was outside. And even if he hadn't lost his key back in Newnes, he still could no longer use it. And even if he had it and used it anyway, and even if he got away with it – even if he was forgiven – he knew that something mysterious lay in their future, something unpredictable, far beyond his ability to fight.

Bon slept in the park on the corner. He awoke to an elderly, jabbing him with a jabbing stick.

Acknowledgements

Gratitude and love to my family, Rachel, Edith, Darcy and Maple.

Thank you to Bill Clegg, Nick Tapper and Grace Heifetz for your patient reading and advocacy.

Thank you to the Australia Council for the grant which helped fund the promotion of my first novel.

About the author

Shaun Prescott is a writer based in the Blue Mountains in New South Wales. His debut novel *The Town* was published in Australia, the UK, USA, Germany, Japan, Netherlands and Spain.